# EVERY SUMMER

# ALSO BY JOANNE DEMAIO

**The Seaside Saga**
*Blue Jeans and Coffee Beans*
*The Denim Blue Sea*
*Beach Blues*
*Beach Breeze*
*The Beach Inn*
*Beach Bliss*
*Castaway Cottage*
*Night Beach*
*Little Beach Bungalow*
*Every Summer*
*Salt Air Secrets*
*–And More Seaside Saga Books–*

**Summer Standalone Novels**
*True Blend*
*Whole Latte Life*

**Winter Novels**
*Eighteen Winters*
*First Flurries*
*Cardinal Cabin*
*Snow Deer and Cocoa Cheer*
*Snowflakes and Coffee Cakes*

# every
# summer

A NOVEL

# JOANNE DEMAIO

ISBN: 9781670298188

Joannedemaio.com

*To my husband, Tony,*
*and daughters, Jena and Mary*

*For our beach time at Point O' Woods,*
*every summer.*

# *one*

### *Early Sunday Afternoon*

EVERY SUMMER, THE SEA HAS cast a sweet spell on Maris' life. From when she was a toddler chasing lazy lapping waves on Stony Point's beach, to the evening she walked the lantern-lit boardwalk two years ago as Jason's bride, the sea has been beside her. Its rhythms comforted; its scent healed.

Every summer, she's walked these sandy streets past painted bungalows and shingled cottages. Waded in the gentle waters of Long Island Sound. Breathed the misty salt air rising off the sea. Some years found her at Stony Point often—like the teenage summers she spent with Eva's family at their home on the marsh. Other years, after college, the most Maris could manage were visits of a few summer days. Still, the beach was always there.

Every summer, Maris has found a way to get herself to the Connecticut shore, to breathe deeply beside the sea and feel every muscle relax. Every troublesome thought fade. Every memory soothe.

Until today.

Until this very minute, when every troublesome thought leaves no room for soothing memories, for relaxing.

Here at Shane's little beach bungalow, Maris sits alone on the half-wall of the back porch. An open-air view of Long Island Sound spreads out before her. Across the water, the August sun scatters a constellation of ocean stars. Stars Maris dare not wish upon until she sees Shane again.

So while she waits for him to return, she does it. She takes a long breath of the redolent sea air. But not in the easy, calming way of summers past. This time? This time she takes a salty breath hungrily, then another, as though she's drowning.

Which she is—drowning beneath regret. And sadness.

Because the way she ended things with Shane fifteen years ago—in an unfinished conversation from a lone payphone by the creek—was wrong, wrong, wrong. She hadn't been fair to someone who simply loved her. Who only wanted to be with her. To marry her.

All these years later, it's still hard to face the truth that she'd broken two hearts back then: hers and his. But *his*, more. That winter day, she might as well have pulled the deep blue sea out from under Shane Bradford.

Now she has to right that wrong.

"*I made a mistake, I made a mistake,*" she whispers so quietly, the words fade in the sea air.

Not knowing where Shane is, all Maris can do is wait in the shade of his back porch. And fiddle with his old sailor's knot engagement ring. And glance around the side of the cottage for his pickup truck. And wait longer. While she does, small waves break on the private stretch of beach beyond the porch, and the sun rises high in the summer sky. An occasional motorboat cruises by. A seagull cries as it swoops low.

Maris checks her watch. The minutes tick slowly past, each one giving her time to imagine what she might say to Shane. What words might explain her callous disregard of his heart back then. Might let on how she feels now. Sliding Shane's engagement ring on, then off, she only hopes she's not too late.

Still waiting, she takes another deep breath of that salt air—air that stings more than it cures these days. She looks around the open porch. Beach grasses spill from a rusted milk can beside an old whitewashed bench. There are vintage crates scattered about, too, some with tarnished lanterns on them. She imagines Shane lights those lanterns after sunset and that their flames flicker in the seaside night. Maybe he sits here in the glimmering shadows. Maybe a bluesy riff rises to the night sky from his harmonica.

Oh, and there! Yes, a happiness jar is on one of the crates. No doubt, Elsa gave it to Shane during his brief stay at her inn. Curiosity gets the best of Maris and she walks over to it. Carefully, she picks up the Mason jar and glimpses what's inside. A smooth skimming stone set in golden sand; some dried seaweed—sea lettuce and kelp; a silver tea-light candle.

Seeing these random pieces of Shane's life unnerves Maris. Enough to get her to leave his rented cottage. Returning the jar to the crate, she crosses the olive-painted porch floor and goes down the seven wooden steps. Because it's not her place to be here—not like this. Not her place to look at Shane's happiness jar, at his personal things. She hurries along the planked walkway beside the bungalow, where lush dune grasses sweep against her legs. In no time, she's back on Sea View Road, heading for her own home. Waiting on Shane's porch wasn't working, wasn't helping. Sitting alone there, her memories, the view of Long Island Sound, the salt air—all of it haunted more than eased her.

"Hey, Maris," a voice calls from behind just then. She looks over her shoulder to see Nick pulling up in the security cruiser. "What are you doing back so early?"

"Back?" Maris slows her step as the car pulls alongside her.

"You and Jason had a big anniversary weekend planned in the Green Mountain State," Nick says through the car's open window. "Shouldn't you still be in Vermont?"

"Oh." She glances toward Shane's cottage. "Vermont … right. Our trip was cut short, actually."

"Too bad. Everything okay?"

"Yeah. It's just that Jason's really backed up with work," Maris lies to Nick. "And the station needed him today."

"Well," Nick tells her as he slowly accelerates, "get on the beach. Grab some rays this fine summer day." As he says it, he gives a wave out the window and drives on.

"Wait! Wait, Nick!" Maris trots along to catch up with his car. "By any chance, have you seen Shane around?"

"Shane? I did, as a matter of fact." Nick lifts the brim of his security cap. "He left in his truck twenty minutes ago. You just missed him."

"Oh, *shoot*." She knew it. She just knew it. He hit the road. After one week at Stony Point, Shane hightailed it out of here but good, leaving behind only his happiness jar, of course. Happiness seems to be pretty elusive around these sandy beach roads lately, wavering out of reach like some intangible sea mist.

"Yep," Nick goes on. "Had a duffel of laundry with him. Asked me where the nearest laundromat might be."

# *two*

---

## *That Afternoon*

THEY'RE ALL THE SAME, THESE laundromats. Being a New England lobsterman, Shane's seen his share of them over the years. Stopping in ports far from home, he's often dropped his duffel filled with seaworn clothes onto random coin-operated washing machines. You've been in one laundromat, you've been in them all. There's the sound of the sloshing washers; the whirring hum of the commercial machines' spin cycles; clothes tumbling in dryers. Dusty grime covers the machine lids. Warm air presses close in the stuffy spaces.

"Can I get some change?" Shane asks the attendant.

Without looking up from a stack of towels she's folding, she motions to the change machine mounted on the wall, near the propped-open entrance door. "Over there."

Shane looks back and sees the coin machine. A soap dispenser is right beside it. "Thanks," he says, taking his handful of singles to the machines. He inserts them there, receiving several dollars' worth of quarters, then the necessary packets of detergent and fabric softener.

Not too many people are here on a Sunday afternoon. A young couple sorts their dried clothes at one of the folding tables. An older woman thumbing through a magazine sits on a chair with metal legs. It's late August and summer is waning. So are the vacationers, leaving Shane with his pick of machines. He chooses two empty ones in a tight area against the side wall. Pulling wrinkled jeans and cargo shorts and shirts from his duffel, he checks the pockets first. Good thing, too. Because in a pair of jeans, he finds Cliff's scuffed-up lucky domino and remembers when he stole it from the commissioner. It was the night a week ago when Cliff had to jump-start his car battery. *Things seem to go my way when it's around*, Cliff told him about his beloved talisman. Figuring he could use his own brush with luck during his two-week stay here, Shane discreetly pocketed the domino and has been holding and flipping it since.

After slipping the domino in his shorts pocket now, he finishes dropping his clothes into two top-loaders, inserts the quarters and gets the wash cycles started. The whole time, a cable-news anchor is reporting the headlines on a wall-mounted TV. Her monotone voice blends with the humming noise of clothes spinning in wash cycles and laundry tumbling in hot dryers.

"Shane?" another voice asks. A familiar one.

He glances back past a line of washers, then looks again.

It's Maris standing there, just inside the open laundromat door. She wears frayed white shorts, a fitted black tank, and her long brown hair is twisted in a low bun. She's tired, and worried. It shows.

"Maris. What are you doing here?" Shane asks, walking around a random plastic chair to get to her. "What's the matter?"

Maris gives a small smile while turning up her hands. "Can we talk?"

~

They head over to wooden stools in the cramped space in front of Shane's two machines. His duffel is on top of one washer, and before sitting, Shane reaches over and pushes open the old window on the wall there. It doesn't help, though. The air outside is as stifling as inside.

"Can't believe you found me here," Shane tells Maris as he sits.

"I stopped by your cottage first. When I was walking home afterward, I saw Nick. He told me you were headed to the laundromat. And this is the closest one."

"So you were pretty intent on locating me."

"I was."

"Okay. What's up, Maris?"

*What's up?* she thinks. Oh, couldn't she give him a lengthy list. First there's Jason packing his bags and apparently leaving her. Then there's her life unraveling this summer. Not to mention her past, haunting her every recent step.

Instead, she only manages to whisper, "I made a mistake."

"What?"

"A mistake. When I left you." She stops then, struggling to find the right words. All the while, Shane says nothing. For too many seconds, as he watches her, he's quiet. Quiet enough to unhinge her further. "It's just that I have to finish something with you. Something that's been eating me up."

"I can see that. But I'm not sure where you're taking this."

"Oh, I'm taking this way back. To that winter day when I called you, fifteen years ago. When I broke off our engagement."

"Maris, that day's long behind us."

"Not for me, it isn't."

"It should be. We were young then. Water under the bridge now."

"Water under the bridge? Seeing you here at Stony Point, it's more like the *floodgates* opened—on my life. On my ..." She'd say more, but just can't.

"Your marriage, too?" Shane asks after a moment.

She gives a slight, teary nod.

"Okay." He turns up his hands. "Go on, then."

Maris *would* take a deep breath to collect herself, but these days she's given up on the whole salt-air-cures-you thing. Instead she gets right to it. "The thing is, the way I ended our relationship years ago was really unfair. Remember how I ran out of coins that day on the payphone?"

Shane nods, and presses the back of his hand to his forehead to dab a bead of perspiration. Beside them, water sloshes in the washing machines.

"Our talk, well it just stopped mid-sentence, when the operator cut us off. And then? Nothing. I didn't call you back. We never spoke. Never saw each other again—"

"Until this summer," Shane finishes.

"Right."

"Things happen like that, though."

"No." Maris sits up straighter. "Not in *my* life, they don't. Not if I can help it." She pauses when a woman looks up at her from a magazine. So Maris leans closer and lowers her voice. Lowers it, but feels the pleading she puts into each word. "There's something you have to know about me."

Shane looks closely at her. He turns on his stool and actually faces her, then takes hold of one of her hands. "All that happened a long time ago. You don't have to explain."

"But I do. Because I left you—and this is the part that still bothers me—with no goodbye."

"Maris. Is that what this is about? Because I *get* it, how it happened then."

"No. Hear me out." Again, she pauses. Breathes. Gathers her thoughts. "I lost my mother with no goodbye, Shane. In a car accident when I was just a child. And then, when I reconnected with Jason a few years ago, I heard his story about Neil dying on the hot pavement, also with no goodbye. And there was Sal, too. Well. You didn't know Sal, but it was the same thing, the way he died in surgery

10

without any of us being able to talk to him at the end. And it's awful. Just terribly sad."

"Life *is* sad, sometimes." Shane leans close, bending to see her eyes. "No getting around that."

"Sometimes there is. I mean, when I saw you a week ago, I realized I'd buried a *knot* of regret these past fifteen years. Oh, I kept myself good and busy to bury that fact—finishing college, throwing myself into a fashion career, moving around the country, getting married. But now I have to finally face it … I never told you goodbye."

"It's okay."

"No, it isn't."

"Maris. We were kids then."

"And I knew better. Because as I grew up, I vowed *never* to leave someone without a proper goodbye. I *knew* what that felt like, and it's not good. But with you? I didn't keep that vow."

Shane pulls back. He clasps his hands behind his neck while studying her. "Maybe it was better that way."

His words surprise her. "*What?*" Maris asks.

"If you handled it differently back then, I would've convinced you to stay. To come to Maine. To marry me." When she interrupts, Shane stops her. "You would've had a different life, Mare," he insists. "You know that."

Maris gives a slow nod. Around them, there's the hum of washers. And the drone of a news report on the TV. Someone slams a dryer's metal door and drops quarters in the coin slot. Maris hears it all before asking what she's often wondered. "What did you do, Shane? After I called you that day."

11

Shane exhales a long breath. "Rattled around the house. Drowned my sorrows, and anger, sitting at a bar that night. The next day, went out on one more lobster trip here in Connecticut. With Noah. It was the last trip of the winter. I went. And I busted my ass."

The way Shane suddenly stands up, leans against one of the washing machines and crosses his arms in front of him, Maris thinks he's done explaining. He wears a tee with the sleeves ripped off, and in those crossed arms, in their heft, she sees every bit of struggle he faced back then. And in a few of those tattoos, shadowed and swirling on his skin, she's sure several dark moments are documented.

"It was so cold on that trip," Shane surprisingly continues. "The seawater froze on everything it touched. Which was dangerous, because it made the boat top-heavy. Which was good for *me*, because as I stood on deck bundled up in that biting wind with nothing showing but my eyes, I gripped a large rubber mallet. And believe me, I spent many hours swinging it, breaking ice off the deck. And getting out all my emotions that otherwise had nowhere to go."

"I'm so sorry, Shane. That I put you through all that."

Shane sits on his stool again, right as the washing machines beside them shift into noisy spin cycles. Both units slightly thump and vibrate while wringing his clothes. "After that last fishing trip, I didn't really know what to do—without you in my life. Lobstering was drying up in Connecticut, so I couldn't just stay here. Was itchy to get out. Get away from everything. So a few weeks later, I *moved* to that house in Maine."

"The one meant for us."

"Yeah," Shane says, running a hand along his whiskered jaw.

"And your father went with you?"

Shane nods. "He was there for me. Helped me through some real dirty days. I was young and scorned and wanted to get out my angst in fistfights. In drinking. Dad kept me out of trouble. Reined me in. And he also kept an eye on the house once I got a job on a commercial boat up north and headed well out into the Atlantic."

As he tells Maris the turns his life took after her heartbreaking phone call that year, the water drains from the two machines beside them. So Shane stands and wheels over a wire basket while Maris opens the machines once they stop spinning and wringing. Together, they lift out the wet clothes and drop them in the basket.

Breaking the quiet between them, Maris asks, "Can you ever forgive me?"

"On one condition," Shane says.

"Name it."

"Help me find a couple of available dryers."

Maris gives him a friendly shove, then wheels the laundry cart across the room.

⁓

Shane wonders if Maris feels it. Feels the intimacy. There's something about the way they stand there, side by side. Their arms move close; their bodies shift. As they reach for the wet clothes—she darks, he whites—and place the items in each dryer, it's like they've been doing this for years. As though they know each other that well. If anyone were watching, they'd think he and Maris were nothing more than a married couple doing the week's laundry.

No one would think that one distraught fifteen-year-old phone call brought her, desperate, to his side today in a public laundromat.

"Seeing you here at Stony Point this summer? It's like you never left," he admits as Maris tosses a pair of gray cargo shorts, then a bath towel, into the dryer.

"Oh, I did leave, though. For years, I had a big career. And travelled the world for my denim campaigns." She pauses, picks up a couple of dark tees and tosses them in. "But when my father died three years ago, I came home to settle the estate. Which was when one incredible secret came out of the closet. One that changed my life."

"Eva?" Shane asks while lifting a few wet boxers and button-down shirts. "Being your sister?"

Maris stops, another towel in hand. "Yes. And she was the only family I had then. A *sister*." She tosses the towel in the dryer before picking up a wet navy polo shirt. "You mentioned, in the shack the other night, that Elsa told you the story?"

"She did. Last Saturday, when I'd first arrived. I was looking at a photograph in the old Foley's back room. Which is when Elsa pointed out who was who and brought me up to date on everyone."

"Elsa." Maris tosses another pair of shorts, this one trail

shorts, into the dryer. "My mother's sister."

"Your aunt, right? The one who sent you that star necklace you always wore back then?"

"Still do." Maris finishes with her dryer, closes the door and lifts the star pendant from around her neck. "But it was Jason who *brought* the stars together for me. Who pushed me to face things and find answers in my life. And Shane, he's still pushing me to do that. Jason's why I'm here today."

"Jason is? You're here for him?"

Maris nods. "He's my family now, too. My husband. And he convinced me that you can't move forward sometimes, if you don't go back, first."

"Totally get that." As Shane says it, he gives Maris a handful of quarters. "My family—Lauren—got me here. Mostly to settle the past with my brother."

"I don't really know the whole story between you and Kyle," Maris lets on while pressing the coins into the dryer. "But will you fix things with him?"

"I'm trying." Shane selects the heat controls on his own dryer.

"You'll be around all week? To have time to see Kyle?"

"Got my cottage rented through Saturday. Then it's back to the boys on the lobster boat."

"I'm glad, Shane. That you'll at least talk with your brother."

"Yeah. Because seriously? I had no idea Jason lost Neil. Finding that out, well, it hit me pretty hard. Makes me want to reconnect with my *own* brother." He motions Maris over

15

to nearby plastic chairs. "You know," he says as he sits beside her. "Before it's too late."

"Kyle was Jason's best man. We had our reception right on the boardwalk two years ago."

Shane leans forward, elbows on his knees, and looks over at Maris beside him. "Sorry I missed that one. And Jason. He makes you happy?"

"He does … So I'm sure you won't believe me, not for one second, when I tell you that he's actually gone."

"What do you mean, gone?"

"I mean that I came home from grocery shopping this morning to a quiet house. That I looked around while putting away jars of mayonnaise and cartons of orange juice and slowly realized he'd left me. Took his crutches and luggage and the dog and disappeared. No note, no message."

"Maris, this is pretty serious."

"It is. I hate to say it, but we really hit a rough patch this summer."

"What *happened?*"

"It's complicated. And I'm not sure where to begin."

"Try."

Maris looks at him, takes a breath, stands up, paces a bit. And he sees it—her effort to try. She turns to him then.

"Jason," she begins. "He's got so much on his plate right now. But still. *Still* he helped Kyle and Lauren this past week. He's really giving, Jason is, doing so much for people until he's depleted. So … he's exhausted. And then?" Maris sits beside Shane again. His clothes tumble in the dryers in

16

front of them. "Then it was our wedding anniversary. But there's another anniversary this month, too. The ten-year anniversary of Neil's death. And of the whole accident, when Jason lost his leg."

"Ah, shit. Sounds like a helluva lot to deal with."

"It is. And to top it all off, with you here? Well, you in particular seem to be catching the brunt of Jason's anger. Or frustration."

Shane, still leaning his elbows on his knees, drops his head for a moment before looking at her again. "Might be a reason for that."

"What do you mean?"

Shane, well, it's his turn now. First he sits up straight, lifts a corner of his tee fabric and dabs his face. Then he stands, runs a hand through his hair and finally looks at Maris. "I sold Neil my motorcycle back then."

"Your Harley?"

After a quiet moment, Shane sits again, taking her hand in his. "When Elsa told me how Neil died in that bike accident, I just knew it. And believe me, I felt awful. Neil died on *my* bike."

"Wait a minute? The same bike we used to ride together down Shore Road? And to Gillette's Castle?"

Shane nods. "I was getting all the cash I needed to marry you, selling off anything I could. Neil'd been hankering for a bike, so I sold him my Harley-Davidson … I don't know, five or six years before he died."

"Oh, no."

"Jason didn't tell you?"

17

Maris shakes her head and fights tears. "No," she whispers.

"Well, it seems Neil died on that bike."

"So on some level, Jason might blame you." Maris stops then, watching only the clothes spinning in the dryer door window before looking at Shane. "But it's *not* your fault, and he'd know that!"

"Listen, Maris. If Jason wants to throw punches at me to get through this difficult month, for you? And your marriage? I'll take it."

"You *would* do that, wouldn't you?"

Shane only nods.

"But there's more." She stands then, pulls a ring from her shorts pocket and holds it out to him.

Shane takes the ring. It's a white-gold sailor's knot with an embedded diamond. A ring he'd never forget. A ring he gave to Maris when he proposed to her one long-ago snowy night on the coast of Maine. He looks over at Maris.

"That ring's rightfully yours, Shane. Take it," she says, before opening a dryer and dropping his dried clothing into the wire laundry cart.

"No, Maris. That's okay." He stands beside her at the open dryer and tries to give the ring back. "You've had it this long, and ..."

Silently, Maris folds Shane's fingers over their old engagement ring. "It'll help," she says with a small smile, "because Jason and I even argued about that. Oh, it's just another thing he had to deal with this week, finding out you and I'd been engaged."

Shane pockets the ring before opening his second dryer. He scoops out his warm clothes and drops them into the same laundry cart. "You mean, Jason really never knew you were going to marry me?"

Maris simply shakes her head.

After closing the empty dryer door, Shane looks long at her. The air between them is taut with tension, with secrets, with words *not* said because too many years have passed. Phrases that will only open a monster can of worms that neither has time for. That at this point, doesn't matter. Finally, Maris wheels the wire laundry cart to a folding table, lifts a pair of cargo shorts and shakes out the wrinkles.

"All this today? You coming here. Talking. Settling the past," Shane says while lifting a piece of clothing from the basket. "It really is for him, isn't it?"

"Partly. Like I said, things aren't good with me and Jason right now. But I'm trying."

"He'll be back, don't worry. Give him a day or two to think things through." Shane sets aside folded pajama boxers on the table. "And let me know if I can help. Because I told you years ago and I still mean it now. I'd always do anything for you, Maris."

Which is all she needs to hear; he sees that. It's in the way she finishes folding a T-shirt and backs away from the table. It's in the way she turns with a regretful smile and gives him a close hug. It's in the soft words she murmurs. "I know, Shane. I know you would."

Shane holds her for the long, painful moment that

*should've* happened fifteen years ago, when Maris couldn't say goodbye. Yes, finally, he holds his first love in his arms before pressing back a fallen wisp of her hair and whispering in her ear, *"Thanks for folding."*

Maris nods against his face; he feels it. She leaves a breath of a kiss there, too, then quickly turns and leaves. Walks straight out the laundromat's propped-open door without even a look back.

Shane watches until she's out of sight. Watches until all that's left are heat waves rising from the parking lot. Behind him, dryers spin loads of wet clothes; washing machines hum and slosh; the mounted TV drones on. When Shane turns to his laundry again, all cleaned and dried, he finishes folding and stacks everything in his duffel, one small pile at a time—tees, shorts, boxers, polo shirts, socks.

All that just happened with Maris—all the talking and looks and touches in a dingy laundromat—he knows what it was: a moment fifteen years coming. A necessary one, too. She maybe knew it more than he did. But walking with his heavy duffel outside, Shane feels a little freer. A little looser. Some rope, some knot, has been untied … setting them both sailing into their own lives.

Before driving off, he pulls that white-gold engagement ring from his pocket. Sitting in his truck, he looks at that sailor's knot carefully, feeling the history of the past fifteen years in all its twisted curves.

# *three*

MARIS KNOWS IT WILL HAPPEN. Jason will call. She's so sure of it that she holds her cell phone in bed that night. Outside, crickets slowly chirp. She turns toward the open window and sees the dark sky. Feels the sea's mist. And waits.

Still, when it happens, when her cell phone rings, she jumps. No amount of waiting, of anticipation, stops her body from startling. So she pauses and takes a breath before quietly answering the call.

"Maris." Silence then, before his voice continues. "It's me."

"Jason."

Their words are few, without intonation. His words telling her that he's staying at Ted Sullivan's cottage at Sea Spray Beach. Her words asking how he ended up there. His saying that it didn't feel right lately, being at home.

21

And in the telling, and the questions, Maris feels it. Feels the horrible, lingering strain between them. Hears the tightness in his throat. The hesitations in her phrases. It's been like this since two nights ago, when Jason came home early from Friday night fishing to find Shane in her writing shack. To find Shane standing close beside her, their words murmured. Their looks, secretive.

How much Jason really saw, Maris can't be sure. Certainly enough to put an end to their Vermont excursion yesterday. But enough to get him to *leave* her this morning?

Regardless, another day's gone by. Another twenty-four hours of distance growing between them, rather than narrowing.

"Neither of us is happy right now," Jason's voice is saying in her ear.

Hearing those words makes her remember Shane's words from this afternoon, in the laundromat. *Jason. He makes you happy?*

And Jason does. He *does*. Like no one else. But recently it feels like he won't even let her say that. Even right now, she can't.

"Three years ago, Maris, I made my life an open book," Jason continues. "Everything was laid out for you. The accident. A stint with addiction. Violent flashbacks. Missing my brother. And one night, right before our wedding, we agreed."

"Agreed?"

"No secrets."

Maris closes her eyes. "I'm not keeping any now," she

says. But more silence comes, a vacuum when she's hoping Jason will help her out. Hoping he'll say, *Okay. We'll start fresh. From here.*

He doesn't. There's only that silence until he says different words.

"I'm just not sure what I trust anymore," Jason admits. "My gut. What I see with you."

"What you see?"

"Friday night. In the shack."

"Jason. How can you not trust me?"

More silence, then. But it's close, this time. So close, it feels like Jason's in the bedroom with her.

"I just want you to know where I am," he says, his words low. "And I've got the dog."

"But Jason—"

"No. We need some time apart. To think."

"What are you saying? Are you coming back? What's your plan?"

"I don't have a plan. Other than taking this time, alone."

"That's not what marriage is—being apart. Just come home." She can't believe the tears he's bringing to her eyes, and whispers the rest. "*I hate that you're not here.*"

"You and I both know it didn't seem that way Friday." If possible then, his voice drops even quieter. "When I walked in on something private between you and Shane. Something unfinished."

"And it's not what you're thinking," she insists. "We'll work this out together, Jason."

"Not right now."

It's there again, in the pause that follows. She feels it, the growing distance between them that she just cannot seem to close.

"We need this space," Jason tells her before ending the call.

Maris looks at the now-silenced phone. In a moment, she sets it on the nightstand and rests her head on the pillow. Warm air drifts in through the open window. That air is damp with the sea, and she pictures the mist rising off the water on this muggy night. The gentle rhythm of waves splashing on the bluff comes to her. Maris stills, and only listens in the darkness. She closes her eyes, too, at the long day's end.

But she knows. Sleep will never happen tonight.

# *four*

### *Monday Morning*

AT LAST, IT'S MONDAY.

That's right, *Monday*, Kyle thinks. Most people are thankful when it's Friday. Not him. Mondays do it for Kyle. Because Mondays mean routine.

And routine is good.

Routine keeps him calm in the face of, well lately, in the face of life. Especially life during this past week following his botched vow renewal ceremony. Which was also the week of his brother sticking around the beach. He and Shane have had some strained talks, but it's routine that keeps Kyle's head on straight. Actually, they could probably all use a little more routine in their lives, with the way this summer's been going.

So this morning, Kyle's up and at 'em. Back to his regular routine as he opens up the Dockside Diner, drops his keys and paperwork in the back office, then wipes down and preps his cooking area. When he goes out to the front counter, his head waitress, Stacy, is already serving customers coffee and muffins from the pastry case. Kyle approaches that case now. Ever since he told Jason that cinnamon gives an energy boost, Jason starts his workweek right here—at the counter with a coffee and cinnamon cruller. So Kyle puts one of those crullers on a plate and sets it alongside a napkin and flatware, reserving Jason's regular Monday seat.

Back in the kitchen, Kyle spins his order-carousel and gets to it. He puts on his apron, lays bacon on his griddle and whisks eggs for scrambling. Once the bacon starts to sizzle, he flips the slices, then pours the egg mixture on the griddle, too. After glancing out to the diner to see if Jason's arrived, he uses his spatula to cut in the scrambling eggs. Does it all without thinking, really. It's all part of his routine.

Ah, yes. Routine. Being back at it, keeping his days regimented with order, with the grind, with monotony even, it has Kyle whistling a tune as he lifts the scrambled-egg edges and checks the bacon. Though early customers continue arriving, still no Jason when he takes another look out over the kitchen's half-wall.

"Yo, Kyle," Rob calls as he comes into the kitchen and ties on an apron. "Place is filling up."

"Yeah. Looking busy today," Kyle tells his cook. "Get the pancakes going?"

"I'm on it."

Kyle scoops the scrambled eggs and bacon onto two waiting plates, adds buttered toast and rings the bell for waitress pickup. He also gives another glance out to Jason's waiting stool.

Then glances again.

Because instead of seeing Jason sitting there—maybe unshaven and looking a little ragged—it's Maris occupying his regular seat. She sits sandwiched between patrons on either side of her. Everyone else is eating, reading a newspaper, sipping coffee.

Everyone except Maris.

Which gets Kyle to clear his stovetop, set aside his bacon press and spatula, and hurry out to the diner while wiping his hands on a towel. "Where's your better half?" he asks Maris from behind the counter. "And hey, how was Vermont?"

"Vermont never happened."

"What?" Kyle glances around. Customers sit at all the counter stools, and he nods to a few regulars. "Jason all right?"

"Actually? He's not," Maris tells him. "That's why I'm here."

"What's wrong?" Kyle moves closer, to better hear in the now-noisy diner. Dishes and silverware clink and clatter. Voices rise. The door opens as more people walk in. "Did he get sick or something? You need some meals to-go?"

"No. It's not that." Maris picks up Jason's cruller and breaks it in half. "I'm worried about him, Kyle. Jason's … out of sorts lately."

"I'll bet." Kyle glances to a customer getting up from a stool beside Maris.

"Thanks, Kyle," the man says as he pats a napkin to his mouth before leaving a tip on the counter. "Excellent grub, as usual."

"Anytime, guy," Kyle tells him with a wave. "Good seeing you." But when he picks up the customer's plates, he gets a better look at Maris. Jason apparently isn't the only one out of sorts. There are shadows beneath her eyes, and her smile? Just not there. Kyle drops the dirty dishes on a tray behind him, then turns back to Maris. "Well, your husband must be run-down, no? Had a crazy week around here. Heck, he practically arm-wrestled me and Lauren out of a bad situation."

"He did, I know." Maris takes a nibble of the cruller. "And with the ten-year anniversary of that accident rolling in, too. Not to mention off-the-charts job pressure with his new show."

"Yeah. I've noticed he's tense about that lately," Kyle says while wiping off the counter where he'd removed the plates. "Like the week before last? He was just spoiling for a fight. At the tailor's, I mean. When we picked up the vow renewal suits. Man, there was no talking to him that day."

"I remember. But—" Maris waits while a waitress fills her coffee cup. "There's more," she tells Kyle then, motioning him closer.

So he does it. Kyle leans his elbows right on the countertop to listen. And waits for whatever bomb she's about to drop.

"Kyle." She briefly shakes her head. "It's just that, well … Jason might have misread some situations this past week."

"Situations?"

"Between me and your brother."

"Shane?"

Maris nods.

"Oh, no."

She takes a long breath. "It wasn't good."

"Aargh." Kyle straightens to make room for Stacy passing with a tray loaded with nearly toppling dishes. "Maybe ... maybe just give him some time, Maris."

"*Time apart.*"

It's the way she whispers those two words—whispers and swipes at her eyes—that stops Kyle cold. "Are you crying?"

"Yes, okay?" Maris picks up a piece of cinnamon cruller, but sets it right down. "Jason's left."

"Left. Wait." As Kyle says it, he first glances back toward the big stove—where he *should* be standing and where orders are *surely* mounting—then picks up the coffee decanter and a clean cup. "Left for where? Work?" he asks while pouring the steaming coffee.

"Left *me.*"

Kyle looks over at her while pouring that damn coffee, which then spills onto his hand. "Are you *kidding* me?" he asks Maris, all while setting the cup down and shaking off the scalding brew. "Like, he moved out?"

"Yes. Jason's gone, Kyle. Packed his bags, took the dog and left."

Kyle, well, what can he say? Oh, he knows damn well what he *has* to say. He motions for Maris to wait a sec as he

29

trots toward the kitchen, grabs the doorjamb and leans in while calling, "Rob! Taking five. Maybe ten, not sure. You got things covered here?"

"Yeah, man," Rob tells him while folding an omelet, then sprinkling shredded cheese on a mound of scrambled eggs. Sausage links sizzle on his griddle beside it all. "I'm good."

So Kyle nods, then walks out and goes around to the other side of the counter. He sits himself on the empty stool beside Maris, turns to her and says in a low, serious voice, "We're going outside to the patio, where it's quieter. Because you're going to tell me what's going on right *now*. And you're telling me *everything*."

# *five*

So MUCH FOR ROUTINE.

So much for keeping his head on straight.

Kyle picks up the highway toward Sea Spray Beach, twenty miles down the coast. His old pickup's air-conditioning is busted, so with one hand on the wheel, he cranks down his window. And wouldn't you know it? He does something he swore he was done with. He lifts a cigarette to his mouth.

Cripe, for the second time in the past week, he just bought a pack. While holding a lighter to the cigarette, he thinks Lauren will kill him if she finds out. But heck, he really doesn't have to worry about that. Because if smoking doesn't have him drop dead of a heart attack first, the emotions of these past days will.

"Damn you, Jason Barlow," he says, then takes a long drag from the cigarette.

The entire way to Sea Spray, with each passing highway sign, and with each random strain of his truck engine, Maris' words run through his head. Especially the part about her and Shane's rushed engagement, back in the day—an engagement Kyle never knew about.

Apparently Jason didn't either. At least, not until this week. And that stinging news had to bite.

As Maris sat at one of the diner's outdoor patio tables earlier, as she pulled her cruller into pieces while not eating a crumb, Kyle heard it all. Heard about the whole fraught Vermont car ride. About the tension in the car. About Shane's sailor's knot engagement ring. About how Maris never told anyone except Eva about the brief engagement—not after the night of that dreaded bonfire when Shane was evicted from their lives.

Still, if Maris is looking to Kyle to fix things, Kyle knows one thing for certain. "*It's a bad situation at the Barlow house,*" he says with a glance in the rearview mirror.

So after tamping out his cigarette, he tries to push more horsepower into his truck's sputtering acceleration. Because if there's another thing he knows, it's this: Jason Barlow has always been a best man to him in every sense of the word.

Now it's time to return the favor.

～

Jason drops his work duffel on the teak deck table. Turning, something catches his eye. It's the dog, sitting on the other side of the slider screen. The German shepherd is sitting posture-perfect, ears straight, watching him through the screen. "Hey, Maddy," Jason says, going back inside. "You can't come with me today." The dog trails his every move as he grabs a big dog biscuit, gives it to her and pats her back. "Behave yourself while I'm gone," he tells her, then goes outside, locks up the slider, grabs that duffel and hurries down the deck steps to the driveway. With a glance at the blue sky, he thinks it's a classic late-August day. He feels the hot sun already; hears the waves breaking on the beach; hears the clicking wind chime of pebbles and wooden starfish strung on fishing line. And walking to the rear of his SUV to toss in his duffel, he hears … squealing tires?

One glance to the road and he sees that it's Kyle. His pickup skids to a stop at the end of the driveway—blocking Jason's SUV—and sprays sand and beach stones from beneath its skidding tires.

"Son of a bitch, Kyle," Jason says while brushing off his clean button-down shirt.

Kyle calls out the open driver's window of his old truck. "I'll tell you who's a son of a bitch. *You* are."

"What?" Jason opens his SUV liftgate and tosses in his duffel loaded with work gear. "What are you even doing here?"

"I had that same thought about you. When your wife stopped in the diner." Kyle leans his arm on the open window as he watches Jason. "I mean, what the hell? Had your cinnamon cruller waiting and instead of you rolling in,

*Maris* is sitting there. Crying, too, and telling me you *left?*"

"For Christ's sake, Kyle." This kind of bullshit is one thing Jason *doesn't* have time for in his stressed-out, overbooked, exhausting life. He eyes the beat-up pickup blocking him. "Move your damn truck already. Busy day."

"Where you going? I'm going, too."

"Don't need a babysitter, Bradford. *Move* it, I said."

Well, Kyle must not understand. Not with the way he shifts in his seat, lifts off the chef apron he still has on, bundles it up and wipes his sweating face. But that's not all. As every passing second spikes Jason's blood pressure, Kyle tosses the crumpled apron aside and, yes, he does it. He lights a cigarette. Holds one out to Jason, too.

"Calm down, Barlow," he evenly says.

"Calm *down?*" Jason walks closer to the truck. His forehead is perspiring now, beneath that glaring sun. A slight headache is pulsing in his temples. "Do you know what my itinerary looks like this morning? My day's booked solid from sun-friggin'-up to sun-friggin'-down. Now, get out of here!" he says, hitching his thumb toward the street.

"I just want to talk, bro. Man to man." Kyle gives a shake to the unlit cigarette he still holds out. "If things are so bad you had to leave home, hell, I get it. You've seen me at my worst. So I'm asking you again. Where are you going?"

"Don't *you* have to work?" Jason asks.

"Made an emergency call to Jerry. He's covering my stove." Still Kyle extends that unlit cigarette.

With his SUV obstinately blocked by Kyle's truck, Jason

blows out a long breath. Snatches the cigarette from Kyle's hand, too. "Give me a light," he says, and Kyle hands him *his* cigarette—which Jason uses to light his own. "I'm delivering site plans to the town for red tape at the Fenwick place," he says through a cloud of smoke.

"Thought those details were ironed out."

"Variances aren't all approved yet. They want to see stats on raising the cottage, and on the placement of pilings under it. Shit on realigning deck stairs, too. Then a stop at Beach Box. Plus a meeting with Mitch Fenwick, later on, for more design talk." Jason takes a long drag of his cigarette, then turns toward his SUV. "But first? Quick Lube for an oil change."

Kyle puts his cigarette in his mouth, squints against the smoke and turns his truck's ignition—which starts the engine on the second try. "Okay, then. Me, too."

⌒〜

One thing Kyle didn't see coming today is things going from bad to worse. But, here we go. He takes the sheet of paper from the counter clerk at Quick Lube.

"Mechanic did an initial inspection of your truck. Found some problems," the clerk tells him. "Wants to know if you'll be adding any of those."

"Are you kidding me?" Kyle scans the list of recommended services: tire rotation; transmission flush; a/c service; belt replacement. Before he finishes the list, his eyes drop to the several-hundred-dollar tab the work would incur. "Nah," he tells the clerk. "Well, okay. Just one. Add the brake fluid."

"What about the tires? They're showing some wear."

"No. For now, just a lube, oil and filter. With the brake fluid."

Walking back to the waiting area, Kyle looks up from the checklist and sees Jason sitting on a gray-cushioned metal chair. He's wearing a short-sleeve checked button-down over navy chinos. But what Kyle notices, especially beneath the fluorescent lights of the oil-change waiting room, is how shitty Jason looks. His hair is unkempt. His face hasn't seen a razor in days. And just how tired is he, with those circles beneath his eyes?

Kyle folds up the oil center's checklist, slips it in his back pocket and takes a seat beside Jason. From his chair, he can see through a large window, right into the service bay. His old bomber's up on the lift. The pickup's looking a little pathetic, too, with its faded paint, a few dings. Question now is just how many more oil changes will it have before he finally trades it in?

When he looks to Jason to tell him about the list of newfound mechanical issues, Jason's leaning forward, elbows on his knees, and not talking much. Not at all, actually.

"Shit," Kyle says—instead of his litany of truck problems. This isn't really where he wanted to get into personal things, at the oil-change garage. But maybe it's good. Jason's completely trapped beside him waiting for his SUV—no wheels, no transportation to get the hell out of here. It's just them, and a random customer watching a TV across the room, and someone standing at the vending machines near the checkout area. "We just did this last week," Kyle tells Jason.

"Did what?" Jason asks without looking back at him.

"You pulled *me* up. Got me out of a really bad place the night of my tanked vow renewal. And it wasn't the first time you've done that, either. Never thought I'd be doing the same for you."

Still leaning on his knees, Jason says nothing. He just drops his head for a second, then keeps an eye on the service bay window.

"You *never* break, man," Kyle says in a harsh whisper. "Came out of that accident ten years ago beat up to kingdom come. No leg. Road burns ripping up your back. All stitched up and a bandaged wreck. Still," Kyle rests his own elbows on his knees and looks at his friend. "Still, life couldn't *break* you. You always pulled through." He drags a hand through his hair. "You always rise, Barlow."

Jason looks at him and barely nods. But after a long breath, and sitting back with his arms crossed in front of him, nothing else.

Kyle matches him, move for move. He sits back, too, so that he can keep his voice low. And so that Jason hears every word he utters.

"Maris filled me in on some shit," he tells Jason. "And man, what shit it is. Hell, even I didn't know Shane was engaged to her. Hit me like a ton of bricks, so I can only imagine, well … I get it, you being pissed. I got mad at

Lauren last week, at how she hid it that she invited my brother to our vow renewal. Felt like a betrayal."

When Jason says nothing, not a word, Kyle gets up and walks to the coffee area. He pours two cups of coffee and buys himself a minute fussing with them. Because he's not sure he's ever seen Jason like this, so damn quiet. Not sure what to make of it except that if this is Jason's life *without* Maris, things have to change. Kyle walks back to him, gives him a coffee and sits again, picking up right where he left off.

"But it's not, man. It's not a betrayal—Maris' old engagement. It's just, I don't know … history." Still nothing, so Kyle sips his coffee and presses on. "But when it's all stacked onto everything else in life, sometimes it just doesn't seem worth the effort to deal with. Get that, too. And hell, you are so *exhausted*, dude." Kyle lifts a foot to his knee, brushes dust from his black work pants, and goes on. "Between work, and the ten-year anniversary more than anything else—reliving that day in your head and thinking of Neil, I'm sure. Well, you probably can't fathom much else."

An older couple walks in and talks briefly to the counter clerk before wandering to the vending machines. They buy some plastic-wrapped pastry before heading to the coffee station. When they do, Kyle doesn't know what more to say to Jason. So he gets up and crosses the room to an assortment of key rings, visor clips and USB plugs. They're nicely displayed in a glass case, and Kyle gives a good look before walking back to his seat. Jason still just sits. He leans forward again, coffee cup in hand, elbows on knees. But he doesn't say anything. Doesn't even look over at Kyle.

So Kyle does it again, too. He matches Jason move for move—this time leaning forward, elbows on his own knees. "Don't go backwards, bro. You're in a good place right now," Kyle tells him, his voice still low and even. "*Really* good, in so many ways. So don't put whatever bullshit's in your head on Maris. She's the best thing that ever happened to you. Believe me, I know. I've seen you before Maris, and after."

The attendant calls out a name, and the man watching TV hurries over to collect his keys and pay the bill. Kyle watches, and waits for anything from Jason. An assurance, an explanation, a *Mind your own fucking business*. Anything. But his friend just sits there, elbows still on knees, head dropped.

"Hell," Kyle says in practically a whisper now that more people are around. "If you need time, fine. I'll stop by, though. Bring you dinners. Whatever it takes, guy. Because news flash? You ain't looking that good."

For some reason, that does it. Barely. Jason tosses him a glance.

"Listen, Barlow. Never thought I'd say this, but I'm worried about you. So you just keep yourself there at Ted's. It's a good place. Maris told me he gave you use of his cottage. Ironic, being Ted Sullivan and all. You know, with him causing the accident. Funny how things come around like that." Kyle leans back then. Leans back in his plastic seat and crosses his arms over his chest. "But if it works for you, well, I'll check in on you." Again he leans forward so that they're face-to-face. "I'll take a ride. Bring you diner meals." He pauses, giving Jason *any* chance he can to even tell him to go to hell. He doesn't. Kyle blows out a long breath in the silence, then says, "Whatever it takes to get you back."

Jason, still leaning on his knees, watches the service bay window. Kyle looks, too, as some sedan is raised on the lift near Kyle's pickup. Life goes on all around them, no doubt about that. All around them, but not with them. Kyle looks long at Jason again, at his shirt taut across his leaning shoulders. At his unkempt hair. Finally, Kyle gets up and goes to a magazine rack on the wall, plucks out a magazine and brings it back to his seat. He flips that magazine over, turns one page, then another, in silence.

# six

## Early Monday Afternoon

OKAY, SO SHANE FIGURES HE and his brother are even now. An eye for an eye. Shane showed up unannounced at Stony Point, put the brakes on Kyle's vow renewal ceremony—and got a sizzling, mouth-scalding, hot-pepper sandwich in return. Slate's cleared.

Cleared, but not resolved. And Shane will be in Connecticut for only a few more days. Which is why he swings by the Bradford house after lunch. Maybe his brother is there. Maybe they can make some headway and talk. He knocks on the front porch door, but the place is buttoned up tight. No one's home. Not Kyle. Not Lauren and the kids. So Shane takes a long look at the house before walking around back. The silver-shingled bungalow has blue shutters. A white wrought-iron bench is in a petunia flowerbed in the front. And in the side yard, a garden hose is coiled among freshly planted ornamental grasses. Behind

41

the house, there's a large shower cabana and an old picnic table. A basket-planter of yellow marigolds sits beneath a pitched-roof overhang, on the back stoop. Some toys are there, too: a glider airplane, jump rope, playing balls, a butterfly net.

But no one's here. So Shane tries the beach next. Maybe he'll spot the Bradfords on the sand. From the boardwalk, he lifts off his newsboy cap and squints against the sunlight. Even though it's late in the season, the beach is crowded. The heat hasn't let up these past weeks, and striped umbrellas and colorful towels line the water's edge.

Well, one thing's for certain—some things never change. Because there's Lauren and her two kids in the exact spot where Shane and Kyle always sat, long-ago summers here. Right in front of the wood bench up on the berm.

"That's my spot," Shane calls to Lauren as he crosses the sand and puts his cap back on.

Lauren turns in her sand chair and waves to him. "Hey, Shane."

He stops beside her seat with a sense of déjà vu. It's an odd feeling, as memories surface right beside the splashing waves. "This was my family's regular spot, growing up. Always sat right here."

"That explains why Kyle is so possessive of it."

Okay, Shane can't help thinking. So this sandy spot actually means something to Kyle. The two brothers stand a chance, then. Shane looks out at Long Island Sound. Sunshine sparkles on the rippling water. "Great beach day."

"Last week before school," Lauren says, setting her

sunglasses on top of her head. "I took off time from the diner to make it a beach week for the kids."

"Mommy, my *tube*," Hailey quietly tells her mother.

"Oh, Daddy's been so busy, he forgot to blow it up, Hay."

Shane crouches beside Lauren and glances at Hailey. Her blonde hair is in two pigtails, and she wears a blue bathing suit with a ruffled neckline. A little shy, she stands just behind her mother. "She's the spittin' image of you," he remarks.

"You think so?" Lauren glances back at Hailey.

"Definitely. And hey, where's that tube? I'll take care of it for you," Shane says then.

Lauren reaches into a tote beside her sand chair. She digs out a brand-new uninflated tube, still in its plastic packaging. "You don't mind?" she asks.

Shane shakes his head and takes it from her, ripping open the plastic and pulling out the wrinkled, airless pink tube.

"Hailey." Lauren reaches for her daughter's hand. "Come say hello. This is your …" She throws a quick glance at Shane.

"Uncle," he says between breaths.

"Uncle Shane." Lauren tugs Hailey closer.

"Pleased to meet you, Hailey. What grade will you be in next week?" he asks, extending a hand to her.

When Lauren nods at Hailey, she lightly shakes his hand, barely saying, "Second grade."

Lauren, wearing a tie-dye tankini, pulls up her knees and

wraps her arms around them. "Hailey's seven," she tells Shane as Hailey sits on a nearby towel and picks up a small plastic horse. "And Evan," Lauren says, nodding to a dripping-wet boy approaching from the water, "is nine. Going into fourth."

"Dad?" Evan asks while lifting off his swim goggles and trotting toward Shane. "Oh, I thought …"

"It's okay, Ev. This is Dad's brother. Say hello to your uncle Shane. He's a lobsterman."

"You catch *lobsters*? Like … on a boat?" Evan asks, stepping closer.

Shane gives another blow into the tube's valve, then pinches it shut. "Sure do," he tells Evan, reaching out to shake the boy's hand. "And what are you finding in the water?" Shane stands and nods to the pails Evan lined up near the breaking waves. "Any lobsters here?"

"No. Just some minnows. A little striper. And a jellyfish, over on the side." Slowly, Evan turns and runs to his pails, yelling back, "And there's either a hermit crab, or a rock I found." He grabs up his plastic shovel and digs the wet sand near a pail.

Shane gives Evan a thumbs-up, then gives another blow into the tube's valve. "I looked for you at your house," he says to Lauren between blows. "Then tried here."

"Looked for *me*?"

Shane nods while maneuvering the inflating tube as he blows more. "Listen," he says, pinching the air valve shut for a second. "I'm running out of time, Lauren. Feeling a little desperate, actually. I've got five days left here. Four, not counting today, before I leave. And I need to make more headway with Kyle."

"He's so busy. With the last week before school and all. The diner's mobbed with end-of-summer vacationers."

"Well, I'd rather not bother him at work again, if that can be avoided." Standing beside her, he lifts the nearly inflated tube and gives it another breath of air.

"Yeah." Lauren sits back in her sand chair and lowers her sunglasses to her face. "I heard about that epic grilled cheese sandwich."

"Figured you would. You can also figure I have nowhere else to turn. You sent me an invitation, so I'm hoping you can help me out. Because I really don't want to leave without talking to my brother. *Seriously* talking." Again he raises the tube to his mouth, takes a long breath and keeps inflating it. "Too much time has gone by already. All these years."

Lauren looks up at Shane. Then looks out at Evan filling his pails with stones and such. Then back at Shane.

And Shane sees it. She's just not sure how far to push things. How much to *arrange* fate for Kyle. Standing there in the shade of her beach umbrella, Shane watches her waver.

"Will you be around, let's see ..." Lauren hesitates. "How about tomorrow morning?"

"Could be." Still holding the pink tube, Shane crouches again when Lauren motions for him to come closer.

"Listen," she quietly says. "Kyle read that exercise helps to decompress, so he takes an occasional morning swim."

45

"Okay."

"Early though. Before he opens the diner."

Shane gives a last puff of air into the tube and closes up the valve, saying, "That could work. I'll be on the beach in the morning."

"All right."

"How early? Sunrise?"

"Pretty much." Lauren hesitates before committing. "Okay, I'll get Kyle to take a swim." As she says it, her cell phone dings and she pulls it out of her tote. "Oh, no."

"Bad news?"

"It's Celia, in a bind. You met her, right? That night at The Sand Bar?"

"Yeah. Seen her around, here and there."

"Huh. It looks like everybody needs Kyle these days." Tilting her phone out of the sunlight, she reads Celia's text aloud. "*Huge Mason jar order came in at salvage company. Need to pick up today and my backseat's jammed. Can't lay it down and order won't fit in just my trunk. Really need a truck. Kyle available?*" Looking at Shane then, Lauren tells him, "And then she says, *Help.*"

Shane wastes no time. He squeezes Lauren's arm while saying, "Don't tell her it's me. But text her back that help is on its way."

"Seriously?" Lauren asks, looking up at him as he stands.

Shane nods, then turns to Hailey still sitting on her beach towel. "Here you go, Miss Hailey. All ready to float in the waves." He gives one of her pigtails a tug, turns and tips his newsboy cap to Evan, then hurries back across the hot, sunny beach.

⌒

Shane watches Celia from a distance. She wears a white tank top beneath denim overall shorts. The overalls are faded and shredded in spots; the tank top, fitted; her hair in a loose side braid. Walking the beach road toward her cottage behind the inn, he sees her fussing with her car. As he nears, she opens a rear door and leans inside.

So Shane goes around to the other side of her car, opens *that* rear door and leans inside, too.

"Oh!" Celia says while pulling on the seatback. "Shane!"

"Hey there, Celia."

She stops then, a little breathless, backs out of the car and straightens, pressing her hand to her forehead. But in a moment, she gets to her seat-struggling again. "I've got this, almost there," she insists with another yank at the back of the seat. "Don't need any help," she adds, tossing a small smile his way.

He leans closer inside the car and tips up his newsboy cap. "But I hear you can use a truck?"

# seven

*Late Monday Afternoon*

THEY TAKE THE BACK ROADS home from the salvage yard. Celia likes that contradiction about Shane. Though his manner is straightforward—his words direct in capturing what he wants to say—he'll also step off the beaten path.

So instead of taking the highway, he drives along a narrow road hugging the coastline. His truck bed is filled with boxes of vintage Mason jars, all of them well packed and secured. The pickup's windows are down, and the salty wind lifts loose wisps of Celia's hair as he drives. There's something freeing about the feeling. About just cruising. The road curves past serene harbors and marsh inlets, where rowboats are anchored in the still waters. They pass silver-shingled cottages, their windows open wide to the sea. A late-afternoon haze hangs misty in the air.

Oh, couldn't she just see all this on the big screen.

Sometimes her life seems so suited for that. Maybe a romantic comedy, the kind she likes to cozy up and watch late on a Saturday night. More often than not, though, her days are probably better suited to a serious drama. Especially the days of the past year, when she loved, and lost love; left Stony Point, and was beckoned back; grieved, raged and accepted; became a new mother, and an assistant innkeeper, all while moving into a gingerbread guest cottage behind the inn.

Actually, none of it was rom-com material. The romance faded long ago, with Sal's death. And the comedy part? Well, there's been little laughing these past months.

So this summertime cruising feels sweet now—after the past year of dramatic days. And the setting? Custom-made for the ease her life has finally found. The silver-screen movie she pictures would be the same one she's recently imagined—*Celia's Return*. But it's not just her return to Stony Point; she sees that now. No, in that title, there's *another* return: her return to everyday simple living. Her return to lightness after a long darkness.

Yes, Celia can just envision the camera assistant raising the clapperboard as Shane drives past ice-cream shacks with striped awnings, and bait hut signs advertising *Live Sea Worms* and *Rods and Reels*. The clapperboard would read *Scene: "A New Day," Take: One.*

And the director? He'd order the establishing shot to focus on the pickup cruising along, while including the seaside vista moving past like a lazy rolling wave. The effect would orient viewers to the beach setting. But more importantly, including the truck in the scene gives a sense of the movie's *journey*—the emotional roads Celia's travelled over the past difficult months.

She drops her hand out the open passenger window now and feels the breeze on her arm. The salt air right here on the coastline is a tonic she breathes deeply. The camera would capture this as it brings her character in closer. It might keep Shane near in the background, too. He wears a loose short-sleeve button-down over a black tee and olive cargo shorts. He's got one arm casually crooked and leaning on the open window, the other steering. And why not include him? In the midst of a summer rainstorm just days ago, it was Shane who helped free a thick knot of grief tied up inside her for a year. Oh, it wasn't a pretty picture, Celia's sure. Her face wet with tears and sadness; her voice angry; her hair and clothes disheveled from the rain and emotion. She remembers the way Shane put his arms around her that day, walling her in. Taking some of her pain right into him.

When she glances over at Shane driving, he senses it, apparently, and tips that newsboy cap of his.

"Mind if I make a pit stop?" he asks. "There's an old friend nearby I'd like to see."

*And … Cut!* the director would call right at that moment.

⌒〜

It's called Lobsterland. The eatery is in an old fisherman's shack built right on the docks. Beneath the August sun, the shack's seaworn white shingles are weathered gray; the eaves and window-trim paint a faded red. Aged fishing net is draped over one side of the building. Two old-fashioned wooden lobster traps lean near the open door. White plastic tables with blue umbrellas are set out beside the shack. An unpainted picket fence lines the edge of the harbor dock. It's as briny a sight as Celia's ever seen. If she didn't know any better, she could be on the coast of Maine as easily as the coast of Connecticut.

Shane parks in the nearby lot. They get out and walk over to the restaurant, until Shane suddenly stops in his tracks. Stops, smiles and opens his hands wide. When Celia looks to see who's got him smiling, an older man wearing wrinkled khaki shorts and a navy tee is *also* stopped still. He's about sixty, with a trim silver beard and unruly silvery hair held back with a red bandana. His eyes, Celia can tell even from where she stands, glisten with sudden tears.

"Hey! It's my boy, Shane!" the man calls out as he strides closer. "Shane from Maine, is that really you?"

Shane meets him halfway and they hug warmly, their hands slapping each others' backs. "Noah, *so* good to see you, my friend."

"What are you *doing* here?" Noah steps back and takes in the sight of Shane—who he apparently hasn't seen in years.

"Family thing. Came home for a reunion of sorts."

"Everything okay, I hope?"

"Sure, sure."

"And this is your wife?" Noah nods to Celia standing just behind Shane.

51

"What?" Shane turns to her. "No—"

"Good to meet you …" Noah brushes his hands on his shorts and extends one for a shake.

"Celia," she says, taking his hand in hers. "Celia Gray."

"Noah. Noah Conti. And what are you doing with this hunk of trouble?" Noah asks her.

Well, whatever affectionate warmth these two have for each other is contagious, because Celia finds herself laughing easily at Noah's question.

"Celia's a friend of mine, Noah. A beach friend." Shane turns to Celia then. "Celia, this is my old friend, Noah. When I was seventeen and full of myself—"

"And you're not any longer, tough guy?" Noah interrupts with a wink of his eye.

Shane waves him off. "When I was full of myself," he continues to Celia, "*and* in trouble with the law, the state stepped in and hooked me up with a mentor. Noah here, well he straightened me out back then. Noah and the Atlantic Ocean did." Again he looks to Noah. "Not sure which of the two was a more formidable force."

"So nice to meet you," Celia tells Noah. And though his eyes twinkle when he nods, she sees it. Sees those decades of life on the water. Sees his leathery skin, the sun and sea leaving it weathered and wrinkled. Sees the grit that those dirty days left behind. Grit, and strength. And something else, too, from living a life he obviously loves. There's a grizzled happiness in his expression; in that casual graying hair beneath that red bandana; in his apparent love for the kid he once took aboard his boat, and saved. For Shane Bradford.

"I worked with Noah on his lobster boat for several years when I was just a pup," Shane tells her. "Straight through until I left here for Maine."

"Got a few more tattoos since I last saw you," Noah comments, taking hold of Shane's sinewy arm and giving a quick look.

"A few tats, a few years of life on the sea …"

"Ah, yes. They go together. And you're staying out of trouble, I hope?" Noah gives Shane's arm a hearty pat.

"It's not easy, Noah. But I'm trying."

"And still lobstering up north?"

"Absolutely. Split my time between local work on Penobscot Bay, and winters on the big boats. In federal waters, a hundred … hundred fifty miles offshore."

"That's pretty hard-core, my boy. You've come a long way from that troubled kid I knew. Proud of you, Shane."

Shane can't seem to help himself—he hugs Noah again. "And what about you, Noah? You still have your boat?"

"I do."

Shane turns to Celia. "This here, Lobsterland," he says, motioning to the utterly charming painted hut and white plastic tables scattered on the dock beside it, "is Noah's blood, sweat and tears. He makes *thee* best lobster rolls on the coast."

"Lobsters ain't local, though. They're scarce around these parts now, so the lobsters I serve? Well Shane, you may have very well caught them. They come from Maine. But I still go out on my boat for fresh fish here, for other menu selections."

"Excellent." Shane takes Celia's hand in his. "We'll stay for dinner?" he asks her.

"I'd love to," Celia says while, yes, still smiling.

"Come on, kids." Noah leads them to the white tables set off to the side, overlooking the harbor. "I'll give you the best seat in the house."

Shane settles in his chair and glances at Celia across the table. She looks casual in her denim overall shorts, and her face is lightly tanned from the summer sun. Her side braid, though, is a little windblown from the ride. She wears gold bar earrings—he notices when she tucks a wisp of hair back behind an ear. And her expression? As relaxed as he's seen since he arrived at Stony Point. Which is a fine sight, as far as he's concerned. One that has him reach across the table and squeeze her hand. When he does, she gives him an easy smile—he notices that, too.

"He wasn't kidding," Celia says after Noah takes their dinner order.

Shane slips off the button-down he wears over his tee. "Wasn't kidding about what?" he asks while hanging the shirt over the back of his chair.

"This being the best seat in the house."

"It definitely is. Could sit here all evening." Their table is right at the edge of the weathered dock. Harbor water laps beside them; fishing boats and assorted sailboats are moored close by; seagulls perch on nearby pier posts, the birds seeming to listen in on their quiet talk. The air is warm; the moment, just right.

Which does something else, too. It has Shane feeling oddly vulnerable, sitting so close to this beautiful woman. A woman who has surprised him much the same way the Atlantic Ocean has—catching him off guard. Keeping him alert. Constantly noticing her.

"Long time no see, I take it?" Celia motions to Noah as he walks inside the tiny sun-faded restaurant building.

"Fifteen years."

"He just lit up, Shane. He was *so* happy to see you. I'm glad we stopped here."

"Me, too. Noah was like a father to me. Back when me and Kyle were teenagers, you know, our mother died. She'd been sick, and well, it was a rough time. Kyle and I were not always on the straight and narrow with no mom around."

"No mom, no anchor?" Celia asks.

Shane nods. "Dad did the best he could, but he had two hotheads on his hands. One of them—myself—did a stint in juvie. Which landed me with a mentor for community service a year later, instead of *another* juvie visit. Of course, now I see that decision was a last-ditch attempt to straighten me out before I became legal. Turn eighteen, and every infraction becomes a criminal record." Shane glances over toward the shingled hut just as Noah emerges, carrying a tray. "My attitude back then could've sunk his boat, poor guy," Shane says, nodding to Noah approaching.

"Here you go, kids. Your drinks, accoutrements," Noah says while setting down paper napkins and plasticware.

"We were just talking about you, Noah," Shane lets on. "Telling Celia I was surprised you didn't toss me overboard some days, years ago."

Noah gives Shane an understanding smile and only pats his shoulder before walking off.

In a dockside lull then, Shane notices something. He notices that Noah and all the commotion of seeing him again? Well, it kept him and Celia occupied. Distracted.

Truth be told, distracted from each other. He and Celia haven't met up in two days, since Saturday. Since that easy afternoon when they had lunch in the cool shade of his back porch. When she questioned who the lucky ones were in this little beach gang—then gave him a startling kiss.

So, here they are again. Together on the harbor, where a distant bell buoy clangs, and a seagull swoops low. The late-afternoon sun is warm; the salt air, pungent. But distractions? None around now.

And their words? Suddenly, few.

Shane sips his ice water, then leans a little closer, setting his arms on the table. "You seemed quiet before."

"What do you mean?" Celia asks.

"In my truck. Driving here. You're a mystery to me, Celia Gray."

She smiles at that. "I was just thinking about things."

Shane sits back and eyes her. "What was on your mind?"

After a moment, Celia tells him. "Memories, mostly. I remembered doing all this." She motions to the coastal restaurant, the harbor boats. "With Sal," she admits. "Cruising around on his Harley."

"The dude drove a bike?"

"A little bit. Sometimes he'd borrow Kyle's truck, too. And we'd drive all these coastal roads. Stop at cheap beach shops. Get takeout. And *always* hit up the ice-cream stands."

"Sounds nice."

"It was. But the *really* nice thing was that with him doing the driving? I could just sit back and look at the scenery. The swaying marsh grasses, the shingled cottages. And driving with you today? I realized I miss those days. They were so easy. Back then, I thought they would never end."

Shane, well he gets it. There have been a few instances in his own life that he'd once thought would never end. So he merely nods to Celia.

"Strike a nerve?" she asks.

"Just saying, I hear you. Sometimes life is such that you can't even fathom something ending. Especially something good."

Now it's Celia's turn; Shane sees it. She eyes him, sits back, tips her head.

"Maris?" she asks.

Shane turns up his hands.

"Have you talked to her?"

"Yesterday. She came looking for me, actually, to clear the air. Things didn't end good with us years ago. I guess it bothered Maris more than she realized."

"You never called her, back then, to fix things? Went to see her?"

Shane shakes his head. "It was just me and the sea for a

*very* long time. But we did talk, yesterday, Maris and I. And it's good now. We're truly old beach friends. Nothing more."

"Funny how life takes us on a ride like that, no?" Celia asks.

"Life. Time. But what happened is that all those years that went by? They did something. Something that helped. Like you told me about sea glass? Time has a way of softening things." Shane looks out at the harbor and feels a certain ease that's settled on him since yesterday. "Softening the rough edges."

"Isn't that the truth?" Celia asks, just as Noah and a waitress breeze by with two food-filled trays.

"*Mangia*, you two!" Noah says after he and the waitress set down their hot lobster rolls, house salads, fries and coleslaw.

"Wow," Celia whispers while arranging her food-laden plates.

"And how," Shane agrees as he stabs his fork at the salad. "So," he says around a mouthful of lettuce, cuke and tomato, "is your daughter back yet? Aria?"

"No. It's such a busy time for me, with the inn's grand opening just about two weeks away. All those Mason jars need to be decorated for the ribbon-cutting ceremony. And there are linens to wash and hang-dry. Curtains to freshen. And rowboat prep, too."

"Rowboat prep? That little vessel seemed sweet just the way it is. I had a very memorable ride with you that one night."

"Thanks," Celia tells him while lifting her lobster roll. The roll is toasted and stuffed with fresh, shredded lobster meat—all of it drizzled in butter. "But the boat has a shade canopy that needs to be installed. Lots of guests have already reserved daytime excursions. So my dad's taking care of Aria for a few days in Addison. Gives me some time to help Elsa. And," Celia says, then briefly closes her eyes at the taste of her lobster, "*that* is the surprise in all this. How my father *loves* being a grandpa to Aria—who'll be back Wednesday morning," she adds while patting a drizzle of that melted butter from her chin. "But it's hard to be apart from my daughter, even for a few days. I always miss her."

Shane nods, then digs into his lobster roll, too.

"How about you?" Celia asks him. "No children?"

"No."

"Maris really left a hole in your heart?"

"For a while, maybe. But it's more my line of work that's the issue. It's tough on relationships. Takes a certain breed of woman to understand what I do."

"That you lobster?"

"Absolutely. The hours are really long, and I'm actually gone for much of the year. In the cold months, on the offshore boats, a trip averages two weeks away, out at sea. Return home for a few days, then I'm right back at it on another trip out. It's the nature of the business."

"But not the nature of marriages?"

"You got it. So for now, I'm married to the sea."

"And you seem to love it, lobstering."

59

"It's what I do."

"Itching to get back?" Celia quietly asks.

"Sometimes. But that little bungalow I'm staying at, and heck, this dinner with you? Nice being right on the water, taking it all in," he says, lifting his cup in a toast to Celia.

She obliges, tipping her cup to his. "You know what they say about all this sea air."

Shane glances out at the harbor, and Long Island Sound beyond it. The sea is blue; the salt air, sweet. "Cures what ails you," he says with a slight nod.

～

"Hurry!" Celia calls to Shane later that evening. After dinner, they'd stopped at Scoop Shop for take-out dessert and now she waits beside the door on his front porch. "The ice cream will melt."

Shane is leaning into his truck and reaching for the ice-cream bag. "Coming," he calls over his shoulder. While hurrying to the porch, he drops his key ring, then scoops it up in stride.

"This Will Do?" Celia asks while taking a look around the porch.

Shane glances at the painted driftwood sign hanging from a string of twine beside the door. "The cottage name," he says as he puts a key in the door lock.

"Huh. This Will Do." Celia follows Shane through the living room, past the blue and green fishing floats hanging in the corner, past the carved sandpipers on the mantel, around the gray rattan sofa, to the kitchen. There, she walks to the door to the back porch. "*This Will Do* makes it sound like the cottage will just … suffice."

"Far from it," Shane agrees while putting their ice cream in the freezer. "The view alone makes it priceless."

"I'll say." Celia looks out the screen door to the open-air back porch.

"Why don't you make yourself comfortable out there?" Shane asks. "I'll grab some spoons and napkins."

So Celia pushes open the screen door and walks outside. She leans on the half-wall and takes in the sight of Long Island Sound. Above it, the setting sun paints a few low clouds pale pink. At the horizon, the vast sky fades to violet. And the deep blue Sound is glasslike at this twilight hour. What it does, that serene view, is mirror exactly how Celia feels right now. Oh, this will *more* than do.

Turning, she notices Shane's happiness jar on top of an old crate. It's right beside the door, so Celia picks it up and gives a look inside the jar. Dried pieces of seaweed edge the sand. To the side, she sees a smooth skimming stone. And there, next to a silver tea-light candle, is a white-gold diamond ring shaped like a sailor's knot. It had to have been Maris' old engagement ring—which Maris no doubt returned to Shane yesterday. Setting the jar back on the crate, one thing's for certain. Shane must see some light in that ring. Some light among the beach friends that still shines from a dark past.

Right then, Shane shoulders open the screen door. "How about a glass of wine first?" he asks, carrying two

61

glasses and a bottle of Verdicchio. "Ice cream later?"

"Perfect." Celia takes the two wineglasses and sets them on the faded white porch table.

"I always like this time of day at the beach," Shane tells her while filling her glass.

"The blue hour?"

"Yeah. Even when I was a kid."

"Lauren mentioned that your family rented a cottage here, back in the day?"

"Every summer. Especially after Mom died, my father always found a way to rent our usual place, a blue cottage over on the marsh." Shane fills his own glass, then takes a long swallow of the white wine. "My old man scrimped and saved so he could at least give his two sons that much." Shane walks to the half-wall and hoists himself onto it, leaning against one of the porch posts. "Give us some reprieve from our home life, which wasn't easy." Again, he sips his wine. "Every summer."

"So this beach holds lots of memories for you," Celia tells him when she sits on the wall, too, and leans on the post facing him. "Have you seen your brother at all?"

"Kyle? A little. Not enough, though. I talked to Lauren earlier, and she's setting something up so I can try again tomorrow."

Celia swirls the wine in her glass and glances out at the darkening horizon. "All you can *do* is try," she quietly says.

Shane finishes his wine, tipping back the last few drops. Their words are few, then, as the sun sets deeper below the horizon. But they're easy words, about summer. And the sea. About how the lobster boat skips like a stone over Penobscot Bay this time of year. As Celia sips her wine, Shane pulls his harmonica from the pocket of the open button-down shirt he wears over his tee. Sitting there on the porch half-wall, he cups the harmonica to his mouth. A few bars of music rise as sweetly as the salt air, the soft harmonica riffs drifting into the night, floating out over the Sound. It lulls Celia, that soft music, as though it's the melody of the summer sea itself.

Lulls her until the music suddenly stops.

"You're cold," Shane says.

"What?"

"You shivered. I saw you. Funny thing about this big open porch. It's just like being on the boats at sea. Sun goes down, the boys' jackets go on." He gets himself off the wall and hitches his head toward the screen door. "Come on inside, out of the damp."

Celia sets her wineglass on the half-wall, but she doesn't move. Instead, she looks from Shane, out to the low setting sun. Then back to Shane, still standing there, but holding the screen door open now.

"*Come on,*" he whispers, then walks inside to the cottage kitchen.

Celia still just watches. Sitting on that wall, she wraps her arms around her bent legs. Keeps an eye on that door, too, where a light just came on in the shadowy kitchen.

Still, she hesitates.

But doesn't she already know. Damn it, damn it. It's just been that kind of day. The kind leading to this moment. A

63

day leading to two choices. Oh, she can wave off Shane, hurry down those painted porch steps, go around the side of the cottage and walk alone in the evening darkness back to her own gingerbread cottage behind the inn. Her secure, comfortable home there. Can walk home to another quiet night by herself. The whole time, she can convince herself that things are good just the way they are, thank you. That she's accepted Sal being gone. That her life has filled up nicely without him here.

She sits back then. Sits back and unhooks her arms from around her bent legs. Swings her legs to the side and slips off the half-wall. Fiddles with her loose overall strap, raising it higher on her shoulder. She stands there longer, leaning against that half-wall. Until she takes one step, then hesitates.

Yes, she can leave. Leave right now and convince herself that she's gone on since losing Sal. Gone on, and her life is fine *just* the way it is now. Safe. Tranquil. Uncomplicated.

Or she can walk through that damn screen door straight to Shane Bradford on the other side.

# *eight*

***Monday Evening***

IT'S A SOUND AS FAMILIAR as the lapping waves. As the crying gulls. Usually Celia thinks nothing of it.

But not tonight. When she opens the squeaking screen door on Shane's back porch, that sound stops her in her tracks. But only for a second. Only until she steps into the kitchen and closes the door behind her.

"Be right there," Shane's voice calls out from elsewhere in the cottage.

What that pause does is this: It gives Celia a minute to get her bearings and look around the dimly lit kitchen. Mismatched dishes are stacked on open shelves near the sink. Dusty baskets of hand towels and napkins sit on the rack of a rickety-looking cart.

She turns, still looking. Trying to familiarize herself with a situation so rife with the unknown. Or maybe with the known. Maybe she knows just what's coming. A quick

65

shake of her head then, before gazing around again. First, up at the old ceiling covered in unfinished, narrow planks of wood. She walks to the kitchen table and brushes her fingers across Shane's short-sleeve button-down, slung over a chairback now. Takes a few more steps over to the side, where there's a tall aqua-colored cabinet. The paint on it is distressed, leaving the wood grain showing through. And there. She turns around. Shane's harmonica and cell phone are on the counter, the cell phone plugged in and charging.

And then? Well, then there's Shane—who she backs right into.

Shane, standing behind her with a long-sleeve denim shirt in his hands.

"Easy now," he says when she backs into him. "Here. Put this on." He holds the shirt up by the shoulders. "You're cold."

"Little bit." Celia slips an arm into one sleeve and waits as Shane straightens it. They get awkward—bumping this way, shifting that—until things line up. "Thanks," she quietly says while reaching her other arm into the waiting shirtsleeve. As she does, Shane helps her out, lifting the big shirt up close around her neck, then moving in front of her. There, his hands take hold of the shirt collar and pull the loose shirt on more snugly.

But those hands, well, they don't let go of that denim shirt. Instead, he tips his head, watches her and very gently tugs her closer.

So … So some things you know. You always know. Like

Celia knew—maybe since their first midnight boat ride—
that she wouldn't resist him. No, oh no. There's no
resisting this moment in the musty shadows of Shane's
cottage kitchen. There's only this. Only standing there in
front of him, and feeling the warmth of his nearness.

When she takes a small step, he gives another tug to the
shirt clasped in his hands. "*Closer*," he whispers, his voice
low.

She takes another step, then a tiny one, until there's no
room for any more. Until his hands shift from the shirt
collar to her side braid—which he straightens over the
denim shirt collar. But he doesn't stop there. Those hands
reach around her neck as he bends and kisses her.

The thing is, this kiss? It isn't hesitant, or teasing, like
the other few kisses they've shared. Those were merely
small tokens of affection, testing the waters.

This? Actually, Celia's not sure she's ever been kissed
this way before. Also not sure she's ever kissed a man back
the way she is now. Because the moment—which had been
quiet, and tentative—changes quickly. Now? Now there's
no thought. No uncertainty. Now there are sharp intakes
of breath. A greediness. And that denim shirt? The shirt
that was so tenderly placed around her shoulders? It's half
off within seconds. Their bodies, their hands, are a sudden
blur of motion. Of grappling, touching.

Particularly surprising to Celia, though, are her own hands.
Her hands tugging up Shane's dark tee. Her hands moving
beneath that tee—feeling the skin of his belly, his chest, his
shoulders—as she lifts the shirt up and over his head.

He stops kissing her only long enough for her to do that—then he's back at it, kissing her mouth, her neck. They move around his kitchen, bumping into the table and nearly toppling a chair before, still kissing her, Shane backs her up to the kitchen counter. His hands, well, then *they* surprise her. They reach around her sides and lift her up onto that counter, then move right back up to cradle her face, his kiss insistent on her mouth. It's all she can do to breathe.

And she loves it.

Loves it even more when those hands of his, those working hands strong from a life at sea, tug off that denim shirt completely and slip down the bib of her shorts-overalls. Slip those buckled straps off her shoulders and lift up her fitted white tank in one fell swoop. Oh, those hands—they leave no time for thinking. For deciding. They simply assert, and damn if she isn't thrilled to give in. And to take right back from him.

Yes, somehow, in between gasps and touches, between murmurs whispering her name and sighs answering back, her hands reach down and unbuckle Shane's leather belt. All while sitting on the counter and kissing him. All while feeling his every greedy touch on her skin, his caress beneath her bra—which he also gets off her—as his hand returns to her breasts.

Until he stops. Stops, his chest rising with deep breaths, his forehead pressed to hers. "You good with this, Celia?" he barely asks, his voice low.

She only nods.

"Come on, then," he says, reaching around her waist while she still sits on the counter, his body standing close.

So she does it. She wraps her legs around his hips, loops her arms around his neck and holds on just as his strong arms lift her *off* that counter and carry her down the short hallway to his bedroom. Somehow along the way, they manage more kisses, more touches as they hurry there. When he sets her on the bed, Shane gets all her clothes off, tugging the denim overall shorts down her legs, slipping his hand beneath her panties and sliding those off, too.

There are no lights on in the cottage bedroom. There is only darkness, which Celia welcomes. It frees her, somehow. As Shane moves over her, she lies back on the mattress, her mouth open to his. His hands, they touch her skin, her belly, her breasts, and in that sweet darkness, his mouth follows each touch. The pleasure in each kiss, in each surprise of his tongue, stirs her in ways she'd almost forgotten. In ways that then have her own mouth move down *his* neck, his shoulder, his chest and belly, as her hands push off his cargo shorts, his boxers. The shorts fall to the floor, his belt buckle clanking on the wood, the clothes a soft thump behind it.

When Celia looks at Shane lying there in the dark shadows, he props himself up on his elbows and motions her closer. She hesitates then, before moving her intimate touches, her scattered kisses back up his body until she's lying fully on top of him, her skin warm against his.

"*Celia*," he whispers. When her fingers trace along an inked drawing on his arm, he stops her with another kiss, all as his hands slide down her back and turn her onto the bed. Moving over her then, his hands, they gently stroke her hair, the side braid nearly undone. And that's his last slow touch as she kisses his chin, his neck, his mouth in a way pleading for him to make love to her—yearning for as much of him as she can get as they move together, as every bit of his body covers her, takes her, once—then again— on this hot August night, in his little beach bungalow beside the sea.

~

Later, they sit on the back porch. A heavy waning moon rises over the black water. That moon drops a swath of gold, leaving glimmering ripples on the Sound. The night is still now; the shadows, dark. Lanterns scattered across the painted floor, and on crates, throw wavering candlelight. He and Celia sit side by side at the weathered table.

"Here," Shane says, lifting a spoonful of his espresso-fudge-swirled ice cream. "Try some."

Celia gently takes his wrist and guides the spoon into her mouth, closing her eyes with the cool flavor. "*Mmm. So good*," she whispers, stroking his arm then, briefly tracing along the shape of a tattoo.

"You're very beautiful, Celia." Shane tastes another mouthful of his ice cream while not taking his eyes off her.

Celia says nothing. Instead she scoops a heaping spoonful of her mocha-chip ice cream and lifts it to *his* mouth.

"Good," Shane says. "But not as sweet as you."

Celia just shakes her head and keeps digging into her ice cream. She's barefoot, and wears only the long-sleeve denim shirt he'd put on her earlier. And her braid? Still there, though the auburn strands and wisps have unwoven so much, it's hard to tell.

Shane finishes his ice cream and gets up from the table. This night has to be remembered, and there's one fitting way to do so. He lifts his happiness jar from a crate and brings it to the table.

"What are you doing?" Celia asks around a mouthful of her mocha chip.

"You'll see." Before sitting beside her again, he pulls something out of his cargo shorts pocket—the same shorts he'd worn earlier in the evening.

"What's that?"

"The punch-out card from the ice-cream shop." He moves it beneath the lantern light on the table so she can see the two punched holes in the card.

"Save it," Celia says. "After ten punches, you get a free ice cream."

"I have a better idea." Shane opens the lid on his happiness jar and leans the card against the glass side, pressing the card into the grains of sand. After twisting the lid back on, he sets the happiness jar beside the lantern.

"I like that," Celia says, still eating. When she finishes her ice cream, she walks to the half-wall and hoists herself up. She hangs her legs over the outside wall and watches the night. Beyond, that heavy waning moon rises above the

71

water. Shane walks over and stops behind her. In a moment, he reaches for her unraveling braid, slides off the elastic and gently unwinds each thick strand. Her eyes drop closed with his touch.

"*Stay the night?*" he whispers into her ear.

Without turning, she raises a hand to his and slightly shakes her head. "I can't."

"Why not?"

"Elsa."

"Elsa?"

"She'll notice I'm not home and might worry. She's like that."

"I get it." Shane lifts his fingers through her unbraided auburn hair, feeling the wavy strands on his skin. "I'll drop off the boxes of Mason jars tomorrow, then?"

"Okay." After a moment, Celia motions to a neighboring cottage. "Look."

Still standing, Shane leans against the half-wall beside her. Lamplight illuminates lace curtains in the neighboring cottage's windows. And solar garden lights glimmer around decorative beach grasses in its yard. "It's a different world here, at night," he says.

"It is. Last summer," Celia's voice vaguely tells him, "when I was still staging homes, I loved to walk these beach roads—daytime or nighttime—to get decorating ideas. But there's something intriguing about an illuminated cottage."

"How so?"

"Oh, seeing inside to their nautical colors, and lazy paddling ceiling fans. Starfish leaning in the windowpanes.

Twinkle lights looped around porch railings. Sheer white curtains puffing in the sea breezes. Who lives there? Are they happy? Sad?" She looks over at Shane, touches his jaw, smiles lightly. "I covered many miles, glimpsing cottage life."

Shane stands there, leaning against the half-wall still. "With Sal?"

Celia nods. Just nods, then looks out at the moonlit Sound.

Shane hoists himself onto that half-wall, too, and sits beside her. But he doesn't face the sea, like she does. He faces his porch, his rented cottage. And takes in the sight of it. When he talks, he doesn't look to her. He's not sure why, either. Maybe he doesn't want to see some sadness about what they just did, inside. Some regret that they'll have to part ways in only days. Some wondering about why they even slept together. Or if they even should have.

Instead, he keeps his voice low when he speaks his thoughts. "That's why we're drawn to each other, Celia. We both know what it is to love someone who isn't there. We get what it's like to wake up every day and for one moment think that the other person's still with us." He pauses, then takes a breath of the damp salt air. "Dead or alive, doesn't matter. And we don't judge each other for that."

"No. We don't."

"And tonight, believe me, I'm aware."

"Of what?"

"That it might not have been me that you wanted, Celia. Inside." He looks at her then. At her gentle eyes, her silky hair, as she sits there wearing only his denim shirt. "But like the cottage name here …"

She squints at him, pausing before whispering, *"This will do?"*

Slightly, slightly he turns up his hands and looks away. "I'll do," he says beneath the dark sky, his words honest. But it's her silence then, that gets him to look at her. And he does, for a few long seconds. Still, that silence is unreadable. And her look, in the night's shadows, is too.

# nine

IF KYLE BRADFORD DOESN'T WATCH it, he's going to blow a gasket. He guesses Lauren knows it, too. That's why she got him up extra early—so that by six in the morning, he's arriving at the beach in his swim trunks.

"*Decompress,*" he says under his breath. "*Just decompress, guy.*"

It might help if there weren't a slew of personal headlines streaming through his mind. The list isn't long, but it's serious enough that it's on a constant loop: Shane being back here at the beach; things not being right between Jason and Maris; he and Lauren avoiding all talk about the elephant in the room. That elephant is the biggest part of the loop—their vow renewal day from hell. And as far as Kyle's concerned, that day needs to be acknowledged, or scrutinized, or tossed out into the sea breeze.

Standing at the top of the granite steps, Kyle stretches

75

his arms and inhales deep breaths of that salt air. One, then another. Lately, these sunrise swims have been doing the trick—yes, decompressing his thoughts. When he walks onto the beach now, the sun is just rising on the eastern horizon, making the sky blush. Even better, Kyle's alone at this hour. It's so peaceful here.

At the water's edge, he drops his folded towel, takes off his tee and mops his forehead with it. It feels like the heat of yesterday lingers, the way it's hot out already. He steps out of his leather boat shoes, too. After tucking his golf cart key into one, he wades into the water. And winces at the cold—something he never gets used to. So he stands there in his swim trunks, acclimating. The gentle current tugs at his ankles as small waves break around him.

Really, Kyle could stop time right here. Alone on the beach, standing in the sea. The sunrise is a masterpiece for his eyes; the lapping waves lull him. He steps out a little deeper, to his knees. There, he dips his hand into the water and blesses himself with his dripping fingers. Hell, his life can use any blessings it can get. Standing there, he swings his hands through the water once more, and dribbles the cool water on his shoulders, his face.

～

Lauren was good for her word.

As soon as Shane gets to the bottom of the footpath, he spots Kyle standing in the shallows. It's the perfect time to talk, right here, with no one listening. No one watching. So

Shane pulls Cliff's domino from his pocket and gives it a flip. A little luck might help him and his brother, both.

After hurrying across the boardwalk, he steps onto the sand. But he notices something while walking toward his brother. Getting closer to the water, Shane can't miss a purple jellyfish bobbing at the surface—which might be just the right icebreaker. So he keeps an eye on the jellyfish as he approaches Kyle from behind.

"Race you!" Shane calls out, getting his brother to give a look over his shoulder. "Move over and give me a swimming lane," Shane tells him as he walks closer. "Hell. You're like an old granny, standing there and tiptoeing in."

"Eh," Kyle says, waving him off and venturing a step deeper.

"Come on." Shane bends to take off his shoes, putting his wallet in one. "Let's do this."

"Where's your swim trunks?" Kyle asks, turning back and eyeing Shane.

"I've got shorts on," Shane tells him while pulling off his T-shirt. "Good enough."

"To the raft?"

"It's not too far for you?" Shane tosses his shirt in the sand and extends his hand.

Kyle squints over at him before emerging from the water. "You're on," he says as he reaches out and gives Shane a firm handshake.

Which is all it takes. Right away, they jockey for positions. When Shane gives his brother a shove, he notices a new cottage standing tall over to the left. It's a shingled beauty, with all the right peaks and gables overlooking Long Island Sound.

"Hold up," Shane says. "Old Maggie Woods renovated her dump on the hill?"

"Like hell." Kyle shakes his head. "New owners had to tear it down and hired Jason to build that stunner."

"Barlow, huh? I should've known."

"Yep. Woods never spent a dime on that mousetrap of hers. You should've seen it, at the end. Looked almost like a caricature, the paint all peeling and faded. The roof sloping inward. The deck railings covered in mold and bird shit."

"Jesus, sounds like an eyesore."

"To put it mildly. That one cottage disgraced the whole beach, man. And her yard? Hell, all the brush and overgrown trees were taking over the neighbors' properties. Pissed them off but good."

Shane considers the stately cottage that has since replaced Woods' hovel. "Remember the old bat standing in the shadows and spying on everyone with those binoculars years ago?"

"Sure do. What a pain in the ass Maggie was. I'm sure she still is. Moved ten minutes down the road. I've heard her new place is as much of a dump as the old place here. Pity *those* neighbors now."

"Yeah, well. Like Dad would say—Good riddance to bad rubbish." Shane does a few stretches, eyeing the water closely now. "Hey, give me some space, for crying out loud."

Kyle does. He moves further left, swings his arms, loosens up.

"On your mark," Shane says, bending into starting position at the water's edge.

Kyle looks over at him. "Get set."

"Go!" Shane yells, bolting into the Sound first and giving his brother a hefty splash before swimming away like mad.

~

*Easy*, Kyle thinks. *Slow and steady wins the race.* He lifts one arm, then the other, swimming smoothly. Gradually, he catches up with Shane. Until, *what the hell?* Kyle stops and stands in the now nearly chest-high water. "Shit. Shit!" he shouts.

Shane stops and treads water in place. "What's the matter with you?"

Kyle jumps back, then swats at his shoulder. "*Ow, ow, ow!*"

"Get bit by something?" Shane calls over.

"Stung is more like it. By a *monster* jellyfish. Hell, it's a big one," he says while dancing to get around it, all while pointing at the water.

"What about our race, you lightweight."

Kyle looks from the dark water where that jellyfish still hovers, then to his shoulder. "I have to put something on this," he says as he turns back.

"Suit yourself." Shane starts swimming to shore, giving

79

that jellyfish and its tentacles wide berth. "I win by default, loser."

Kyle glances back at him, then keeps walking toward the beach. The sun is rising higher now, and an early morning mist moves across the sand. "*Decompress, like shit*," he tells himself.

"How's that sting feeling?" Shane asks when he emerges dripping from the water and catches up on the sand.

"Burns like hell."

Shane steps closer, eyeing Kyle's shoulder. "Like a hot pepper might?"

"What?" Kyle shoves him away. "You prick. You *knew* that jellyfish was there, didn't you? Got me over into my … *swimming lane*," he says while air-quoting the words.

"Let me see where it got you." Shane laughs and walks closer again, dripping seawater the whole time.

Kyle glares at him first, then turns and shows him the red welt on his shoulder. "Damn it," he says, looking around. "Got your license on you? Or a credit card?"

"What?" Shane heads to his wallet tucked in his shoe. "Why?"

"I read it's the easiest way to scrape off the stinging tentacles." Kyle takes a plastic gift card from Shane and scrapes the edge of it over the sting. "I've got to get home and treat this," he says, tossing the card back to Shane. "Thanks for nothing."

"Anytime, brother." Shane salutes him, picks up his shoes and heads off in the opposite direction.

And if the sting can get any worse, it does a half hour later when Kyle's sitting at his dining room table. Lauren stands behind him, pressing a cool compress on the irritated shoulder.

"*Huh*," Kyle whispers as he sits there reading the newspaper while Lauren dabs.

"What?" Lauren pulls off the compress. "Did that hurt?"

"No, no. It's this. Look." He points to an article he's reading. "New study shows that second-born children are more likely to be troublemakers." He pushes away the paper. "Damn straight."

When Lauren leans closer to the sting for a better look, Kyle glances back at her right as she gives a small laugh.

"You asked for it, you know," she says.

"*What?*"

"If you can dish it out, you better be able to take it, Kyle."

"What are you talking about?"

Lauren walks around him, crosses her arms and squints at him. "A few hot peppers snuck into a grilled cheese sandwich? Shane served you back a stinging jellyfish."

Kyle looks long at her standing there in only a buttoned-up denim vest over black cropped jeans. Then he grabs the compress from her hand and dabs his shoulder himself.

"Point for Shane," Lauren tells him as she goes into the kitchen to start breakfast for the kids. "Tie game."

Kyle says nothing. Because damn it, she's right. Shane got him good. And Kyle's not sure which stings more—the actual tentacle sting, or that his brother evened the score.

In a minute, Lauren's back. She has a bottle of aloe lotion and pours some on a soft cloth, then rubs it on Kyle's sting. Right away, the lotion cools the burn and Kyle relaxes in his seat.

"Hope it doesn't bother you while you're at the diner," Lauren quietly says, still lightly rubbing his shoulder. "And that it feels better before we go to Elsa's tonight."

Then nothing, not until Lauren bends low to give him a kiss. She presses her lips to his cheek first, then turns his head and kisses him deeply—enough to get him to moan right into it, all while reaching his arms around her and sitting her in his lap.

"*Nothing a little lovin' can't fix, no?*" he whispers, to which Lauren swats him with that aloe cloth.

But she does one more thing, too. She kisses him once again, then brushes his jaw with her fingers and heads back to the kids' breakfast in the kitchen.

# ten

## Later Tuesday Morning

CELIA KNOWS. OH, DOES SHE know. But somehow, it didn't stop her.

Yes, she knows that Shane's days at Stony Point are numbered. She knew it last night in his bedroom. Knew it when he walked her home well past midnight. They crossed the night beach, then veered off to the hidden path to Elsa's inn. And it was like their secret was out, the way the dune grasses whispered around them. The moon knew, too. Waning, but still nearly full, it wisely smiled down on them. Then there were those tiny stars above, winking illicitly at the two of them. It felt like the whole world knew what Shane did with her behind his closed cottage doors.

Knew that they threw themselves into one fleeting summer affair.

But Elsa *doesn't* know—and *can't* know—so Celia's cautious with her words today.

As morning sunshine streams in through Elsa's kitchen garden window, Celia sits at the massive marble island. Jute twine, and folded yards of burlap, and rolls of lace ribbon cover the island surface. There are scissors and glue and tea-light candles, too. Everything they need to decorate many, many happiness jars for the inn's grand opening.

Elsa stands at the sink, spritzing her herb plants there. "So how is it that *Shane's* delivering the Mason jars?" she asks.

"Shane? He saw me yesterday, fussing with the backseat in my car—which was jammed. So he offered to pick up the jars in his truck."

At least that much is true. Still, as she talks to Elsa about Shane, Celia neatly lines up their jar-decorating supplies. Anything, she's doing *anything* to distract her from actually meeting Elsa's eye. Because she's afraid. Afraid Elsa will see some truth there. Or notice Celia glancing away while talking. Hiding some secret. Everyone knows Elsa picks up on that sort of thing. So Celia keeps her hands busy unrolling ribbon and stacking burlap pieces by color—tan, sage and white.

"But why didn't he bring the jars here yesterday?" Elsa persists as she pours a cup of fresh-brewed coffee.

"It was late. And we didn't want—oh, wait! That must be him now," Celia says, going to the window when she hears a vehicle pull into the driveway. "I'll help carry in the jars."

"We'll stack some in the dining room," Elsa tells her while adding cream to her coffee. "And some right here in the kitchen."

In her rush to get outside, Celia brushes against a stool at the island. She rights it and gives a quick glance back after straightening that darn stool. Of course, Elsa is still standing near the coffeepot. Calmly standing there, coffee cup in hand and watching Celia go.

Okay, and her raised eyebrow is *duly* noted.

In hurrying down the inn's front stairs to Shane's pickup, Celia smoothes her navy tank top and brushes a wrinkle from her cropped white jeans. Lately it feels like she's walking a tightrope—with her beach friends and her past on one side, and this recent black sheep on the other. She wavers between them, loyal to both now. Problem is, her beach friends won't be.

Shielding her eyes from the August sun, she watches Shane lowering the pickup's tailgate. His light brown hair is cut short, but a shadow of whiskers covers his face. He's got on khaki cargo shorts today, with boat shoes. And the sleeves of his black tee are ripped off and ragged at the shoulder. As he slides a box of jars close to the tailgate, Celia sees the tattoos covering his arms. Inked drawings that, in bed last night, she drew her finger along like following a maze. Which is what their relationship feels like—a maze, turning this way, surprising that way.

"Hey, Celia," Shane says when she walks around the truck and stops beside her. When she leans in for a better look at the jar inventory, he kisses the top of her head. And it's funny what can happen in the span of two seconds, maybe three. Funny but sweet, the way the sensation of that kiss gets her eyes to drop closed, her mouth to smile, before she turns to him. All in a few seconds, all their own. Celia sneaks a light kiss back, hers on his mouth, before her fingers gently brush his whiskered jaw.

What it all does, those scarce touches, is set the tone. While they talk about the morning; and Shane mentions his sunrise visit with Kyle on the beach; and Celia lets him know Elsa is all set up for jar-decorating; and Shane says he missed Celia after she left last night, those scarce touches continue. Scarce, but seeking something. Some reassurance. Some answer to their silent doubts.

Still, when Celia tries to finally lift a carton of Mason jars, Shane stops her.

"No, no," he says, unhooking her fingers from the edge of the box. "I'll get that. You hold the door for me."

He follows her to the inn's front porch, where she opens the door and calls out, "Elsa! First box is coming!"

"Oh, terrific!" Elsa hurries down the hallway to them. "Good morning, Shane," she says when Shane steps inside cradling a packed box in his arms.

"And a fine morning it is," he tells her back.

"Follow me." Elsa motions him down the hall toward the dining room.

But Celia waits there at the door. She hears their voices making small talk; hears Elsa thanking Shane for delivering the jars; hears Shane's voice reassuring her it's no problem.

"Aria will be back tomorrow," Elsa is saying as she

follows Shane to the front door now. "So we'll get this decorating for the ribbon-cutting ceremony done today, and get all this glass safely put away before the baby's home."

"We'll be busy," Celia tells Elsa. "The truck is *full* of boxes."

"Oh, let me have a look!" Elsa follows Shane outside, and by the time Shane returns carrying another box, Elsa's asking, "Have you seen Kyle at all?"

"We actually had a swim together this morning."

"*Magnifico!* I'm so happy," Elsa tells him on her way to the kitchen. "Kyle's stopping by with Lauren and the kids tonight. We're having dessert and a little visit." As she says it, Elsa is pulling Mason jars from one of the boxes and lining them up on her kitchen island. "And you still have three more days here, Shane. So I wish you two the best. *Famiglia* is so important."

This time, when Shane comes down the hallway again, he's alone. Which gives him the perfect moment to sneak a kiss on Celia's cheek as he passes through the front doorway. When he brings in a third box, Celia joins him in the dining room, where she begins sorting through the various jars.

"Do you think we can finish these today?" Celia asks Elsa over her shoulder. There are vintage wide-mouth jars in the dining room; shot-glass-sized jars covering the marble-top kitchen island; some crystal jelly jars near the sink; clear jars and pale blue, too.

"I think so." Elsa picks up a piece of burlap and wraps

it around one jar. "I just have to run out for cupcakes after lunch. I thought Lauren's kids would like that tonight. But I won't be long."

"Mrs. DeLuca?" another voice calls out then from the front door.

"That must be Cliff," Elsa says. "He needs a photo for the Stony Point newsletter, Cee."

And when Cliff walks into the kitchen, Celia glances there as Shane stops him. "Commissioner," Shane says, standing in front of him. He takes a camera from Cliff's hands, saying, "You've got two strapping arms, and I've got more boxes to carry in."

"What?" Cliff asks, just as Shane sets the camera on the counter and turns Cliff around.

"I think that'll be the last of the boxes, Elsa," Celia mentions before counting the jars in the opened cartons. "Rick really came through, down at the salvage yard."

"We might have to wash some of these, first," Elsa is saying in the kitchen, right as Cliff sets another box of jars on the counter there. "Cliff?" Elsa asks in a moment. "Why in the world do you have on garden gloves?"

"Oh, these." He holds up his hands right when Celia walks in to count Cliff's jars. "I was in a rush to get here and forgot all about them."

"Were you raking?" Elsa asks. "And wait, are those actually *mine*?" She steps closer and puts on her leopard-print reading glasses for a better look.

"I borrowed them," Cliff says. "When I was here the other day. Needed to pull out some leaves and brush from beneath the trailer. I swear I've been hearing something under there. Some animal shifting around. Scratching about."

"Did you find anything?" Shane asks, walking into the kitchen.

"No." Cliff pulls off the gloves and tucks them in his back pants pocket. "Nothing."

"Well, gentlemen." Elsa sits on a stool at her kitchen island. "Thank you for your assistance. Celia and I have *much* to do now."

Cliff reaches for his camera on the counter. "Hang on. Before I leave, I need that picture we talked about, for the newsletter. This way, I can invite the beach community to stop by for the inn's ribbon-cutting."

"Cliff, I'm in my *work* clothes." Elsa motions to her leggings and loose sleeveless blouse.

"No matter. You're always beautiful. Come on, now," Cliff insists as he raises the camera to his eye. "Picture day."

Elsa looks at Celia, who shrugs back to her. "In the dining room, then," Elsa relents. "Near the tall windows."

"Elsa," Shane says from the doorway. "Before you start, I'm going to take off."

"What?" Elsa motions for him to follow her. "Nonsense, Shane. You helped with all this and should be in the picture." She waves a hand at the boxes of jars covering her dining room table. "I'm the hostess, and you *have* been my guest."

Celia, well, she looks at Shane resisting and shakes her head. "Oh, Shane. There's no arguing with Elsa. Come on," she says. "It'll be fun. And it's good publicity for the inn."

"Publicity?" Shane asks.

"Let's face it, Shane," Elsa assures him. "You *do* get people talking around this little beach community."

"In that case," Shane says while joining them, "I'm in."

Celia and Elsa stand side by side, and Shane moves behind Celia.

"We need lots of smiles," Cliff informs them while focusing his camera. "Ready?"

Shane, Celia feels it then, he puts an arm around her waist and bends to her ear. "*Walk after lunch?*" she hears whispered close.

"One," Cliff says, adjusting his stance.

Celia silently nods and quickly gives Shane's hand on her waist a squeeze.

"Two," Cliff is saying.

"*Meet me on the boardwalk,*" comes to Celia's ear, Shane's voice low.

"And … *Sorridi!*" Cliff calls out, right as Shane gives Celia a slight tickle on her side. "Smile!"

# eleven

SITTING BENEATH THE SHADE PAVILION on the boardwalk after lunch, Shane fidgets with a braided leather cuff on his wrist while keeping an eye out for Celia. Not for long, though. Within minutes, she steps onto the far end of the boardwalk, most likely after taking the secret path from Elsa's, then crossing the beach.

So she slipped away. Shane wasn't sure Celia would, not with all those glass jars waiting to be wrapped and twined and filled.

But she did.

He stands and watches from the shadows beneath the pavilion as Celia approaches. Her step is light. She changed into mesh capri leggings, a long tank top and sneakers. A straw fedora is on her head.

"Got your walking shoes on," Shane says when she stops beside him.

"Definitely." Celia takes his hands in hers, gives a quick look around and sneaks a light kiss. "Let's walk and talk?"

"Sounds good, Celia. You know, I've been away from here for a long time." He unhooks his sunglasses from his shirt collar and puts them on. "Lead the tour on one of those cottage walks you told me about."

And so she does. They head down the Stony Point boardwalk and turn onto the sandy beach roads. The thing is, Shane's had some doubts since last night. Some wondering if the night was nothing more than two lonely people spending a few hours together.

Some wondering if Celia had any regrets.

Now Celia's voice lulls him like the calm seas do. How he's been missing that. Missing being on the lobster boat these late-August days when Penobscot Bay is sheer as glass; the air, warm; the sunset skies, pink. These are the times when the summer moon rises heavy over the bay, the moon seeming so close as its golden light spills on the water. The longer Shane's away from the sea, the more he thinks about it.

But all those longings sweep aside while walking with Celia. While listening to her soft voice mention different cottage names.

"Heron House," she's saying. "And over there," she tells him, pointing to a white bungalow sitting atop a sloping hill, "is Summer Winds."

Shane looks at the cottage needing a fresh coat of white paint. Sheer curtain panels hang in the windows, the curtains wafting like sails in a salty breeze. Trailing ferns cascade from shabby window boxes.

"That's the first cottage I staged here, last summer," Celia explains. "It's where I met Elsa. She stopped by to water the window boxes and we got to talking."

"The rest is history?"

"Pretty much."

Doesn't Shane know that history now, too. A year later, here's Celia—practically a widow, and a single mother raising a new baby alone. Shane walks beside Celia down one beach road and up another. She points out garden whirligigs—one of a robin with spinning wings. They wave to passersby headed to the beach, sand chairs and umbrellas in tow.

"Before last summer, I only staged houses in Addison, and wasn't familiar with the cottage vibe. So walking these fairy-tale streets, well," Celia says with a sigh, "it gave me coastal ideas to bring to my work."

Shane gets it, the whole fairy-tale streets thing. These painted bungalows and shingled cottages with their waving flags and clinking wind chimes, they'd have you think you stumbled upon some utopia. That life's as easy walking these streets as it is anchored in the calm bay in Maine. And sometimes, like right now, it is. Easy, easy, easy.

But not always. The tide, at sea or on land, always turns.

He discreetly takes Celia's hand in his as they pass a silver-shingled cottage with gardens of red geraniums. "You must love walking here with Aria now."

"Oh, I do. The sound of the stroller tires gritty on the sandy roads. The seagulls and salt air. It all lulls her right to sleep."

"You miss her."

"Always. My father's bringing her back tomorrow."

"Good. Hope I can see her this week."

Yes, easy, easy. A slow stroll, the afternoon air sunny, bees bumbling lazy over marigolds. A golf cart passes them; they veer around a speed-limit barricade. A few teenagers with tubes slung over their shoulders walk toward the beach. Flip-flops flip; voices ebb and flow like gentle waves.

When they turn onto the road near the marsh, Shane slows his step. "Now *this* is a very familiar street to me," he says.

"Why's that?"

"There's the cottage my father always rented for us, growing up." He nods toward a blue-painted cottage, on the left.

"Which one? With those yellow flowers?"

"That's the one. Kyle and I spent time, every summer, right there." Shane takes in the sight of the ocean-blue cottage. It's aged well. The shingles are the color of the sea; clusters of brilliant yellow flowers grow against the side of it. "Lots of memories inside those blue walls."

"Tell me one," Celia says.

"Okay, let's see." Shane walks a few steps closer and briefly lowers his sunglasses. "*Holy smokes*," he whispers then.

"What?"

He stops and points to a small white-framed window. "I can't believe it. See that sailboat propped behind the glass?"

"Sure."

"What a blast from the past. Me and my brother, oh man, we were just boys. We always took that very boat to the marsh across the street. Attached a string to the boat and put it in the water. Then we'd set it sailing in the hot summer sunshine."

"Sweet memory," Celia murmurs, looking at the little boat in the window.

Shane takes a step closer to the cottage. There's a fresh coat of white paint on the window trim. But the toy boat? Its white sail is weathered; its red hull, faded. "The stories we made up, kneeling on the banks of the marsh. That little boat bobbing in the water," he tells Celia beside him. "Pirates. And sea monsters coming after it. Heck, on rainy days, we'd play with it right in that same window, pretending stormy seas were rocking the vessel."

Celia tips up her fedora and squints at Shane.

"What?" he asks.

"So you were close with Kyle back then."

"Definitely." He nods toward the cottage window. "Playing with that boat? That's how we met the Barlows, too. In the marsh. One day, they stumbled on me and Kyle there. I still remember how they pelted our boat with rocks." Now Shane points to the marsh across the street, where the lush late-August grasses are tinged with gold.

"Rocks?"

Shane nods. "Grenades. They were pretending to be soldiers. Jason and Neil hung out there in the marsh a lot. Neil always wore his father's boonie hat from 'Nam. And they both wore camping vests loaded with canteens and supplies, playing out war stories. Throwing rock grenades in the water. Me and Kyle would join in sometimes." Shane stops talking then, and draws a hand along his jaw. "What a trip."

"It's really sad," Celia tells him as Shane reminisces. "You've lost a lot of time with your brother."

"Fifteen *years*. Have a nephew and niece I know nothing about, too." Lingering in front of the old blue cottage, Shane shakes his head. "*Shit*," he whispers.

"Hey." Celia squeezes his hand. "You *still* have a few days here. Maybe you and Kyle can talk more."

"Maybe. But that chance is beginning to feel like sand slipping through my fingers. My brother's so busy with the diner, and his family. It's hard to connect."

As he says it, an older man comes around from the blue cottage's backyard. He's spraying a hose and stops in the side yard, giving those yellow flowers a drink.

"Listen." Shane leans close to Celia. "Go with me on something," he quietly says before turning to the man. "Been admiring your place," Shane calls out, walking over to the side of the cottage. "Got lots of memories here."

"That right?" the man asks over his shoulder, still spraying those flowers.

"Yeah. My father rented this cottage, when I was a kid. Every summer. Been about twenty years now, since I've been here." Shane walks closer and looks the cottage up and down. "Amazing. Place looks the same."

"I haven't changed a thing." The man stops spraying,

tips up a baseball cap he wears and looks at the cottage, too. "Throw a fresh coat of blue paint on it from time to time. It holds up against the salt air."

Shane nods. Nods, then pulls his wallet from his back pocket. "Name your price."

"Shane!" Celia says from behind him. She catches up to him and takes hold of his arm. "What are you *doing*?"

"*Remember, Celia*," he barely whispers, leaning close. "*Go with me.*" She only nods, but stays right at his side as he tells this surprised man, "Must be a figure that'll do it."

"Come again?" the man asks, setting down his hose nozzle.

Shane lifts his sunglasses to the top of his head. "You must have some amount set in your mind. Some magic number. You know … a dollar amount just enough to let it go."

"*What?*" The man steps back. "Are you serious?"

"Never been more." Now Shane crosses the lawn toward that white-trimmed side window.

"My *cottage*? You want to buy it, just like that?"

"No." Shane hitches his head toward the small window, its trim bright white against the deep blue shingles. "I want that sailboat. Right there."

It just happens then, the way Celia pinches Shane's arm at the same time the man gives a quick laugh while saying, "Son of a gun! That old boat?"

"Means a lot to me." Shane stands still, holding his wallet open. "Every summer growing up, me and my brother set that very vessel sailing on the marsh."

"No kidding." The man, he looks from the sailboat

propped in the window, then to Shane. "Wait a minute. You one of the Bradford boys? Kyle, is it?"

"Not Kyle. Shane."

"How do you like that? I'm Walter." Walter hurries to Shane and gives his hand a good shake. "I *remember* your dad. Quite a guy. But he had his hands full with you two whippersnappers those days."

"That he did."

"He around?"

"No, sir. My father passed away. Been gone fifteen years now."

"Oh, sorry to hear that. I used to chew the fat with him when he showed up for the cottage key." The man steps back, hand to his chin. "And what about your brother?"

"Kyle." Shane motions in the direction of Back Bay. "He actually bought a place here at Stony Point, down on the bay. With his family. I'm visiting for a few days."

"And you're all grown up now. This your wife?"

Shane kisses the top of Celia's head. "This is Celia," he says.

"Nice to meet you," Celia tells him, shaking Walter's hand, too.

And Shane sees it. Beneath the brim of her fedora, there's a twinkle in her eye as she does it. She *goes* with him.

After their introductions, Walter looks back to Shane.

"So, my friend. What's it going to take to set that boat sailing my way?" Shane persists.

Walter waves him off. "Put your wallet away. The boat's yours."

"Seriously?" Shane asks.

"It's just been collecting dust propped in that window. I'll get it for you." He motions for them to wait as he trots toward the cottage's front door.

"Really?" Celia asks, leaning close to Shane then. "You thought having a *wife* might sweeten the pot?"

"Worked, didn't it?"

As he says it, Walter returns. The sail of the boat peeks out the top of a canvas tote he carries. "It's yours," he says, giving the tote to Shane. "I'm happy for you to have it."

Shane salutes him as he backs toward the street. "Means a lot, guy. *Truly* appreciate it."

Walter nods. "You two take care. Enjoy your afternoon." As he picks up his hose, he adds, "Stop by anytime."

"Bye now," Celia calls, giving a light wave as she walks with Shane on the sandy road.

~

And so it goes. Again. Life suddenly turns. Sets you on a different course.

They head to Shane's bungalow on Sea View Road. Sitting in the shade of his back porch, they have a cool drink. A quick one, though, because Celia has to get back to work. Afterward, once she returns to the inn, Shane takes that red sailboat into his cottage bedroom. There, he props it on his dresser top—carefully leaning the toy boat against an old painted box filled with dusty seashells.

Standing alone, he backs up a step, looks at the little

sailboat and adjusts one of its canvas sails. Somehow, it feels like seeing that blue cottage today, and having that boat again, well it could be a start to something. To maybe getting his brother back.

# twelve

*Tuesday Evening*

IF ANY PLACE COULD BE haunted, Kyle thinks it would be Foley's back room. Anything can summon the ghosts in those four walls—a creak of the wooden floor; dust swirling in the glow of the jukebox; the dim lighting over the booths. Sitting there now, can't he envision spirits dancing, or cards being dealt, or drumsticks rat-a-tatting on the old tabletops? Especially since Jason preserved the original room in the inn renovation. It's like time dropped the whole beach gang off in this room in their teens and never came back to pick them up. To bring them to adulthood.

No. Sitting in a refurbished booth after pushing open a sliding window, all it takes is Elsa to do that. She sweeps into the room now, which gets Lauren flying out of their booth and giving her a long hug after Elsa sets down a tray of frosted cupcakes.

"Celia told me she sent you all back here! How are you

both doing?" Elsa asks when she holds Lauren at arm's length, then looks past her to Kyle. "Okay?"

"We're fine now, Elsa. Just fine," Lauren says, right as Hailey comes up beside her.

"I thought about stopping by your house after the vow renewal day came and went," Elsa tells them while brushing her thumb over Hailey's cheek. "But gave you some space instead."

"Believe me, space helped," Lauren admits as Kyle stands and hugs Elsa, too. "Things have quieted down, and Kyle's, well … decompressing. Right, honey?" Lauren asks while stroking his arm.

"Trying to. I'm getting some exercise to calm my nerves," Kyle explains when they all return to the booth.

"Daddy goes swimming," Hailey says before joining Evan at the dinging-and-blinking pinball machine, where he's hitting the flippers to keep a ball in play.

"Yes, of *course*. I saw Shane today and he *said* you two went for a swim!" As Elsa says it, she pats Kyle's shoulder.

Which gets Kyle to wince—right as Elsa's words bring him back to the tribulations of his very adult life. Gone are the long-ago memories of sweet times in this place: hanging out on the deck beneath the light of the moon; getting half lit with a few cold ones after a hot day in the sun with the gang; feeling Lauren's body press close in a slow dance near the jukebox.

Instead, Kyle winces *and* tells Elsa, "Swim? More like Shane put me right in the path of the biggest jellyfish in Long Island Sound."

"Jellyfish?" Elsa cautiously sits across from Kyle. "Shane did that?"

"Oh, yes. Absolutely," Kyle assures her as he pats his stinging shoulder.

"It's a sibling thing," Lauren puts in. "You know how brothers can be."

Kyle nods. "His way of paying me back for something."

When Elsa sits back looking confused, and turning up her hands, Lauren nudges Kyle.

"Elsa," he says. "I can't get into the whole story, especially with the kids here. But ... well you know Shane and I stopped talking when my father died."

"They had a big argument," Lauren quietly says as she leans across the table to Elsa. "Estate issues, and well, things were said—"

"Before distance and time stretched that argument into one *long* rift." Kyle simply shrugs then. "But while Shane's at Stony Point, we've seen each other here and there. Like this morning."

"And we're still hoping for *some* resolution this week," Lauren says, more to Kyle than Elsa.

Elsa reaches over and squeezes his hand. "And I'm wishing on an ocean star for you two brothers."

"What's that noise?" Hailey suddenly calls out from where she stands at the jukebox.

"What noise, princess?" Kyle asks.

Her voice comes in a cautious whisper. "*Listen!*" As she says it, a whooshing *hiss* fills the room.

"Oh, that's nothing, dear." Elsa gets up, takes Hailey's

103

hand and walks to the doorway, with Evan following close behind. "It's Celia! She's steam-cleaning the inn's curtains. See?"

Celia turns in the room across the hall and gives a friendly wave, then presses a handheld steamer so that it emits a hissing puff of steam.

"Hey, Cee!" Lauren calls while leaning from her booth and waving back.

"Come on, kids," Elsa says, leaning low. "I got us some yummy cupcakes. You sit in the booth behind your mom and dad. There's a deck of cards there, too. You can play Go Fish."

"And we brought something for *you*," Lauren tells Elsa once the kids are settled in with their cupcakes, juice and playing cards. "You were going to be the justice of the peace for our vow renewal. *And* you let us use your *inn*, even though you're so busy." Lauren pulls a plaque from a bag beside her. "Well, after everything fell apart, we still couldn't let that day pass without thanking you." She hands Elsa the gift.

"Is this driftwood?" Elsa asks.

"It is," Lauren says. "Kyle got it right from the beach, and I painted the message and strung rope on top. To hang it on the wall. Do you like it?"

Elsa runs her hand across the gray driftwood and murmurs the painted words. "*The best memories are made gathered 'round the table.*" When she looks at Lauren and Kyle, tears fill her eyes. "It's just beautiful."

"Look." Lauren points below the words. "I painted

dune grasses on the bottom. They remind me of your secret path to the beach. And a seagull, soaring above."

"Well, I absolutely *love* this sentiment," Elsa declares.

"Same here," Kyle tells her as he gets up and grabs a few cupcakes and napkins from the counter. "Because many epic evenings have happened right around *your* dinner table, Elsa. Especially when you try out new inn recipes on all of us."

"But Lauren." Elsa looks up from the driftwood sign. "You really didn't have to do this."

"We wanted to." Lauren reaches over and clasps Elsa's arm, just as that steamer makes a hissing chuff in the next room.

"After what we put you through …" Kyle adds, biting into a vanilla-frosted cupcake.

"Oh, it was terrible," Lauren insists. "Don't deny it, Elsa. To have everything fall apart, after all the *work* you did prepping for that vow renewal. So now?" Lauren picks up her own cupcake, a chocolate-frosted. "We'd do *anything* for you. To make amends."

Elsa squints at them both. And gives a small smile. "Anything?"

"Anything," Kyle says before pressing the last of his cupcake into his mouth.

"Hold that thought." In two seconds flat, Elsa's up and out of the room.

"What?" Lauren asks while watching her go. In the sudden silence, the only sound is of Celia's steamer in the inn's gift shop down the hall. *Hisssss. Pfffft.* Lauren looks at

Kyle as he wipes his hands on a napkin. "What do you suppose Elsa has—"

But she doesn't have time to say more. Not when Elsa promptly returns with her leather ledger. She sits across from them again and opens it on the booth table.

"Elsa?" Kyle asks. "No, wait. When I said *anything*—"

"I took you for your word. So we're scheduling a vow renewal redo." Elsa motions to the open ledger. "As you can see, I'm booked for the inn's September grand opening, but in the weeks afterward?"

"Oh, I don't know." Kyle nudges the ledger toward Elsa and sits back in the booth. Quite honestly, the farther he can get himself from that botched vow renewal night, the better.

"Kyle." Lauren touches his face. "*Breathe*," she whispers.

"Listen." Elsa reaches across the open ledger and squeezes both their hands. "I see how strong your love is. And that love needs to be celebrated, especially with your two beautiful children." She nods to Hailey, who's watching Celia *puff* and *hiss* across the hall.

"Don't mind me," Celia says, entering the back room now. She pats Hailey's head, then walks to the side wall and fusses with the window curtains. "I want to get this steaming done before Aria's back tomorrow."

"Hailey," Lauren tells her daughter. "Sit with your brother and let Celia finish. You can watch from the booth."

When Hailey sits again, Celia walks close to her booth and plugs in the steamer. "Here, hon. You can try." She leans to Hailey, but aims the steamer in the opposite direction. "Help me press the button?"

Hailey reaches her tiny hand over Celia's finger as Celia presses, and a noisy puff of steam rises like a cloud.

"Can I try?" Evan asks.

When Celia gives him a turn, Elsa gets back to business. "Now, Lauren. What's your actual anniversary date?"

"September twenty-third. In about a month," she says around a mouthful of cupcake.

Elsa picks up a pencil and hovers it over that date's square.

"Wait!" Kyle grabs Elsa's arm, just as Celia sends a shot of hissing steam over the far window's curtains. "I mean, we might want the ceremony earlier. Before the kids are settled back in school. And homework starts up. And soccer practice begins."

Oh, Kyle doesn't miss it, the way Elsa warily squints at him before relenting. "Well," she says, slowly closing the ledger. "You let me know. And soon."

Kyle's sure *Elsa* doesn't miss it either, the way he takes a really long breath, as though there could never be enough air to calm his frazzled nerves. "Honestly, I just don't know if I can plan a vow renewal again. I mean, the stress …"

*Hisss. Chufff,* goes the steamer across the room.

"Don't *worry*," Elsa tells them. "We'll keep it low-key this time. Simple." She leans closer and asks hopefully, "Don't you think you owe it to each other?"

"If we have a redo," Lauren says, running her hand along Kyle's arm, "it *has* to be kept small."

"Real small," Kyle adds. "Just our inner circle here. *No* extended invites."

"Okay," Elsa says. "I can work with that." Again, she opens her ledger.

"Still, I don't know." Kyle wavers. *Already*, he thinks. *Already* he's stressed out with the thought of it all. "I mean, Jason's my best man, but he'll be so darn busy once that Hammer Law is lifted. Plus he'll be running on overdrive with *Castaway Cottage* filming."

*Pffffft. Hisssss*, sighs from the steamer, closer this time.

"Well, you just check with Jason and Maris *first*, then," Elsa tells them, looking from Lauren, to Kyle. "To be sure."

Kyle looks at Lauren, who raises an eyebrow when she looks at him.

Which only gets Elsa to drop her voice. "What now?"

*Ah, man*, Kyle thinks. *There really are no secrets at this beach.* Elsa's onto them. And so is Celia, the way she's suddenly hovering closer, hissing that darn steamer at the topper curtains on a window right next to him.

But it's Lauren who breaks the silence. "*You haven't heard?*" she whispers to Elsa.

A long *hisssss* comes as Celia watches Lauren now, all while drawing her steamer down a nearby curtain panel.

Elsa shakes her head.

"Fine. I'll tell you. But it's just between us," Kyle says. "Jason and Maris split up."

"*What?*" Elsa nearly falls back in her booth seat.

Lauren nods and takes *Elsa's* hand this time. "Jason actually moved out."

From behind them, only a long, excessive, puffing steamer *hisssss* fills the room.

# *thirteen*

---

## *Tuesday Night*

Nothing's worse than indecision.

Doesn't Jason know it. Because all day—from checking the planner app on his phone first thing this morning; to getting in his SUV and heading to the CT-TV studio in Hartford for a meeting with his producer, Trent; to getting back to Ted Sullivan's deck and fine-tuning an elevation concept for the Fenwick place; to tossing out scrapped paper sketches and setting aside the fat markers; to stopping at the White Sands shotgun cottage where there's no Hammer Law and demo *is* underway—his indecision undermined every thought.

Should he, or shouldn't he?

The question distracted him at traffic lights, so that other drivers sounded their horns for him to get moving. Had him checking the time on his phone far too often. Took his appetite so that he couldn't finish his lunch. Had him drive past the Stony Point railroad trestle—but *not* turn in beneath it.

Now, at day's end, that indecision still eats at him. Should he go see Maris, or shouldn't he? If he doesn't do something about it, there'll be no sleeping tonight. So he takes Maddy for a night walk along Sea Spray Beach. Maybe that'll help. The waters run deeper here than at Stony Point, the waves stronger, the wind sharper. The dog, splashing through the shallows, either picks up on that energy of the sea—or on Jason's conflict.

A conflict that comes to a head right on the beach, actually. Because walking along it, a cool wind lifts off the water, beneath a waning moon. The sight of that moon slung low in the dark sky, and the touch of the wind, remind Jason of one thing and one thing only—his wedding reception. Especially when he and Maris danced on the candlelit sand at Stony Point. He wore a black tux; Maris, a satin-and-lace gown. That night, a thin crescent moon also hung low, casting little illumination. But Mason jar lanterns dangling from decorative piers glowed along the beach. Sweeping drum brushes from a jazz combo on the sand kept the night's beat. And when a salty breeze lifted off the dark water, Jason took off his tuxedo jacket and draped it over Maris' shoulders. He held her face and kissed her then, before continuing their slow waltz on the beach.

That's the memory in his thoughts now, walking on this night beach.

Only that. Only Maris dancing in her gown, with his black jacket slung like a cape over her shoulders. Her hair was in a chignon; her braided gold chain and star pendant around her neck.

All of it, he remembers. The wisp of hair he brushed off her cheek. Her whispered nothings in his ear. Their bodies close.

A wave breaks at his feet just then. In its hissing retreat, Jason swears he hears Neil's far-off voice. *Seriously, bro? What the hell are you doing here tonight?*

And it's enough. All of it. The tormenting indecision of the day. The sweet memory of Maris in his arms that misty summer night. And his brother's spirit in the splash of a wave.

It's enough for Jason to whistle for Maddy, who lopes down the beach to him. She's got a dripping stick of driftwood clamped in her jaw; her tail is swinging.

"Let's go," he tells her as he veers up across the beach back to Ted's cottage. Finally, finally, his decision's made. He'll do it. He'll go see Maris.

Because it was exactly two years ago *tonight* that he danced with her beneath that sliver of moon, beside the sea.

Two years ago on *this* day that he stood at the altar and watched her walk down the aisle of St. Bernard's Church.

Two years ago that in his own vows to her, he told Maris how lucky he was to walk alongside the sea with her. To watch the stars above it together, and know life better when he does.

So he hurries back to Ted's cottage now. Crosses the deck, gets the dog settled inside, and grabs up his car keys from the countertop. Gives them a small toss in the air, decision made. His cell phone dinging right then with a text message convinces him he's doing the right thing. He reads the words from Kyle: *Happy anniversary, dude. 2 yrs ago right now was an epic night. Hope you + Maris are at least together tonight, and make it to yr 3.*

That's right. It's his wedding anniversary, after all. No matter what, no matter the hour, on this one day Jason will drive back home to Stony Point—if only to sit with his bride for a few minutes, maybe on the bench on the bluff. The waves will break, and he'll just hold her hand and remember.

⁓

Maris turns on few lights at home this evening. The glow from the jukebox in the alcove casts some illumination into the living room. But it's not enough light for her to see. So she switches on a table lamp next to Jason's chair. That's better.

For a moment, she stands still, her hand resting on the upholstered chair. In the dining room, she can see the bouquet Elsa sent today. The vase of flowers is on the table, beneath the dim lantern-chandelier. Tucked among the bouquet's greens are blue hydrangea and white cosmos blossoms. *Cosmos*, Elsa wrote in the card, *is the traditional second anniversary flower, symbolizing harmony. And the hydrangeas?* she noted. *Look at the blossoms. Each petal forms a tiny star, just right for a tiny wish today.*

A tiny wish. Maris hasn't made any wishes lately. *A wish,*

*a wish*, she whispers while walking to the mantel now. Her white conch shell sits next to a carved seagull mounted on mini-roped pilings. Anniversary cards are propped there, too. Cards from Lauren and Kyle; Paige and Vinny; Jason's mother; Cliff, even. There's also a hurricane lantern on the end of the mantel, beside a framed photograph. Maris picks that picture up now and runs her fingers over the image. It's of her and Jason, dancing on the evening beach two years ago, tonight. Tiki torches and candlelit Mason jars illuminate them beside the sea. Jason's dark hair is wavy in the misty air. A sliver of crescent moon hangs over the water. A jazz combo on the sand plays a slow waltz. Maris can still feel the sensory moments of the dance: the salty scent of the sea; the touch of a sea breeze on her skin; the whisper of Jason's words in her ear.

Two years.

How can a few days undo all that she sees, feels, remembers in that photograph?

It can't. Not if she doesn't give up.

So she makes her decision. She sets down the photograph, gets her cell phone from the kitchen and goes out to the deck. If she's going to talk to Jason today, on their wedding anniversary, she wants it to be outside, under the same starlit sky they'd danced beneath.

~

Grabbing a sweatshirt off the back of a kitchen chair, Jason goes outside to the deck and locks up the slider behind him.

With a glance at his watch, he thinks he can be at Stony Point in twenty minutes. He's been gone three days now, and tonight especially, he needs to see Maris. To touch her face. To hold her. But before heading down the stairs to the driveway, he crosses the deck and leans on the railing facing the sea.

And breathes.

And checks his cell phone, joggling it in his hand for several moments.

Running his knuckles over his jaw then, he turns around. Turns, but still leans on the deck railing. Still holds those keys.

Keys which he eventually drops on the teak patio table before pulling out a chair and just sitting there. Watching the waning moon rise over that sea.

～

Sitting alone outside on the deck, Maris hears small waves breaking on the bluff. When her phone suddenly rings, her eyes drop closed and she does it—she makes that hydrangea-petal wish. Wishes that it's Jason calling.

It's not.

It's Eva calling from Martha's Vineyard. And rather than get into the nitty-gritty details with her sister on her vacation, Maris only listens after the call goes to voicemail.

*Hey, sis. Happy anniversary! Two years already, so happy for you. You're probably out to dinner right now, but I wanted to call. Hope things are better for you guys since we talked Saturday. Call me later, okay?*

114

Maris slides the phone away. If only it were Jason who had called. It might've helped things to talk, even a little. How she misses his voice. In the backyard beside her, the big maple tree rises in dark silhouette against the night sky. There's a slow chirp of lazy crickets on this warm night. She finally looks at her cell phone again, pulls up Jason's number … and hesitates. And thinks of a few *days* ago, not two years ago. Thinks of their strained and failed road trip to Vermont last weekend, an excursion meant to celebrate their marriage.

Far from it, the tense words they flung at each other only sent them home.

Sent their simmering argument and punctuated silences to the kitchen, to their bedroom.

And ultimately sent Jason packing. He's miles away from Stony Point, and from her.

With all that in mind, she looks at Jason's number on her cell phone screen, flicks that screen off and sets her phone on the patio table.

Out over the Sound, the same moon rises, in the same sky they'd danced beneath two years ago—Jason's tuxedo jacket over her shoulders, her wedding gown's small train brushing the sand.

A memory, and nothing more.

# *fourteen*

## Early Wednesday Morning

WHEN JASON'S ALARM CLOCK WAKES him, he reaches for it and turns it off. A little more sleep will do him good. So lying on his back, he tosses an arm over his eyes.

But only for a minute. Because the day waits for no one, and Lord knows his every minute is booked. So he sits up, lifts the sheet, swings his legs over the side of the bed and gets to it. Stands right up, and falls promptly—and heavily—to the floor.

The sound alone is more frightening than the fall. There's a violence to the whole thing, to the way he crashes down—grabbing at something, anything, so that his arm hits the nightstand, which knocks over the lamp. The thumping bang of his body landing on the hardwood actually scares him. And gets his heart pounding as he lies there wondering if he's injured now. After a minute of catching his breath, he slowly moves his arms. Hands. Legs.

And foot, God damn it. *One* foot.

It's been years since this has happened. Since he's woken up and *forgotten* he's missing half a leg. Woken up and jumped right out of bed—ready to walk over to his dresser, or the bathroom, or the window—then taken a nasty fall across the floor instead.

Propping himself up on his elbows, he still hears that godawful sound of his body hitting the floor. Hears the dog, too. Her collar jangles as she scrambles up the cottage stairs and stops in his doorway. Stops, then walks slowly to him, her head down, tail slowly wagging.

"It's okay, Maddy," Jason tells her as he manages to pat her head. If he can just crawl to his bedside chair, he'll get his bearings.

Except there is no bedside chair here at Ted's place.

"*Shit*," Jason whispers, letting himself sink back to the floor. Again he throws an arm over his eyes. And feels his heart still beating too hard. *Shake it off*, he thinks, just as the German shepherd's wet nose nudges his hand.

It strikes him then, why it happened. Why he got out of bed the same way he did for all of his life—prior to the motorcycle accident—when he still had both feet. And those two feet would hit the floor running.

It's not that he's in an unfamiliar bedroom. It's because of yesterday. It's because things aren't right with Maris, not to mention the whole anniversary screwup and the way he let that day pass.

It's because he's not thinking straight—as his fall nicely reminded him.

After struggling to stand, he shuffles back to the bed, sits and notices the mess now, left over from his trying to *break* that fall. The alarm clock and green-glass bedside lamp are askew on the nightstand. He reaches over to right them, then straightens the nightstand, too. Finally, he has to orient himself after that damn plummet to the floor. So he does nothing but sit on the bed to calm his heart rate while looking around the room. The walls are paneled with whitewashed boardwalk planks, and thin white starfish line a high shelf running across the far wall. Another lamp, and a basket of seashells, is on the painted Shaker-style dresser.

With a long breath, Jason spots what he needs—his forearm crutches leaning against the wall near his bed. Not close enough to grab without taking a few hops. Which he manages. But when he reaches for the crutches, one falls to the floor. Keeping a hand on the wall for balance, he leans down and scoops up the crutch, hooks both of them on his forearms, and makes it into the bathroom. He'll feel better after a shower.

"Damn it," he says, looking into the glass-enclosed shower stall. He forgot to buy a stool to sit on. And the old webbed chair he used yesterday in the outdoor cabana just won't cut it inside. Next thing you know, he'll be scratching up Ted's new shower floor. So he looks around for a stool, checking the other bedrooms, a closet. But, nothing. And there's no way he'll risk slipping, standing on one leg in this unfamiliar shower. He could always shower again in the cabana outside, but he'll lose too much time hauling his stuff out there now.

So he skips the shower, takes off his tee and—still on his crutches—washes up the best he can in the sink instead. When he dries off afterward, he holds the towel to his face for a long moment, pressing it close over his eyes and just breathing before lowering it and seeing his reflection in the bathroom mirror. Which gets him to draw a hand over his unshaven jaw, then turn and head back to the bedroom to put on his leg before shaving.

Except his prosthesis isn't there.

Still in his pajama shorts, he goes downstairs. Well, here's a difference between living at Ted's and living at home: Here, Maddy's not nipping at his crutches as he maneuvers the stairs. Instead, she watches him from the bottom. Her tail thumps the floor; she whines; sits; stands again.

Out of sorts, Jason thinks. Just like he is.

Still on some home-autopilot, he instinctively turns into the living room to put on his leg. Except here—*unlike* at home—there's also no prosthesis in the living room. So he heads to the kitchen, where he actually left his prosthetic leg leaning against a chair. If he could just get the leg on already, he'd feel better. Balanced. Sitting now, he takes the silicone liner and sock from the chair and holds them to his stump. The process is such habit as he aligns everything, rolls the materials up to his thigh, then carefully smoothes it all out. Finally, he presses the prosthetic limb onto the end of his left leg before standing and getting all secure and in place.

Next, the dog—who's been shadowing his every move

ever since he crashed onto the bedroom floor. He fills her bowl, only to have her promptly scatter the kibble all over the floor. "Slow *down*, Maddy," he warns, then gets a dustpan from the utility closet, sweeps up the dry kibble and dumps it in the trash.

"Coffee, coffee," Jason says quietly after putting away the dustpan and opening the kitchen blinds. The past two days, he had coffee out: with Kyle at an oil-change garage Monday, and alone at a café down the road yesterday. But he doesn't much feel like sitting at a restaurant table again. So he checks one upper cabinet, then another, looking for coffee filters. "Come on," he says under his breath, before opening a drawer and finding them. Okay. Now, a coffee scoop. Naturally, it might be in the flatware drawer. He opens one drawer to find potholders and hand towels. The second has forks, spoons, and yes, a coffee scoop. The rest is easy: scoop out coffee and get the coffeepot brewing while he goes upstairs and shaves.

And nicks himself. But good, he realizes when he turns his face and sees the cut in the mirror. "*Damn it*," he whispers while ripping off a piece of toilet tissue and sticking it on the bleeding cut. Doesn't help matters when he looks more closely in the mirror and sees how haggard his eyes look.

But if he gets busy putting on some outfit or another he won't have to think about that. In the guest bedroom, he grabs a button-down from the closet and a clean pair of shorts from the dresser drawer. Problem is, he usually gets dressed *before* putting on his leg. So now he sits on the bed

120

and easily takes his pajama shorts off, because they're loose-fitting. Putting on the cargo shorts is more of a struggle as he gets one leg started, then manipulates the khaki shorts over his artificial foot and up over the prosthetic limb. That done, it's back downstairs for coffee. Of course, he's already behind schedule, dicking around with this drawer, that cabinet, no shower stool—and falling out of bed.

And he's back at it in Ted's unfamiliar kitchen, opening one cabinet, then another, before finding a coffee mug. Next up? Toast, at the very least. There's got to be a toaster around here somewhere. But when a quick glance proves otherwise, he waves off the breakfast thought, telling himself, "Eh, hell with it."

Coffee will suffice for now. So he sits down at the table. Sits there and sips his coffee. Another sip, before adding a reminder to his cell phone: *Hardware store for shower stool.*

As he types in the message to himself, Jason can't help but notice his overloaded inbox. There are emails from Trent, Mitch Fenwick, something from the town zoning office, a new client, contractors. The number of unread emails is enough to get him to set aside the cell phone and just drink his coffee.

Until that damn phone dings with a text message this time. A message from Elsa that he cannot ignore. He reads her clip words: *Name a time and place good for you Friday evening. We need to talk and I won't take no for an answer.*

No greeting, no niceties. Okay, so she's onto his absence, and *doesn't* like it. Leaving the phone there in front of him, Jason finishes his coffee before finally answering Elsa with a time and a place.

That done, he slides the phone to the side, closes his eyes and raises his fingers to softly pat his tired eyelids.

And so his day begins.

~

*If she'd thought the hurricane was frightening during the day, nighttime gives new meaning to the storm. With the power out, the cottage rooms are black. Outside is black. The sea is black.*

*So is the sound. It's that ominous, the blowing wind. In darkness, the wind seems almost supernatural, the way it whistles. And that whistle is what spooks her. It makes her think some spirit's following her down the cottage hallway, and up the stairs. That low, foreboding whistle has her glancing over her shoulder. Or like now, quickly closing the door behind her, then leaning on it to keep the spirit, the whistle, out.*

*At least a candle burns steady on her dresser top. The candle flame throws barely enough light to get her bearings. But she does, still leaning on the door and looking around the shadowed room. Her overnight bag is on a chair near the closet. An extra blanket is folded at the foot of the bed. And on the dresser, beside the candle, is a tarnished silver vase. It's pitted and faded, but filled with the most beautiful saltspray roses.*

*Oh, that seems months ago, not days, when she and the other women here took shears and clippers and went out on the dunes. They cut all the flowers they could before the hurricane struck. Now those wild roses are scattered throughout the cottage. They're slightly wilting, but their fragrance lingers. On her dresser, the candle flame beside them flickers in a bit of wind that makes it through these old cottage walls. When that flame wavers, shadows dance inside the room.*

*But it's the light knock on the door behind her that gets her to jump.*

Maris pauses her fingers over the laptop keyboard, then hits the Save button on the latest chapter of DRIFTLINE. Rolling her chair back, she checks the pewter hourglass to see how much sand is left to fall. It looks like a few minutes' worth, but it's hard to tell. The old shack is dark this morning. She didn't light any of the lanterns, and draped a light blanket over the window to keep out the sun. It helped to channel that darkness, as she wrote about it.

Wrote about the flowers, too. She gets up now and walks to the table where she left the tarnished silver vase filled with days-old hydrangea blossoms and wild beach roses. More than a week has passed since Jason picked the flowers for her. Last Monday, before any of them even knew Shane was still here, Jason put the wildflowers in that silver vase and left her a note, wishing her a good writing day. The flowers are faded now; the blossoms, drooping. She bends close and inhales. Yes, their scent still lingers.

Back at her desk, Maris flips the hourglass for another hour of writing time, just as someone knocks at the shack door. Her heart stops, because it can only be Jason. Jason making up for not getting in touch yesterday, on their wedding anniversary.

"It's open," Maris calls before spinning around in her swivel chair. "*Elsa?*" she asks.

Elsa stands there wearing a black sheath tank top with faded ripped jeans. She has on big sunglasses, and thin gold bangles hang from her wrist. From the doorway, she just gives Maris a sad smile.

"Oh, Elsa." Maris sits back with a long breath. "You know."

⌒〰

Oh, does Elsa know. It was all in her hug, and in her sympathetic pat on Maris' back. But the look Elsa gave her said she wants answers.

So on their way to the house, where Maris then brings a coffeepot and mugs outside to the deck, she tells all. *Yes, Jason left. On Sunday. Sea Spray Beach. Ted Sullivan's cottage. No, he hasn't been back. We have no plans yet. Barely talking.*

Grabbing a box of powdered doughnuts from the kitchen counter, Maris heads back out through the slider. "Not like your inn cuisine," she says as she sets down the box beside their two coffee mugs.

"That's all right." Elsa lifts out a doughnut and bites in, then rubs her fingers together to get off the sugary powder.

"I really only have an hour, Aunt Elsa. I have to get back to my writing."

"Maris." Elsa lifts her cat-eye sunglasses to the top of her head. "How can you even *think*, with Jason gone?"

"Ironic, isn't it? But it's like my emotions are just what the story needs. The words don't stop." Elsa takes another bite of the doughnut, and Maris sees it. She remembers

124

Jason telling her that Elsa is a closet junk-food junkie. And here's proof, the way Elsa digs into that sweet store-bought doughnut.

"Is the book almost done?" Elsa manages around a mouthful of pastry.

"Pretty soon. The first draft, anyway."

"And what do you hope to do with it when it's complete? How will you get it published?"

"Right now, I'm *only* focusing on finishing it, and on doing right by Neil's manuscript. I'll explore my publishing options when the time comes."

"Okay." Elsa takes another bite of her doughnut. "Okay. And what are your options with Jason?"

It's the way she says it, with such sadness, that breaks Maris' heart. She knows that Elsa loves Jason, too, like a son. "How did you know he left?" Maris asks, instead of answering.

"Kyle and Lauren visited me last night. It just came out in conversation. But don't blame them for telling. They meant no harm, and are more worried than anything else."

Maris nods. She still has the text message Kyle sent her Monday after talking with Jason at some oil-change garage. She's read the message so often, it's memorized. *Not good, Maris. Not good. Could not get through to Jason.* The message scares her still. It must've scared Kyle, too.

"I get it," Maris tells Elsa now. "I get why they told you. But please. Please don't let Eva know, if you should hear from her."

"She's still at her parents' place on Martha's Vineyard?"

"Yes. Eva, Matt and Tay made a vacation of it, until the end of the week. And if Eva finds out Jason left, she'll hightail it right back here."

"I won't let on." Elsa leans forward and clasps Maris' arm. "But tell me, why *did* Jason really leave? Did he find out about your engagement to Shane?"

Maris sips her coffee. "He did. But it's not just that." She thinks of last Friday night, when Jason walked into her writing shack when Shane was there. When the air was charged with tension, and history, and love, too. Yes, love—all left over and twined together with her and Shane's past. But she can't tell Elsa that. It's too private, too much. "Look, we've both made mistakes," Maris admits. "Jason has. I have."

"Mistakes?"

Maris only nods.

"And it's personal?"

"It is."

"You know you can tell me anything, Maris."

"Not this."

Elsa takes that in and sips her coffee. After a moment, she talks more. But about the summer now, and how it's been hard on Jason.

"Which is why," Elsa says, "I *still* suspect his leaving is more tied in with *Neil*, than with Shane."

"I'm really not convinced of that."

"Let me explain something. It might help you understand."

"Go ahead, Aunt Elsa. Please."

"Okay. I lost Sal last year. And still I can think, *Oh, I*

*remember last August when Sal was around, laughing at his birthday party.* Or, *A year ago, Sal was here when that tree limb fell on the deck.* Or I can still *hear* him telling me, *I'll be seeing you, Ma,* right before he went into surgery."

"So what are you saying?"

"That my memories are *fresh*. That it sometimes still feels like Sal just, I don't know, went back to work on Wall Street. Like he's not gone forever, because the memories are *that* close. But after ten years? What will I have left then? What memories won't have faded away with time? I'll lose even those— remembering what Salvatore looked like, how he sounded. And it *won't* be easy." She gives a sad smile. "Like I'd imagine Jason's experiencing now, with Neil's loss, a decade later."

Maris slightly nods, then gets up and leans on the deck railing. Seagulls swoop over the distant bluff. When she turns back, Elsa is watching her.

"What is it, dear?" Elsa asks.

"I get it, what you said just now." Maris looks long at her aunt while tossing around a thought that's been on her mind lately. "But how would you feel if on some level, you felt *responsible* for Sal's death?"

"*What?*" Elsa whispers. She crosses the deck to where Maris stands. "Are you saying that Jason was responsible for Neil's death?"

"I'm *not* saying he was. But *Jason* might think so."

"Why?"

Maris looks out at the dewy morning lawn before answering. "Okay. I'm going to confide in you ... something very, very private."

127

"Maris?"

"Jason was *driving* Neil's bike that day." The brief silence from Elsa isn't surprising, as she processes what Maris just said. A silence that gets Maris to simply nod.

Elsa's shocked words, when they come, are scarce. "No, no."

"No one knows. It's not even in the police reports."

"Oh, Maris."

"It's true. And this is *strictly* between you and me."

"Of course."

Elsa says little more while Maris tells her bits of the story: how Neil tossed Jason the keys that day; Neil's last words in Jason's ear; Ted's car coming up behind them; a whirlpool of roaring; Jason wrenching the motorcycle a few feet over; the force of Neil's weight on his back.

But as they stand there on the deck, looking out at the sea, Maris feels Elsa's hand clasp hers on the railing.

"Will you go see him at Ted's?" Elsa finally asks.

Maris understands. What more can Elsa say? And of course, she'll expect Maris to reply with, *Yes. We'll talk. I'll be with him through this.* The thing is, Elsa *hasn't* seen Maris plead with Jason to come back. Hasn't seen her unload her worries on Kyle.

Didn't see her wait all day yesterday for some word from Jason on their wedding anniversary. Anything.

"Listen," she tells her aunt. "It was Jason's choice to leave. I love him, but I'm not going to beg." The distant cawing of seagulls rises from out over the bluff. And a sea breeze lifts off the Sound, blowing wisps of her hair. "If Jason wants space," Maris says, "then space is what he's going to get."

# *fifteen*

THE SALT IN THE AIR feels heavy. Almost tangible, without a sea breeze stirring it around. Shane stands at the water's edge and looks at the lavender horizon as the sun sets. It's the twilight hour—the moment when the sea seems to calm; the air stills. A frozen moment, almost, holding on to the day. He walks along the sand beneath the high tide line and scoops up a few good stones. They're smooth, and just the right shape for skipping over that glass sea.

Before throwing a stone, though, he stands and just looks out at the water, the sky, the wispy clouds. The nice thing about skipping stones is that it clears his head, sending troublesome thoughts right out over the sea, too. So Shane does it. He hooks his arm in a side throw and sends a stone flying. Fly it does, skimming over the Sound's surface, straight out, then veering left.

Joggling a few more stones in his hand, he keeps walking toward the rocky ledge at the far end of the beach. The lone cottage on stilts there rises from the sand. Pausing, he hooks another flat stone out into that sweet salt air, right at the surface of the sea. It does too many skips to count, leaving a plume of sea spray in its wake.

Followed by another flat rock skipping right past it? Practically putting Shane's stone to shame? He turns and sees Kyle just behind him and pointing to *his* still-skipping stone.

"Creamed you," Kyle tells him.

"Shit, man." Shane shakes his head and looks again to where the stone zigged and zagged. He also gives a nod to an approaching couple wading in the shallows. All the while, his brother bends to pick up another stone. At the same time, a jogger comes up behind Kyle, announcing, *On your right.*

"Good night for a run," Shane tells the jogger, who waves in return when he runs past. Shane keeps walking then, the small waves breaking at his feet. He's still holding a few stones, but doesn't throw any. Not until Kyle gives a light whistle, hurrying to catch up with him. So Shane waits while throwing another stone over the sea.

"Sup, dude?" Kyle asks when they start walking, side by side.

"Finally got out on the water." Shane tips up his newsboy cap and looks over at Kyle. "Tooled around on the Sound with Noah today. Remember him?"

"Your old captain?"

"That's right."

"What's he up to these days?"

"Owns Lobsterland now," Shane tells him. "Little seafood shack couple towns over. We caught fresh fish for his menu."

"Not a bad gig."

"You just clock out from the diner?"

"Half hour ago. Sweltering behind the stoves today." Kyle throws another stone. "Felt like a walk before heading home."

"Yeah." Shane can see Kyle's in his work clothes: black pants, black tee. "Where's your wife? Kids?"

"At Lauren's folks'. Probably just finishing up dinner." Kyle grabs up another flat rock off the sand. "What about you?"

"What about me?"

"You never married? No wife back in Maine? Kids of your own?"

"No."

"Ever come close?"

"Only once."

Of course Kyle knows. They both do, without saying anything. Shane's *once* was Maris.

"Been in a few relationships. You know," Shane goes on, walking the packed sand. "But it's a trade-off, lobstering on the boats. Being gone for long spells. Doesn't work for some women."

"Maybe someday."

Shane tosses up a stone and catches it midair. "So …

you got a few minutes?"

"I could. Why? You want to clear the air?"

"Something like that."

"Okay. But first, come on." Kyle gives the rock in his hand a shake. "Bet I can out-skip you, tough lobsterman always out on the ocean."

"Bullshit. I'll skim circles around you."

"Do it, then."

Out of the shadows up ahead, a scruffy dog gives a random bark at them. The woman walking it pulls the dog close, apologizing to them as she does.

Shane salutes her, then resumes walking the water's edge.

"Yo, Shane."

Shane looks back over his shoulder.

"Chicken?" Kyle asks, getting into throwing position.

"Like shit." He returns to Kyle's side. "Go ahead, before it gets too dark to see."

So Kyle does, giving his all to the throw. Of course he has a perfect stone, too, sending it skimming atop the water in skips too many to count. "Your turn," Kyle tells him as he brushes off his hands.

"Something riding on this?" Shane asks as he pulls a stone from his jeans pocket and turns sideways.

"Seriously?"

"Yeah."

"Jeez, you remind me of someone. Friend of Elsa's son, always betting … Well, anyway," Kyle drifts off as two women walk by, chatting and giving a wave. "You got a brew at that cottage of yours?" Kyle asks Shane. "Too crowded to talk much here."

"No. I'm out. We'll grab a six-pack. Loser buys."

"You're on. My truck's in the lot here, I'll drive." Kyle motions for Shane to go ahead and skim. So Shane lifts that stone, two-handed, to his chest as though he's a pitcher about to throw the winning ball. He studies the dark water lapping at their feet, turns and flings his stone—sending it spinning over the water. When he looks at his brother, Kyle's texting on his phone.

"I know, I know," he says to Shane while plucking out his message. "Let me just tell Lauren where I'm headed. And that I'm buying."

◦~‿

"What's this?" Shane settles in the passenger seat of Kyle's old pickup. He cranks open the window, then lifts a box of raisins from the console between them. "Snack food?"

"Oh, those. Give me some," Kyle says, extending a hand as Shane shakes out a few raisins. "Lots of antioxidants in them. Fiber, too, to improve blood sugar levels. Which keeps you calm. Zen, you know?" Kyle tosses a few raisins in his mouth before starting the engine. "It's either raisins, or smoking."

"No contest." Shane helps himself to a few raisins, too, as Kyle drives the winding beach roads. "Hey. I hear that Sal fellow was really taken with these wheels."

"Oh, man. Salvatore. Thought this was the perfect

beach vehicle," Kyle tells him. "Bought it from me, too." They wave to Nick standing guard before driving beneath the trestle and turning onto Shore Road.

"What? Sal *bought* your truck?" Shane asks. "What do you mean?"

"Promised me that when he came back to Stony Point, it would be with a bank check to buy this old klunker. When he never made it back alive," Kyle explains while rolling down his window, "I never gave it a second thought. Not until weeks after his funeral, when that bank check was delivered to me. A check Sal wrote out and left in safekeeping before his surgery. Just in case." Kyle takes the winding road slowly, cruising past crowded seafood joints, and marshes backlit by the low sun. "So I've got 40K burning a hole in my bank account."

"Are you *kidding* me? *40K?* For this bomber?"

"No joke," Kyle assures him, slapping the cracked dashboard. "Sal was a Wall Street hotshot. And according to his pal, Michael Micelli—the guy you remind me of, and who delivered the check—well, Sal's net worth was shocking."

"God damn." Shane looks at Kyle, looks away, then back at him in utter disbelief.

"One of these days I'll go truck shopping," Kyle is saying as he turns onto a dusty beach road lined with tiny cottages, and seasonal shops selling overpriced tubes and plastic sunglasses and such. He parks his truck right in front of one of those shops. "Come on," Kyle tells him, getting out and checking his watch before leaning back in the truck. "I want to get something for the kids here, before they close."

Shane gets out, too, eyeing the little shop filled with beach junque: plastic sand pails and comic books and cheap flip-flops and terry swimsuit cover-ups. Kyle quickly picks up inexpensive binoculars for Evan, and a felt-animal sewing kit for Hailey.

"All set?" Kyle asks over his shoulder while at the register. "Package store is down the block. We'll grab the beer there."

"You go ahead. I'll meet you at the truck."

Kyle squints at him, then heads out. "Suit yourself."

Once he's gone, Shane walks around the little shop, its wooden floor creaking beneath his step. He passes jigsaw puzzles, and playing cards, and shelves of penny candy, not really certain what he's looking for. Until he turns a corner onto baby things. The shelves are filled with cardboard books and stuffed animals and piggy banks and plush baby rattles. He stops at a bin of infant headbands. Large loopy-ribbon bows are attached to the soft and stretchy fabric.

"*Perfect*," Shane whispers, brushing through the selection. He picks up a headband the color of the sparkling blue sea and heads to the register. "*Just perfect.*"

# *sixteen*

---

### *Later That Evening*

SO THIS IS IT. *THIS* is what Lauren's vow renewal invitation intended: two brothers talking. Having a heart-to-heart. Duking it out. Getting past, over, around some insurmountable rock wall between them. Butting heads. Whatever.

It's about to happen. Shane can feel it. Now's the time. There are no temptations here to sway them otherwise. To issue payback. No dish of mouth-burning hot peppers; no nearby stinging jellyfish; no people mediating; no barriers. Not here, on his open-air cottage back porch. Shane glances out the window to where Kyle's standing at the half-wall. His black work clothes are wrinkled after a long day behind the stoves, and he patiently waits. Waits and takes in the view of Long Island Sound. There are no beach-walkers, no joggers, no barking dogs to interrupt. It's just the two of them now, and a few beers.

And, oh yeah, a mountain between them.

So Shane grabs a couple of cans but stops on the way out. Stops short and snatches up Cliff's lucky domino off the counter. He gives the talisman a good flip in the air and drops it in his jeans pocket before shouldering open the squeaking screen door.

"You're here because of a typo." It's the first thing Kyle says. Leaning against that half-wall, he takes a beer from Shane, snaps it open and has a long swallow.

Shane does the same, standing there on the porch. A shot of whiskey might be better for what they're about to hash out—a rift as deep as the Atlantic Ocean—but beer's better than nothing.

"A typo?" Arms crossed, Shane leans against a roof post. He tosses his newsboy cap on a nearby crate as evening settles in. The sun has set, and a neighbor's sea-garden is lined with flickering lanterns. Beyond, a quarter moon hangs low over the Sound.

"That's it. A typo." Kyle lifts his can in a pseudo toast. "Surprised?"

"I'm here at Stony Point because of a ... *typo?*"

"Yeah. I was putting away paperwork after me and Lauren moved to the new house, and I noticed my name was spelled wrong on our marriage certificate. It was Elsa's idea to fix the error with a vow renewal."

"Sounds like something Elsa would come up with." Shane takes a swig from his beer can. "She's a good person."

"With good intentions."

137

"And all went well until your wife sent me an invitation to your vow renewal ceremony?"

"Pretty much, man," Kyle says, sitting on the half-wall now. He leans back against a roof post, crooks a leg at the knee and rests his hand holding the beer on that knee. "Then the bomb went off."

"Meaning I showed up."

"After the last time we talked, fifteen years ago, never thought I'd see you again. Didn't think I *wanted* to, either."

"But your wife *arranged* this," Shane says, his voice low.

"She did. Invited you without telling me."

"Yeah, well … Lauren had her reasons. And I'm here. So let's cut to the chase, Kyle."

"All right. I'll cut to the chase."

But he doesn't; not at first. First Kyle tips up his beer can for a drink. Looks out at the water. Drags a hand through his hair. Getting all the other detritus out of his head, Shane's sure, before getting the job done. The rift closed.

"What happened to my share of Dad's estate?" Kyle finally asks. "Last you and I talked, right after he died, you told me some bullshit about there being nothing."

"Still telling you that, too. And it's *not* bullshit."

"Don't give me that crap, Shane. Dad owned that house we grew up in for decades. Sold it and went north to live with you in Maine? There's no *way* he didn't sink that cash into *your* house on the harbor, set you up in your life there."

"I remember when you accused me of that fifteen years ago. You thought I played Dad for a fool. Stole the old man's estate."

"Yeah. And you told me to go to hell. To get lost, and don't come back."

"I did." Shane, still leaning against a porch post, sips from his beer can. "But *only* after you wouldn't listen to me."

"Because some of those finances were rightly mine. Dad would've wanted it that way, and you damn well knew it then—and now."

"I *tried* to tell you what happened, but you were so riled up, Kyle, I couldn't even get the words out edgewise. Not with the way you started shoving me around, throwing a few punches."

"With good reason." Kyle stands now. He paces the olive-painted porch floor. Takes a long swallow of his beer. Lifts the corner of his black work tee and dabs at perspiration on his face. "I was a steelworker back then, don't you get it? In and out of work. There was even talk of closing the shipyard here, which would've left me high and dry." He drags a hand through his hair and turns to Shane. "I needed that money more than you know. Me and Ell, we were pretty serious. But I needed some stability before she'd commit. A bank account would've helped. And you *kept* Dad's finances from me, asshole. Put it down on that house, maybe. Blew it. Gambled it. Drank it. I don't know. Shit, all I know is that I seriously needed that cash."

"Maybe you did." Shane tips up his can for a long swallow of beer, then looks out to Long Island Sound beyond the open porch. "But maybe what we both needed, to stay brothers, was time."

"What?" Kyle sits on the half-wall again and leans against a post facing Shane. "To stay brothers?"

"It's the only reason I'm here. In Stony Point. To stay brothers. So you going to listen to me *now*? Or you going to be that same twenty-four-year-old hothead and blow a gasket again?"

From where he sits in the shadows, Kyle silently eyes Shane. Fifteen years ago—oh, doesn't Shane know it—his brother would've taken those jacked arms of his and thrown a punch or two right about now. Would've called Shane out. Would've shoved him right over that porch half-wall.

This time, Kyle doesn't. This time, he just sits on the porch ledge, leans against the post and motions to Shane that he's got the floor.

Shane's voice is low in the night as he talks to Kyle. Low, and serious. Dire, even. Ominous as he begins a seafaring story.

"Me and the boys were out at sea about a year ago. In the fall. It was a two-week trip on the big boat, and getting cold miles offshore. Came upon another boat in distress one day. Serious distress, when the vessel's main engine failed. Land was a long ways off, leaving that boat idled there in the Atlantic, so our captain agreed to tow her back to port. The crews got the situation under control, set up the towline between the vessels and began the slow

journey. By now, the sun was about to set, and we had miles
to go. Captain told me to keep watch on the operation, and
left the deck lights on for the night's trip. Which was good,
because awhile later, I noticed something funny with that
towline. Slight at first, but I paid attention—"

"Shane, seriously? I thought we were going to ... *cut to
the chase*," Kyle says, air-quoting the words.

"Shove it, man. I'm making a point."

"And taking a helluva long time to get there."

"Just go with me on this. And you should appreciate this
story, being a former shipbuilder."

"Fine. Carry on, then."

"Anyway, the towline ..." Shane continues. "Now
remember, these were two ocean-faring vessels. So we're
talking *substantial* towline rope, stronger than a good-sized
steel cable. And at one point on my deck-watch, I noticed
a change. Drops of water were suddenly flying off that
rope. Something wasn't right, the way those drops were
shooting off it. It was because the damn rope between the
two boats got way too tight. Happened so quickly, the
winch operator couldn't even slack it. And I knew. I just
knew. The pressure on that towline became lethal, and that
rope was about to blow. There was barely time enough for
me to warn the boys and bail. Because when that towline
snapped, if I was in its way, I was about to take my last
living breath. The force of that snapping rope would slice
me in half. No lie. So I yelled to the crew and ran like hell.
Never took cover as God damn *fast* as I did in those few
moments. *Moments*, Kyle. Never took my eyes off that

towline either, as I hit the deck. Not until I couldn't even *see* that towline anymore. That's how *fast* it flew back when it actually snapped. It turned *invisible*. And I had no fucking clue where it was even headed … until I *heard* it. Sounded like a gun going off when it hit the steel boat. Wasn't until I followed that nightmare sound that I saw I'd be okay. Saw right where it hit."

"And that you *weren't* in its path." Kyle hadn't moved from where he sits. He just listened, until now. "That's some serious shit going down on that boat."

"Happened last fall," Shane tells him again with a nod. "Seas were getting rowdy as the sun set, waves coming up. Lucky me and the boys made it through."

"So one quick decision kept you alive."

"No, man." Shane hoists himself on the half-wall and sits quietly for a second. "A *decade* on the ocean kept me alive. If that had happened in my early lobstering years, I wouldn't have noticed those damn drops of water spraying off the rope. Wouldn't have sensed something amiss. Hell, probably wouldn't have been paying as close attention. And no *way* would I have gotten myself out of that rope's deadly trajectory. I'd have been killed and gone a long time now."

"And what's *any* of that got to do with us?" Kyle asks.

Shane looks out at the Sound. It's as dark as it was that treacherous night last fall. "Fifteen years ago, you and I were both in a bad way. I was actually engaged to Maris—"

"Heard something about that, the past few days."

"It's true. And I'd scratched together *every* damn penny to put down on that Maine house, on my *own*. *No* handouts.

*No* help from Dad. That little house was going to be our first house—mine and Maris'. But she ended the relationship at the last minute, right before we were to elope. So I was reeling, ready to take out *anyone* who crossed me. And you had your own issues with your line of work. I get it, steelwork's a tough racket, dude. Employment's volatile. And being out of work is one of the worst life stresses."

"What are you saying?"

Shane stands, clasps his hands behind his neck and looks up at the night sky. After a long breath, he looks Kyle straight on. "I'm saying that Dad's dying was *our* towline that snapped. And we had to get the hell out of the way, or that whole scene would've taken us down. Killed our relationship. So we made *split-second* decisions that put fifteen *years* of distance between us. Years of silence, and living, and experience, and maturity. Jesus, you name it. And maybe *that's* what we needed—lots of time—for me to set the record straight, *and* for you to listen."

"And it all comes back to the money."

"Sure does. Of which, there was none."

"You're telling me Dad didn't know what happened with you and Maris, and didn't set you up in a new life to basically keep you out of prison?"

"No, I'm *not* telling you that. He knew about me and Maris, that's for damn sure." Shane walks to the faded white porch table. He pulls out one of the mismatched wooden chairs, swings it around backward and sits on it, crossing his hands over the chair's back. "But that's it."

143

"Why else would you even let him live there with you, if he wasn't financing your life?"

"Had no choice." Shane gives a short laugh. "The day I was leaving Connecticut for Maine? I tossed the last of my things in my truck. Turned around and there was Dad, standing on the front stoop. Coat on, suitcase in hand."

"What?"

Shane nods. "Oh yeah. He got himself in my truck and explained a few things on the drive north. Dad? Hell, he was drowning in debt, bro. Years of paying Mom's medical bills did him in. Second mortgage on the house. Loans. If he didn't put the house on the market when he did, bank would've foreclosed. I'm lucky he had a small life insurance policy to somewhat cover his funeral expenses."

"You're serious."

"I am. There *was* no estate to lock you out of. Dad was at the end of his rope, financially. Still have all the paperwork, if you ever want to come to Maine and go through it."

Kyle just stares at him for a long second, then stands and waves him off.

"Something else you said back then always stayed with me, Kyle."

When Kyle paces in the night's shadows, his voice is low. You'd barely hear it if you weren't listening. "And what's that?"

"You said it was my fault Dad died when he did." Still sitting on that swung-around chair, Shane squints through the darkness at his brother. "That I burned through his money, then left him alone for weeks at a time when I was out on the Atlantic."

"I remember."

"You really think I'm that heartless? That I didn't leave him food and cash and an itinerary and have the neighbors check in on him?"

Kyle crosses the porch and sits on the old white bench. A lantern glimmers beside it, casting shadows on his face. "No," he finally says. "Not now, I don't."

"Let me assure you, brother. Paint a picture for you, to ease your own mind." Shane goes to sit on the half-wall and motions to the sea beyond. "Dad spent his last few months sitting on the docks outside my house. He helped repair lobster traps with some of the old salts up there. Coiled rope while waiting for my boat to come into port. Breathed that salt air off the Atlantic. Even worked part-time in a doughnut shop right on the harbor." Shane just turns up his hands then. At this point, it's all up to Kyle. He can believe him—or not. "You know, how Dad came up with *any* money to rent that little blue cottage when we were growing up is beyond me. But he *did*, every summer, maybe just to give us *some* decent memories as kids. And that he did? Made it worth it for me to bail him out. To give him a place to live in Maine. Pay off some of his debt. The guy was only in his sixties, and I thought he had years ahead of him. We *both* did. But don't worry, Kyle. Those last few months were pretty damn sweet for the old man."

Something changes, then. The way Kyle takes a shaky breath, gets up from the bench, walks to the half-wall and looks out at the low sliver of moon over the sky. Drags a hand through his hair, and eventually looks over at Shane. Shane can see it. He can see the change. The tears Kyle fights.

The fifteen years apart, fifteen years of living, that let Kyle finally see the truth.

~

When Shane goes inside to get them both another can of beer, Kyle is suddenly exhausted. He feels the heavy weight of regret. The weight of being wrong. The weight of ego, slights, heartache, and stress between him and his brother when their father died. Back then, it's no wonder some emotional towline snapped.

Closing his eyes against the fatigue, he believes Shane. It's not easy, either, because it also means Kyle's to blame for much of their rift. Which led to the whole beach gang's collective shunning of the man. But of *course* his father's savings were wiped clean. Their mother had been sick a long time, and their father lost a lot of ground at work, caring for her. It's why he scrapped together enough cash for that little blue cottage every summer. Without it, his and Shane's good memories would've been few.

When the screen door squeaks and Shane walks through with two more cans of beer, Kyle looks over at him from where he sits on the half-wall. "Still here," he says.

Shane hands him a beer. "Me, too." He sits on that wall, near his brother. The dark water of the Sound spreads out beyond them. A mist rises from it, wisps of it reaching them now. "I know we lost fifteen years, Kyle. Gone. I didn't see you get married. Wasn't there when your kids were born. But hell, I'm here now." He stops then, and neither says anything for several moments. "Jason and Neil?" Shane finally says. "They'll never get to see each other again. Nothing, ever."

"It's rough, I know. Shit, were they dealt a bad hand."

"Yeah. So I'm *here*. Here, and ready to see the *rest* of your life."

"Eh." Kyle sips his beer. "A lot of my life sucked back then, let me tell you. Went through my share of hard knocks." Those, Kyle keeps to himself. He doesn't tell Shane how he once *lost* Lauren—to Neil. How it was all Kyle could do to get his diamond ring back on her finger after Neil died. How Evan isn't even his own son, but is Neil's. "You didn't need to see those chapters," is what he says, instead.

"Well, here's to a new chapter, man." Shane holds up his beer can in a toast.

Kyle obliges, raising his own can. "Damn hard to admit something is right—being here, talking to you," he says, "when you want it right *another* way. But it *is* right." He motions between himself and Shane. "*This* is."

"I hear you, bro." Shane takes another long swallow of his beer. Looks out at the sea, where the Gull Island Lighthouse beam flashes in the night. Looks at Kyle across from him on the half-wall. "I hear you."

# seventeen

## Thursday Midmorning

EVEN THOUGH MARIS HAS BEEN alone for days now, it doesn't feel it. Not with the way someone's always at her door, knocking, rapping, cautiously calling her name. Elsa at the shack door, *tap-tap*. Lauren dropping off a warm dinner plate at her kitchen slider, *knock-knock*. Even Cliff at her front door, asking if there was anything Maris needed from the grocery store, *rap-rap-rap*.

The friends just don't let up on her, or on Jason. Behind each question asking how she's doing, Maris hears the concern. Sees the visitor quickly look past her shoulder for maybe a glimpse of Jason in the house. Maris can't miss the optimistic expression that drops when she tells them otherwise. That he's not here.

Oh—love it or hate it—there's nowhere to hide in a little beach town.

But the thing is, with each knock, each rap, each tap,

Maris' first thought—always—is that it'll be Jason. It's a hope that has her spin in her seat, trot to a door. Yet every time, that hope is dashed.

And now? Again. Someone's at her front door this Thursday morning.

Like always, when the knock comes, she hurries from making a second pot of coffee in the kitchen, rushes down the hallway, through the foyer and opens the heavy wooden door.

"Oh! Shane?"

⁓

"Maris." Standing on the front porch, Shane twists the leather cuff on his wrist. "I hope I'm not interrupting anything. Your writing, or, I don't know—"

"No! Of course not." Maris stays inside, holding open the door. "Is everything okay?" she asks.

"It is. Everything's good, actually. But I'm stopping by, well, I'm actually here to say goodbye."

"Really? You're leaving already?" She opens the wood door further. "Come inside. Please!"

Shane steps into the dark foyer. There's a small table there, with a basket on it. Keys, and sunglasses, and a scarf spill from the basket. A dog's leash is curled on the table, too.

"You're leaving *today*?" Maris asks.

"No. I'll be hitting the road early Saturday. At sunrise. It's a long ride back to Maine, and I need to square things away at home before boarding the lobster boat Sunday. My crew will be waiting. So I'm making the rounds to say goodbye to folks."

Maris crosses her arms in front of her, pauses, and smiles. Her fingers toy with her gold star pendant. "I'm glad you stopped by."

"Well, I know just how important goodbyes are to you now."

"And usually not easy," she says, swiping at a quick tear. "But important."

Shane nods and takes off his newsboy cap. "It was really good seeing you this summer, Maris. And, you know … I hope to read that book of yours and Neil's one day," he says, fidgeting with the cap in his hand. "You keep going with your writing, you hear me?"

"*I will*," she whispers. "And, well, regardless of everything, Shane … the difficulties of these past weeks, I'm really glad you came to Stony Point. And that we talked."

"Me, too." He glances to the door then.

"Listen! I just put on a fresh pot of coffee," she tells him. "Have a cup before you go?"

He hesitates, takes a long breath and looks past her shoulder. "Maybe for a few minutes."

"Come on." She waves her hand for him to follow as she heads to the kitchen.

So he walks down the dark paneled hallway, coming upon a living room first, on the left. A hurricane lantern and framed photographs and tin stars sit on the mantel over a massive stone fireplace. But what he can't miss is a side alcove, where a vintage-looking jukebox glimmers in the shadows. "Now that looks awfully familiar," Shane says, veering over to the alcove. "Isn't this the original Foley's jukebox?"

"Sure is." Maris joins him at the jukebox and brushes her hand over the glass dome. "Everyone here, the whole gang? They pitched in and bought it off Foley's old owners, before Elsa bought the cottage." Maris quiets for a moment while looking at the record selections. "It was their group wedding gift to us."

"*Nice*," Shane says. "And where *is* your better half, anyway? He around?"

"Jason?" As she asks, Maris pats the jukebox, then heads back to the hallway.

"Yeah." Shane catches up with her in the kitchen. A window's cranked open over the sink, but the room's warm. A tower fan in the corner blows around the still air. "I want to at least *try* to say goodbye to him." He gives her a regretful smile. "You know, old friend and all."

Maris motions for Shane to sit at the table, then lifts two mugs out of a painted cabinet. "That would mean a lot."

Shane tips his chair back and glances out through the slider, past a weather-beaten deck to the big brown barn out back. Random, colorful fishing buoys hang from its outside walls. "So where is he? In his studio?"

"No," she vaguely says while pouring their coffees, then setting them on the table.

"Out on a job? I can come back, Maris."

She stops then, right there, while bringing a carton of

cream to the table. Just momentarily stops in the middle of the kitchen. Stops and shakes her head.

And Shane sees it, right away. Sees it as she sets the cream on the table and sits in a chair across from him. There's some sadness in her eyes, and it breaks his heart. Because a part of him will always love her.

"Jason never came back," Maris says, her voice soft, her hand turning her coffee cup.

"*What?* Since Sunday?" Quickly, Shane counts the days on his fingers. "It's been five days now."

Maris only nods.

"This does *not* sound good. And I hate to see you like this, Mare. Can I help?"

"Oh, Shane." She gets up and brings a store-bought box of doughnuts to the table. "I don't think anybody can help. It's complicated," she says while nudging the open box his way. "And no one can seem to break through to him."

So people have tried, he realizes. Shane lifts a powdered-sugar doughnut from the box, looks around for a napkin, and gets up to grab a few paper towels. When he sits again, he breaks the doughnut in two and dunks half in his coffee. Holding it aloft, he looks at Maris across the table. She wears an olive V-neck tank top over ripped-denim Bermuda shorts. Her hair is swept to one side, and that star pendant hangs from a braided gold chain around her neck. At once, utterly put together, and utterly devastated. "This is pretty surprising, Maris. From what I've heard around these parts, you two are solid." He bites into the dripping doughnut half.

"I thought so, too. Until recently."

"Well," Shane says around a mouthful of doughnut. "Where is he? And more importantly, are you *sure* he's all right?"

"No, I'm not. Kyle went out to see him, and he says the same thing."

"Wait. Out to see him? *Where*, Maris? Where's your husband holing himself up?"

"Down the coast, twenty miles or so." Maris stirs cream into her coffee and takes a sip. "A place called Sea Spray Beach."

"In a hotel?"

"No. He's staying at a cottage he renovated a couple of years ago. It belongs to one of his clients. Ted Sullivan. An unlikely friend, actually."

"Unlikely?" Shane dunks his other doughnut half in his coffee, then bites in.

"Ted Sullivan." Maris' voice is so serious then, she has his full attention. "Ted is the man who drove his car into Jason and Neil."

Which is enough to almost get Shane choking on his doughnut. "Jesus Christ, are you *kidding* me?" he finally manages after washing down the pastry with a large mouthful of coffee. "And Jason renovated this guy's cottage?"

"Top to bottom. The project even won Jason a coveted coastal architect award."

"Well, I'll be damned. And now Jason's *living* there?"

"Long story, Shane."

153

"Aren't they all."

"This one, especially. That motorcycle accident, when it happened, was really, really hard on Jason. And now's the ten-year anniversary."

"Maris, come on. This is a little ridiculous, no? Leaving you because of it?"

Maris shakes her head. "There's more, Shane. Other things that I just can't—"

When she simply turns up her hands, and her sentence fades off, Shane finishes it in his head. *Other things that I just can't get into with you. Things about you and me. About secrets. About mistakes. About Friday night, in the shack.* He can figure a lot's going down between her and Jason—more than he knows.

But Shane doesn't go there. Doesn't cross that line she just laid down. Instead, he only says, "Still, Maris. Leaving you and staying there—at that Ted's place? It doesn't even make sense."

"Maybe not to us." She sips more of her coffee before walking to the slider and looking out toward the bluff. In a quiet moment, there is only birdsong floating into the room. Finally, Maris looks at Shane from where she stands. "But back then? I wasn't there. You weren't there. Things happened to Jason that nightmare day that we will *never* know, or understand."

"If you say so." Shane slides his coffee cup away, stands and goes to Maris at the slider. He puts his hands on her shoulders and looks her straight on to ask the only question that matters, with Jason here or not. "But you're okay?"

She only nods.

"Maris. You're sure?"

She squeezes one of his hands on her shoulder. "As okay as I can be."

Shane looks from her, to the Barlow backyard. Beyond the brown barn, he sees a corner of the old silver-shingled shack there. "Were you writing out there this morning?" he asks.

"I was. What else can I do, at this point? Just came in for another coffee when you showed up."

"Okay, then. I won't keep you from your work." He tucks her brown hair behind an ear. "Listen. Jason will be back, I'm sure. He has a beautiful wife. I know you guys hit a rough patch this summer, but I can see you've got a *really* good life here. Your family's around. Eva, your aunt. And you deserve it all, Mare." As he says it, he gives her a close hug. Gives her the goodbye she needs. "*You take care now,*" he whispers into her ear.

"You, too," she says. "You, too, Shane."

He sees it, the way she steps back and tries, *tries* to appease his worry with a smile. He looks at her, touches her cheek, then grabs his cap from the table, walks outside through the slider and leaves.

# *eighteen*

*Thursday Afternoon*

IT JUST DOESN'T SIT RIGHT with Shane.

Not as he sweeps sand from his back porch.

Not as he brushes leaves and cobwebs out of the outdoor shower enclosure.

Not as he crosses those chores off the *Before You Leave* checklist tacked on the cottage refrigerator.

Not as he empties a couple of dresser drawers into a few small boxes.

Still doesn't sit right, not as he makes a sandwich out of leftover cold chicken salad from the fridge, adding slices of fresh tomato and onion. Not as he sets chips and a native peach on the sandwich plate and eats his lunch out on the porch.

Not as he looks out at Long Island Sound sparkling beneath the midday sun.

Maybe it would've helped if Maris said more. But it was

156

obvious that she couldn't go there with him, with their history and all. A history that might be part of her problem with Jason.

Still. Jason Barlow walking away from his life at Stony Point? And his *wife*? *Don't get it, don't get it*, Shane thinks, shaking his head as he brings his lunch things inside and washes off his plate. Problem is, there really aren't too many people he can talk to here.

But there is one.

So he reaches to the shelf near the sink and grabs Cliff's lucky domino, gives it a good flip and catches it midair.

⌒⌣

An hour later, Shane finds himself knocking on another door—this one a screen door looking into a gingerbread cottage. He sees inside to the living room's white board-and-batten walls; to a seashell-encrusted vase and a mini wire lobster trap on a painted end table; to Celia, wearing a loose chambray button-down half-tucked into frayed black shorts—and headed his way.

"Shane?" she asks.

"Hey, Celia."

"Good to see you," she says, opening the squeaking door and stepping out onto the front porch.

"You, too." Shane steps closer and presses a kiss into her auburn hair, a kiss nobody would notice. "You busy?"

Celia glances over her shoulder. "Updating the inn's website while Aria's napping."

"She's back, then?"

Celia nods. Smiles, too. "My father brought her yesterday."

"Good. Because I actually got her something."

"You did?"

He hands Celia a small bag. "For when she wakes up later."

"Shane? What is it?"

"Just a little present," he quietly says as she lifts out the bowed headband.

"Oh! That is so precious!" She looks to him and briefly touches his whiskered jaw.

And he gets it. Their voices are quiet; their touches, restrained. They have to be, with too many close neighbors, and passersby, all around them.

"*Thank you*," Celia whispers, setting the bow back in the bag.

"I thought of Aria when I saw it." He looks past her into the small cottage, then back at her face.

"I'm still surprised to see you here," Celia tells him. "Is there something you needed?"

"Actually, yes." He hesitates, glancing over his shoulder. "But it's nothing. You're busy."

"Not too busy for you. What's the matter?"

"Just needed an ear."

"What's wrong?" she cautiously asks. "Did you finally talk with Kyle?"

"I did. Yesterday. It went pretty well, actually. But it's not that."

"Do you want to come inside?"

"Eh, not a good place to talk here. Too many eyes." With that, he motions to Elsa watering her nearby hydrangea bushes, and to Cliff pulling up to the inn in his security cruiser. "Listen, Celia. I'm going back to my cottage to soap down my pickup, and check the oil for my trip home. Maybe you can take a walk by later with Aria? When she's up?"

"Okay." Celia quickly squeezes his hand. "Okay. I will."

The day is hot, and indecipherable from every stifling day before it. That August sun doesn't quit, its rays beating down on dry lawns and evaporating birdbath water and withering marigolds. It's the kind of summer that seems like there's no end in sight, even though September is only days away.

Shane lifts his arm to his forehead to brush away the sweat, then picks up an old garden hose that leaks at the spigot. He aims the hose nozzle into a yellow plastic bucket he found inside, in a broom closet. No sooner is the bucket filled with soapy water than Shane hears Celia's voice. He looks over from where he stands in the driveway. Celia's getting out of a golf cart she parked curbside.

"Someone once told me—" she calls out to him, then lifts her guitar case out of the cart.

"Sal?" Shane interrupts.

Celia nods. "That many hands make light work."

"Smart man."

Celia walks down the driveway and sets her guitar case beneath a tree before looking around at the dripping hose, and foamy bucket of water, and fat yellow sponges.

"Where's your daughter?" Shane asks.

"Elsa's watching her." Celia loosely cuffs her chambray shirtsleeves and plucks a sopping sponge out of the bucket. "I'll help wash, okay? And you tell me what's going on."

Shane nods, pulls a rag from his back pocket and crouches to clean his wheels. He wipes the rag over the silver rims. "I just came from the Barlows'."

"Oh, stop right there," Celia says, soaping the driver's door beside him. "Is Jason still gone?"

"You knew?"

"It's the whole grapevine thing. Pretty amazing how very few secrets there truly are here." She looks at him crouched beside her.

"And what do *you* make of the split?" Shane asks while working on a stubborn grease mark on the tire rim. "Of Jason taking off."

"I get it. I took off last year, after Sal died. Sometimes you just have to go somewhere alone to lick your wounds. To heal."

"*Heal?* Celia, his brother's been gone for ten years now."

"True." Celia dips the sponge in the soapy pail, then lifts it to the truck's side. "But don't forget, Jason had over two decades with Neil. All I can say is that I had two *months* with Sal last summer, and the grief after he died was unbearable. I can't imagine what it would feel like to lose him with twenty years of history."

160

"Point taken," Shane agrees. "But still, to leave your wife because of it? Seems pretty low. Or unfair, anyway, to Maris."

"You know, I hate how Jason's getting painted in this awful light. Everyone's judging him based on this one crazy week, and the emotional decisions being made. He's so much more than that."

Shane stands and steps back, eyeing the soapy truck. "How so?"

"Come on, give the guy a break. On top of that ten-year anniversary of the accident, I'm sure Jason just found out about you and Maris being engaged, like everyone else here did. And he's not allowed to react to any of it?"

"So you're saying he's held to a different standard than other people here."

"Seems to be. Just let him have some space. He'll come around."

"What about Maris?"

"Maris knows Jason better than *any* of us. She'll understand what he's doing."

"And maybe none of it's any of our business?"

"It *isn't*," Celia admits, lifting the hose and spraying the soap off the side of the truck. "But that's the way folks are here. We all *care*. Which means we meddle, and look out for each other, and bring over cooked meals, and lend an ear." She looks over her shoulder at Shane. "Last year, when I left Stony Point after Sal died, I moved back home to Addison. Thought it was a permanent move, too, until one night Jason showed up at my door."

"That's right. I think you mentioned that before."

Celia nods, and keeps spraying as she walks the length of the truck. The water droplets glisten in the bright sunshine; her cuffed shirtsleeves are wet. "Jason convinced me to come back here. For Elsa, for the others. But for myself, too. And I *did*. It wasn't easy, and I've had mixed feelings about it. But I'm still grateful to Jason. He has this way about him that cuts through to the truth." She drops the hose and picks up the soapy sponge again. It drips a bit on her shorts, dampening the frayed hem. "He's actually Aria's godfather—"

"Come again? Jason is?"

"Oh, yes. *Everyone* wanted to be Aria's godfather. You missed the contests the guys all had this summer, vying for that title. There were bocce tournaments, fishing contests, bingo and tubing competitions ... you name it."

"And Jason won."

Celia nods. "*And* he gave Aria a gift I'll never forget, on her christening day. A brass ring he grabbed from the Sound View Carousel. He included a beautiful note wishing my daughter a brass-ring kind of life." She pauses then, scrubbing around a door handle. "And I realized just what that meant. If you think about it ..."

"Explain it to me, this brass-ring life." Shane steps closer and soaps the truck beside Celia.

"Well." Celia squints over at him. "A brass-ring life isn't really an *easy* life. Because you have to *reach* for that brass ring. And *try*. And try *again*. And nearly fall off the horse as you grab for it. And go home, dejected. But wake up another day to try again. So when you *do* grab onto it, the happiness is earned, and deserved."

"The best kind?"

"The kind that gets you through the rest. So maybe right now, Jason's in the midst of *the rest*," she says, air-quoting the words, sponge in hand. "But I believe he'll come around."

Shane looks at Celia long enough for her to stop scrubbing.

"What?" she asks.

"You say that with some conviction."

"Because I mean it."

Shane tips his head. "Are you maybe a little bit in love with Jason Barlow?"

"Hey!" Celia flicks soapy water from her sponge at him. "*No*, Shane. I mean, do I love him? Sure, like I love all the gang here. But I'm not *in* love with Jason."

"Okay," Shane says, holding up his hands—sponge and all—in defense.

"Listen," Celia goes on. "It's just that Jason's actually one of the most selfless people I've encountered. I mean, come on. He was up all hours last weekend trying to save Kyle and Lauren's marriage? As if that's his responsibility?"

"I didn't know."

"Well, he did. So maybe now he's tired and just needs space to clear his head. Maybe his leaving is as simple as that." Celia stops washing and looks at Shane beside her. Her voice drops. "I didn't have that kind of space to deal with my emotions this past year. And let me tell you, it can really mess with you—not having that space. You saw me, last week on that rainy day."

"I did, Celia."

"I came undone after bottling everything up for a long time."

"Okay, I get that. Lord knows I've dealt with my share of emotion in my own way, out on the ocean. But I still …"

"Still, what?"

"I keep coming back to one question. And that's if I maybe said some things to *push* Jason over the edge." As he says it, Shane pictures last Friday night—less than a week ago—when Jason walked into the fishing shack to find him there, alone with Maris. Alone and obviously tangled up in a very private moment. Shane knows, as he's sure Jason does, where that evening might have led if Jason hadn't walked in. Shane and Maris had been standing in the shadows, Maris close and touching his jaw, his face, as she whispered to him. As they felt the past fifteen years melt away while standing inside a musty fishing shack that might as well have been on the Maine docks as on the Barlow bluff. The night was warm; the air, misty; the years, erased.

"Oh no, Shane." Celia reaches for his hand. "You didn't."

All he can do is nod. Nod silently, because seriously? That night in the shack seems a world away from the place he's at right now. This place with Celia. So much *else* has happened this last week—including a long talk with Maris at the laundromat. A talk that set his past entanglement with her sailing away, setting them free.

"It's just that …" Shane begins, dipping his sponge into the soapy bucket, then looking at Celia. "I'm not sure if Jason might be at this Ted Sullivan's place for the wrong reasons."

"*Shane*," she whispers. "You *really* said things to him?"

He blows out a quick breath. "Said things. Did things. It's all one of those long stories. Who pushed who? Who asked for what? Who goaded, who fought back? So I don't know if I maybe have *something* to do with Jason's leaving."

Celia squeezes out her sponge and sets it in the sun. "There's only one way to find out." She takes his sponge from him and sets it down, too. "You have to talk to him."

He squeezes his eyes shut and turns away. "*Aargh.*"

"What?"

"I was hoping to spend a couple of hours with *you*. Grab a grinder, maybe?"

Celia simply shakes her head, her eyes not leaving his.

Shane watches her. Sees a strand of her auburn hair slipped out of its low twist. Sees her chambray shirt dotted with water. Wipes a spot of soap off her cheek. "At least a jam session, then? Before I set out to find Barlow?"

～

Shane's not sure what does it. Is it being with Celia on his back porch, with the sea just beyond?

Is it that he has only another day here, so every fleeting minute takes on new meaning?

Or is it that in talking about Jason and Maris, he and Celia actually allayed any doubts they might have had for each other?

Whatever the reason, this jam session is the finest he's

ever had, on land or sea. Below deck on a boat or in a seedy beach bar—nothing tops this one.

Celia sits on the porch half-wall, guitar on her lap. Shane also sits on the wall, facing her. Leaning against a roof post, he cups his harmonica to his mouth and the two instruments weave in and out—the wave of one rising just as the other retreats. Perfectly in sync. Celia's fingers move over the six strings with ease. Her silver thumb ring glistens in the sunlight. And her glimpses at him are nothing less than sweet. So he plays on.

Until Shane hears a familiar tune he can't place, try as he might. So he sets down his harmonica, gets comfortable and instead just watches Celia strum. Her fingers slow; her touch is gentle on the guitar. Still, he can't place the song she plays until she *sings* her version of it. Which completely takes him aback, especially the way she slows the song, her voice breathy. Her emotion, real.

*Twinkle, twinkle ocean star ... How I wonder what you are.*
*Floating on the sea so light ... Like a diamond shining bright.*

The way she delivers those special words, well, it could bring him to tears. When she veers her guitar strumming into an interlude as sweeping and flowing as the sea itself, Shane adds his own harmonica riff. And somehow, the song seems sad and hopeful, all at once. When she sings the last verse, he sets down his harmonica once more.

*Twinkle, twinkle ocean star ... How I wonder what you are.*

There's a quiet moment when she stops playing. Just sets her hand over the strings, dips her head and briefly closes her eyes.

"Your spin on that song is beautiful," Shane tells her. "Do you sing it to Aria?"

The question gets Celia to give him a long look, one that's filled with story, and private memory. "I've sung that song to a lot of people." She checks her watch then. "Oh! I promised Elsa I wouldn't be long. I really have to go and get Aria."

"Okay, no problem." He walks over and helps Celia off the porch ledge, taking her guitar as she stands and straightens her chambray button-down.

"Good luck with Jason?" she says when setting the guitar back in its case.

"Thanks." Together, they start down the seven painted porch steps. "Listen, Celia. Are you free later?" Shane asks from behind. "I'd love to have you and Aria over for a cookout."

"That sounds nice …"

When she pauses and looks over her shoulder, Shane sees it though, before she says it. Sees her polite smile declining his invite.

"But I'm actually cooking with Elsa tonight," Celia says. "We're fine-tuning her first Sunday dinner recipe for when the inn opens. Got to make it just right, you know."

"Oh, I'm sure it will be. But I'll see you before I leave Saturday?" Shane asks when she continues walking down the steps.

Celia turns back once more. "Of course," she says with a wave, then heads to the planked walkway there and the golf cart beyond it.

"Wait!" Shane hurries down the steps after her. At the walkway, he stops and cradles her face, brushing aside a loose wisp of her silky hair. And he sees it, some change in her hazel eyes. Some difficulty, now that the end is in sight. Now that Saturday is around the corner. So beside the cottage, far from any prying eyes, he first takes her guitar case and sets it down. Silently then, he leans in and kisses her. His hands, they touch her soft skin as he lengthens the kiss, as he senses her breath catch in sadness as she kisses him back. "Thanks for the song," he tells her, stroking her jaw, his hand slipping to her throat, down her arm, wanting to hold her right there but knowing he can't.

Celia says nothing. She just gently cups his face before picking up her guitar case, turning and walking away.

# nineteen

SHANE KNOWS HE CAN FIND it. For the nearly two weeks he's been at Stony Point, it's become really clear which cottages are Barlow Architecture originals. They're the stuff of dreams. Of glossy magazine spreads. They're the beach cottages that look even better with each passing summer; with each season of sea breezes; with misty mornings and hazy evenings drizzling dew on the shingles, the gables.

Driving a sandy road at Sea Spray Beach, Shane keeps a lookout for Ted Sullivan's cottage. Low, craggy dunes line one side of the street. Beyond them, Shane's sure, is some breathtaking view of Long Island Sound. But it's the other side of the street that has his attention. He drives past several cottages—some shingled, some painted—each with a prominent second-level deck or balcony facing the water.

And there it is, the cottage he's looking for. Shane

almost missed it, the way it blends right in with the surrounding dunes and neighboring seaside homes. But he can't miss the Barlow touch. The new cedar shingles the color of golden honey. The wide white trim. The brass wall lanterns glimmering in the early evening light. It looks like there's a big deck, too, and a stained glass window on the second level. The window's image is of a great white egret standing in the shallows. Stunning. And clearly a Barlow original.

Shane also recognizes Jason's SUV in the driveway. So, Jason's here. Shane wasn't sure if he'd find him or not. If Jason would be out to dinner. Or nursing a brew in some honky-tonk beach bar after work.

He's not.

Still, Shane parks his pickup behind Jason's vehicle, then sits for a minute to get his bearings. To take a good long breath of that salt air, which is sharper here at Sea Spray. He notices that right away. Another breath and he gets out of the truck and heads up the deck stairs. As he does, he hears waves breaking and glimpses the beach across the street. Like the salt air, the waves are also stronger here than at Stony Point. That's what happens with no forest or rocky outcropping protecting the beach from the open Sound. While taking in the view, though, he hears a voice—Jason's voice—coming from up on the deck.

"Wasn't expecting you today," Jason says from where he's sitting at a teak table. "What's the dinner special, Kyle?"

"Not Kyle," Shane throws back while paused on the

steps and watching Jason work on some blueprint, or architectural sketch. He's bent over his papers, his hand quickly delineating lines and angles on the drawing.

Jason silently looks over his shoulder, then tosses down a black marker he'd been using. At the same time, a German shepherd lying at his side scrambles to its feet. When it gives a quiet growl, Jason grabs the dog's collar and pulls it close.

"Jason," Shane says. The sun is low in the sky, and lanterns are scattered on a wide railing, on small tables. One lantern shines directly on Jason's workspace. Shane takes another step.

"Stop right there," Jason tells him.

So Shane does. He'll do whatever it takes to get through to his old friend, if only for Maris. He stops on a stair and leans on the railing. "Not here for trouble, Jason."

"Doesn't look that way to me."

"Come on, guy. I just want to talk. For a few minutes." Shane takes another step up.

"I told you once already," Jason warns him. But he doesn't get up. Doesn't walk over. He just turns in his chair, one hand still holding back the growling dog.

"We used to be friends, man." Shane still leans on the railing. He makes no move to get any closer. To sit with Jason. To maybe have a beer with him. Something.

"That was a long time ago."

"And I need to have some words with you." Shane glances around the deck. The design is impeccable, with its stainless-steel grill in an elaborate cooking station. And there's that teak table, with a massive white conch shell centerpiece, moved out of Jason's way. In its place are cottage sketches on sheets of paper, and a few black markers, and an architectural scale. A badass calculator. And then, there's Jason watching him closely. "I'm coming over, damn it," Shane says as he steps onto the deck.

"No, you're *not*," Jason tells him, his voice rising now. "I'll come to you."

Shane tosses up his hands and waits there. As Jason orders his dog to stay, he reaches for something Shane can't decipher in the shadows. Not until Jason stands and gets them situated. They're forearm crutches. He walks closer then, the crutches tapping on the deck floor. Beneath the cargo shorts Jason wears, his residual limb is clearly visible. Shane sees up close how the left leg was amputated below the knee. It's the first time he's seen Jason without his prosthesis.

"Shit, Jason. That's why I'm here, too," Shane tells him, motioning to his leg.

Jason stops and just stands there, leaning on his crutches. "Is that right."

"Once I left fifteen years ago, I was gone," Shane says, still standing in place. He glances over at the dog giving a nervous whine while sitting near the table. "I wasn't looking up Maris. Wasn't keeping tabs on Kyle. No one. I've been on the ocean and didn't think I'd see *any* of you again. Not until I got Lauren's invitation." He stops talking. Just stops, mid-sentence. "Hell. I never knew about your accident until last week. And about how you lost Neil. And your leg."

"Maybe you're lucky."

"No. No, what I am is *really* sorry. You've been through the wringer, man."

"Don't need your pity."

"It's *not* pity." But Shane sees it. Sees that he's hitting a brick wall here. Maris was right. So was Kyle. There's no getting through to Barlow. So Shane sits himself down on the top deck step. He turns, though, toward Jason— stopped and leaning on his crutches. Behind him, teak chairs are cushioned in blue-and-white stripes; whiskey-barrel planters spill over with red geraniums and vinca vines. But Jason? He's looking plenty beat standing there in his wrinkled shorts and some ratty college tee.

Just then, Jason walks over to the railing and looks out toward the beach. When he does, there's a blur of movement crossing the deck. Tail low and wagging, the dog scurries to Jason's side. "Down, Madison," he tells it, and the German shepherd drops at his feet. "And you, Bradford? You can get your sorry ass out of here before I get you out myself," he tosses over his shoulder.

"Ease up, guy. I'll be gone for good Saturday, soon enough. Just a pleasant memory for everyone to talk up for a while. And before I leave, I figured I'd give you something substantial to keep. Some advice. You know, as a parting gift."

"I'm losing my patience with you."

"Like I said, Jason, I didn't come here to fight."

"Nah, you came here to play the bigger man card."

"Jesus, no. What the hell's wrong with you?"

173

Jason turns then, leans on that railing and faces Shane straight on.

"Listen," Shane presses. "I'm here for another reason." From the top stair, he stands and takes a step in Jason's direction. When he talks, his voice is low. "I'm here to tell you not to make the same mistake I did."

Jason gives a short laugh. "I wouldn't come close to making the mistakes you've made."

Shane just shakes his head. Maybe this isn't worth it. Maybe his words are only falling on deaf ears. Maybe Barlow's about ready to shove him right down those deck stairs. But still, Shane persists. He takes another step in the fading evening sunlight. A step bringing him near enough to see the raised scar running along Jason's jaw, even with a couple of days' whiskers there. Near enough to see some fatigue on his face.

"You're actually *precariously* close to repeating what I once did," Shane tells him. "My mistake? I let Maris go."

Jason says nothing. Gives Shane nothing to throw back at him. He just silently watches him.

"She's crazy for you," Shane continues. "She's also devastated, man. And hell, you can *fix* things with her. The ball's in your court. Just make the move, for Christ's sake."

Well, the restrained words that come out of Jason next? They're even worse for the thick silence that precedes them. "You waltz into town for two weeks and are going to tell me how to run *my* life? Go to hell."

"You got it wrong there, guy."

"Wrong?"

"I'm *not* telling you how to run your life." Shane turns to the deck stairs to leave. He descends a few before stopping and looking back over his shoulder. "I'm telling you don't fuckin' blow it."

⁓

Jason watches Shane leave, then gets the dog a bowl of fresh water and gets himself a can of cold beer—which he holds to his perspiring face. When he does, he closes his eyes for a long moment. The misty salt air hangs heavy. The heat doesn't let up. Finally, he snaps open the can and takes a long swallow. Only then does he get back to work, picking up his markers to detail a revised elevation sketch of the Fenwick place. And blows out a long breath, as though he'd been holding it the whole time Shane was here. Okay, and takes another swallow of his cold brew, right as his cell phone rings. He slides it across the deck table and sees that it's his sister calling.

"Paige," Jason answers.

"Haven't seen you since the botched vow renewal. How's it going, big brother?"

"Yeah, it's going." As he says it, he pulls closer his most recent elevation sketch and darkens a few lines.

"The kids start school next week, can't believe it. Where'd the summer go?"

"No kidding."

"Talked to Mom in Florida. She was on her way out to a movie with a friend. Said the theaters are nice and air-conditioned. Especially in the Florida heat."

"Feels like Florida here."

"Definitely. So hey, I haven't heard much about Kyle and Lauren since we packed up our cottage and went home. They doing okay?"

"They're working through things, pretty much. Calming down."

"Well, good! That's good. I'll let Vinny know. He's been so busy coaching already, for the fall swim season. Oh, and listen. We'll see you at Neil's Memorial Mass on Sunday, right?"

"I'll be there," Jason says while shading in part of the front elevation. He has to adjust the door placements on the Fenwick cottage. Bring them into balance with the new windows.

"The weather looks good, too. Maybe we can all hang on the beach afterward?" Paige asks.

"I don't think so, Paige." Jason sets down his marker and leans back in his chair. "Mass is enough for me. Not feeling much more than the church and brunch this year."

"So you and Maris are just going to lie low that day?"

"Yeah." Jason pushes some papers away and takes a sip of his beer. "Ah shit, Paige. It's just that—"

"I *knew* it. I just knew it."

"Knew what?"

"Something's up with you. You're too distracted."

"I'm *working*, Paige. But you're right," he admits, rubbing the back of his forearm. It stings when he does, and so he looks to see a nasty bruise taking shape there. Must be from his fall out of bed the other morning. "Things aren't good."

"What do you mean? Is Maris okay?"

Jason thinks about Maris. About the word Shane personally delivered to him about her. She's *devastated*. Devastated, damn it.

"*Jason!* I said, is Maris okay?"

A pause, then, "We're kind of not together right now." As he says it, he closes his eyes. Because he knows damn well what's coming next.

"*What?*" Paige hisses at him. "Not *together?* What the heck did you *do?*"

To which Jason says nothing—not that she gives him any time to.

"Oh, I could *pummel* you," Paige fires off. "Because there's no way this is Maris' fault. Where are you?"

"Well," he answers, tossing up a hand and thinking of Shane's visit, "it's no secret now. Ted Sullivan's place."

"Seriously? You're staying at *Ted's?*"

"He's away, and letting me use the cottage."

"Oh my God."

"What, Paige?"

"Jason Barlow, tell me you're not doing this again."

"Doing what?"

"Taking down your *life*. I'll be there ASAP."

And that's it. The phone goes silent as he's sure his sister is already out the door and on her way.

# twenty

### *Thursday at Twilight*

IT'S LATE, AND WHEN PAIGE breezes in, the outfit she's had on all day shows its wear: her chambray shorts are wrinkled; her black pullover's long sleeves, shoved up; slip-on loafers, scuffed on her feet.

But Paige being Paige, *she* shows *no* wear. Instead, it's like there's a whirlwind in the kitchen. She carries a salad and plate of chicken-and-spinach lasagna from home, berates him nonstop while she heats it in Ted's microwave and sets out silverware and napkins, then sits with Jason at the kitchen table for an hour. Jason can tell it's her way of being sure he actually eats something. The recessed lights are set low; the slider's open to the warm sea air outside. While Jason eats, his sister finally quiets and listens to him.

The thing about Paige is he's never kept anything from her. She's seen him at his worst, and at his best. From coming fresh out of the motorcycle accident—utterly beaten down and his body half bandaged—to getting married two years ago. From being addicted to pain meds, to receiving the Connecticut Coastal Architect Award.

And now this—seeing his state of mind when he lets on he might lose Maris. And rather than face that in Stony Point, he left there.

"*Lose Maris?*" Paige whispers while toying with two chain pendants hanging around her neck. "Why?"

"Why?" Jason asks, lifting a forkful of the cheesy lasagna. "For one thing, my own demons—which kicked me in the ass this summer. Maris has seen me pretty down, dealing with them. It's been tough," he says around a mouthful of food, "thinking about Neil and reliving memories at this anniversary. Every summer, it feels like he's getting farther and farther away, like a fading reflection in some rearview mirror."

"It's been ten years," Paige only says, giving his arm a squeeze.

Jason nods, then drags a slice of bread through mushrooms and white lasagna sauce on his plate. "There's more, too," he admits. And those three words open a floodgate. His voice just flows, slow but steady, as he tells Paige everything. Tells her all about Shane Bradford and his engagement to Maris and a secret diamond ring and private talks in the shack, talks that were escalating to something more—the air was *that* charged—when Jason walked in.

"But you think she'll *leave* you? Isn't that extreme?"

Jason spears a forkful of salad. "No. Because no matter what, Maris never fully realized what she signed on for, marrying me. I'm an amputee with a boatload of baggage. Right from the get-go, I've hated for her to see me deal with certain things. Flashbacks, triggers. Even a random sadness."

"But why? It's who you are."

"Why? It feels private. And I'm not at my best during those times."

"Does she mind? Does she tell you to get over yourself?"

"Never."

"So why do you think she'll leave?"

Jason sets down his fork, wipes his mouth with a napkin and pushes his plate aside. "Because there's another guy who rolled into town with *no* baggage. One who is unattached."

"Shane."

"He was once very much a part of Maris' life, and still can be. I don't want to witness that, when it happens."

"Witness what?"

"Witness the moment Maris walks out on our marriage."

"Come on, Jason." Paige eyes him closely. "And anyway, looks like *you* beat her to the punch."

"What?"

"Think about it." Paige's cell phone dings with a text message. "It's Vinny," she says, standing and reading the text. "I really have to get home. And you *know* what you have to do." She walks around the table and moves aside Jason's crutches. Bending to hug him, she whispers in his ear, "*Talk to Maris.*"

*Talk to Maris. Talk to Maris.*

The words play on a reel in his mind as Jason puts on his prosthetic leg. As he looks at his cell phone charging on the kitchen countertop. As he rinses his dinner dishes and silverware and glances at the phone again. As he gathers his papers on the deck, and his markers and scale, and puts them away inside. As he turns on a few more lights in Ted's cottage, slips his phone in his cargo shorts pocket and grabs Maddy's leash.

*Talk to Maris. Talk to Maris.*

Jason's not sure he can right now. If at the end of a long day, he just doesn't have it in him. So he'll go to the one place that can rid Paige's words from his head; can stop them from nudging him to make that call. He whistles for the dog and they go outside to the deck, down the stairs and onto the beach. A long walk along the high tide line always works. It's the one place on this blessed planet that eases his gait, and eases his mind.

For Maddy, too, apparently. Before Jason even crosses the beach, the dog runs ahead and splashes into the shallows. She barks playfully, then snaps at a breaking wave.

And it's that breaking wave that has Jason pause on the packed sand below the high tide line. That has him turn to the sea and the violet horizon in the distance. That has him wait for another wave to slosh onto the sand.

*They're right, you know.*

The words come as the wave retreats back into the Sound with a long hiss. Well, he's no fool. They're either words from his brother's spirit, or words Jason is just craving to hear, manifesting in beach sounds.

"They're right?" Jason asks.

*Paige. And Shane, too*, his brother says, or the breeze lifting off the night water whispers.

Jason waits, then waves off the words and starts to walk the beach. "I don't want to hear it, Neil," he quietly answers.

*Talk to Maris*, his brother insists, right as a distant foghorn wails into the misty night. *Come on, bro.*

Still, Jason only walks. When the dog lopes too far down the beach, he gives a sharp whistle.

*Suit yourself, Jay*, he hears as Maddy's collar jangles when she trots past him.

Then? Nothing. Not for several steps. There are only the waves breaking stronger here on this unsheltered beach. No rocky outcroppings, no forest ledges shield it from the strength of the open waters.

And no more voices whisper in the frothing water, either. Nothing.

Squinting to the dusky horizon, Jason pulls out his phone and does it. He calls Maris.

～

"Maris." There's a pause before she responds; Jason notices that as he slowly walks the night beach.

"Jason."

"How are you, Maris?"

"Not good."

No pause there; he notices that, too. It gets him to stop walking and just talk. "What's the matter?"

Her voice is soft. Controlled. "Everything's the matter."

"Everything?"

"Jason. With *us*."

"Us." He looks out at Long Island Sound. Drags a hand through his hair. "I don't know. Maybe if I come see you?" he quietly asks. "For a half hour even?"

"*No.*"

That word? That word she whispers. He barely hears it. And says nothing in return.

"No. It's late," she continues. But only after a few seconds, as though she was wavering. Closing her eyes, maybe. Picturing a talk. "You have an early day tomorrow, I'm sure."

In the silence that follows, he hears very little. Maybe Maris taking a breath. Maybe not. Wherever she is in their house, there's no noise. No TV turned on. No jukebox playing. No dishwasher running. Nothing.

"Where are you?" he asks her.

"*What?*" Her voice, still a whisper.

"In the house. Where are you?" He stands waiting on the high tide line, waiting to hear her voice, when a wave breaks close to him. A bit of sea spray reaches his legs. "Maris."

"I don't know what I can say to convince you that it's not what you're thinking. With Shane. With our marriage."

Problem is, Jason's already convinced otherwise. Words

can't undo what he's heard, what he's seen, what he feels. "You don't have to explain, sweetheart. Neither of us does. Because after this past week, I'm just not sure this is going to work anymore."

"This?"

"Us." Saying it, giving voice to those words, his throat tightens. "Loose ends with Shane."

"But Jason—"

"There are other things. My own demons, Maris. You, shelving your denim career. Things've changed."

"Wait. Are you saying you don't want me to finish Neil's book?"

He shakes his head. "I don't know what I'm saying. That's why I needed this space."

"But you're shutting me out."

"No. It's just that … That's not what I …" Silence, then, for a few seconds. For the time it takes another wave to break. And in that one breaking wave, his whole life feels like it's breaking.

"Jason."

"There's nothing … I should go, Maris."

"Okay," she says.

When he disconnects the call, Jason's not sure of something. His thoughts can veer two ways. Either this is the summer they both got lost, or the summer they both stopped trying.

# twenty-one

*Late Friday Morning*

Fresh OFF THE LINE!"

As Celia says it, she's carrying in a basket of sun-dried bedsheets. She heads to the inn's laundry room, where Elsa waits with Aria. The baby lies in her portable play yard and watches an animal mobile clipped onto the edge of it. A felt elephant, lion and zebra slowly spin around.

"Oh, there's nothing like the smell of sheets hung to dry outdoors," Elsa says as she flips up a sheet and lets it waft down.

Celia picks up the other end of the sheet, and together they fold it in half, then half again. They keep folding until the sheet is tucked into a tight square, before Celia sets it on a long table beside them. Even the inn's large laundry room has been redone. Its palest-gray beadboard paneling is the same silvery color as the commercial-grade washer and dryer; matching gray shelves are built in over the

185

machines. There's a sink, too, a big one, with stainless faucets. A striped upholstered chair is in the corner; twig wreaths hang on the wall; paned windows look out onto the inn's grounds.

"This is the prettiest laundry room I've ever seen," Celia quietly says, right as Elsa picks up another sheet from the clothes basket.

"It is. If we have to do a little drudgework in here, I at least want the room to be nice." When Elsa flips open that sheet, Celia bends and picks up her two corners. "You're a little quiet today, Cee," Elsa says as they tug out the wrinkles.

"Just tired," Celia tells her. "Aria was restless last night."

"It's no wonder, in this heat." They fold the sheet in half. "Take her for a nice walk after lunch, before her afternoon nap."

"I think I will. Have her get some fresh outdoor air."

"Oh, and Aria's new headband is *so* darling, Celia. It has tiny *sparkles* in it, when you look close."

Celia glances over to Aria cooing in her playpen. The baby has on her new blue summer headband, its loopy bow soft on her head.

"Your father spoils her when he babysits," Elsa is saying as they fold a queen-size sheet in half again. "Grandpops do that."

And grandfathers just *might* do that, Celia thinks as she finishes folding and walks over to where Aria lies, pumping her tiny arms. So Celia will let Elsa believe that Celia's father *did* buy the headband. No need to correct Elsa and admit it was actually from Shane. No need to open a whole can of personal moments that will simply raise Elsa's eyebrow once again. What Celia and Shane have between them, no matter how fleeting, no matter how brief—their summer affair—is too private to share. Instead, Celia just smiles and reaches down to touch Aria's hair, and the bowed headband, too.

"*Mmm*," Elsa sighs while holding another sheet to her face. "You can just smell the summer air right in the fabric." She walks over to the play yard, where Celia still stands. Gently, Elsa lowers a bit of the sheet to the baby's face. "Maybe Aria can smell that sweet scent, too."

"Nothing like it," Celia says. "*Aria di mare*. The sea air."

"Do you smell that, sweetie?" Elsa asks her granddaughter. "The sea air in the sheet?" As she says it, she lets a piece of the fabric tickle the baby's cheek.

The morning goes easy like that, as they fold the inn's sun-dried bed linens. Their eyes drop closed with the fresh scent of each sheet they lift. They stack the folded linens and pillowcases on the laundry table, talk softly, spin Aria's felt-animal mobile. When Elsa's cell phone eventually rings, Celia tells her that she'll keep folding. "Go ahead and answer," she says, nodding to Elsa's phone on the table.

Elsa hurries over. "*Yes* ..." she says with some caution into her phone. "Yes, this is Elsa speaking." More silence, then, "Oh, *yes*! Of course! Mitch ... *Fenwick*, is it?"

Celia holds a folded end of sheet beneath her chin, and lifts up the other end to neatly finish. All the while, she listens to Elsa chat.

187

"Jason *mentioned* you'd be calling. Can I put you on speakerphone, Mitch?"

"I hope I'm not interrupting, or keeping you from anything," Mitch's voice suddenly comes through the phone speaker.

"No, not at all," Elsa reassures him while lifting a pillowcase from the basket. "I'm folding sheets fresh off the line and don't want them to wrinkle."

"Ah, you'll be sleeping soundly, I reckon."

"They *do* do the trick," Elsa agrees. "Now refresh my memory … what can I help you with?"

"Your nephew, Jason—"

"Nephew-in-law," Elsa interrupts.

"Beg your pardon?" Mitch's easy voice fills the room.

"Through marriage," Elsa explains. "Jason's married to my niece, Maris."

"Yes, of course. And my cottage is the next castaway for his TV show. He said your inn reno premiered the show …"

"It did! Earlier this summer."

"Right, right. Well, Jason thought you might share some of *your* experiences dealing with a renovation *and* a film crew?"

"And what an experience it was!" Elsa snaps the pillowcase in half.

"Which is why I was hoping to meet with you before the Hammer Law lifts and our demo begins. My daughter and I … well, mostly myself … feel awkward in front of cameras. Looking for any tips, or … or *advice*, before the hammers swing and the cameras roll."

Celia is oddly comforted by some southern inclination to Mitch's voice. His pitch is smooth; his words, paced. It's a voice very soothing, somehow. Elsa must feel the same way, because when Celia looks over, there's a slight smile on her face.

"It'll have to be before Labor Day weekend, Mitch, which is the grand opening of my Ocean Star Inn," Elsa explains. "After that, my life will be all *avanti tutta*!"

"And what's that now?" Mitch asks on speakerphone.

Now, wait, Celia thinks while folding another sheet into a square. If she's not mistaken, there's some smile in *Mitch's* tone, too.

"*Avanti tutta*. It's an Italian phrase my son used to say. Full speed ahead." Elsa sets down her folded pillowcase and pauses, looking out the window in the direction of the beach, and the Fenwick cottage. She tucks a loose strand of her caramel-highlighted hair behind the blue bandana on her head. "So I'm thinking this Monday, maybe?"

"Perfect. Why don't you swing by my place to see where they'll be filming?"

"Oh, I'd love to!" Elsa suddenly looks around the room in somewhat of a panic. "I just need to check my calendar and pencil you in."

"*Go!*" Celia keeps her voice hushed while waving her hands toward the door. "*You go. I'll finish here.*"

Elsa quickly squeezes Celia's hand, then grabs her phone, takes it off speaker and rushes toward the inn's reception area. Her chatting voice carries back to Celia from the long hallway.

With the laundry room to herself now, Celia walks over to the baby's portable play yard. She bends low, whispers a few words to Aria and brushes her silky brown hair beneath that sweet headband. Then Celia gets back to the business of sheets. The business of sheets, and thoughts of Shane.

Lifting another sheet from the basket, Celia holds it to her face and inhales that, yes, that sea air scent that cures what ails you. Because suddenly it feels like something *does* ail her. Some hint of sadness, maybe. Or some empty feeling touching upon her heart.

She holds that sheet there to her face, breathing the scent a few moments longer, and okay, pressing the soft fabric to her suddenly damp eyes, too.

# twenty-two

## *Friday Afternoon*

THERE ARE WAYS TO TELL lies, without actually lying. Oh, doesn't Celia know this. You just circle around the truth. It's kind of like a verbal tiptoeing, the way she's been careful to not draw any attention to her masked lies lately.

Like today, for instance. Because, yes, she'll *take* Aria for that afternoon walk now—just like she told Elsa earlier. Truth. Absolute truth.

Before Celia leaves, though, she stops in her bedroom in the little guest cottage. There's one thing she has to do first, before walking. She dips her fingers into a crystal dish of sea glass on her dresser. Her fingers, they brush through the soft-edged pieces and scoop up a handful. There are greens, and whites, and some blues in her palm. The blues are the most rare. Carefully, she tips the bits of sea glass into a piece of soft netting left over from the inn's Mason

191

jar decorating. Her fingers pull the netting closed and secure it with a strand of twine before she heads to the baby's room.

Aria, Celia can tell when she lifts her from her crib, is already drowsy. Her body is lax, her eyes heavy. So Celia settles the baby in her stroller, nestles a plush seagull beside her and heads out for her afternoon walk. Truth.

All truth, just like she told Elsa this morning while folding those sheets. Because Celia *wasn't* lying. She just verbally circled around more of the truth—which was that she *would* be walking, yes. Gone *unsaid* was that she'd be walking down Sea View Road to Shane's little beach bungalow. To his weathered cottage by the sea.

It isn't until she's halfway there that she realizes she's been fighting tears the whole time. Because she's also circled around a painful truth to herself. *Yes*, she'd be walking to Shane's cottage. Truth.

The truth she circled around, denied, squelched, was that she'd be visiting him for only one reason: to say goodbye. He's leaving Stony Point in the morning.

Nearing Shane's cottage now, Celia leaves the stroller on his lawn and climbs the steps to the front porch. Standing at the door, she gives a few knocks, then backs away, waiting. *"This Will Do,"* she whispers, reading the cottage name on a piece of driftwood hanging beside the door. Oh, the aptness of that name doesn't escape her. This little beach bungalow more than sufficed for her and Shane's time together these past two weeks. Their grinder lunch; their guitar-and-harmonica jam session; her emotional breakdown; their glasses of wine; private talks; stolen kisses. A quiet minute later, she bends to take a look inside the front windows to the living room. Beyond, a bit of the kitchen is visible, too. That tall, aqua-painted cabinet. The kitchen table.

But no Shane.

So she wheels Aria down the boardwalk-planked walkway to the back porch. The stroller tires thump over each plank; sweeping dune grasses whisper beside them.

"Over here, Celia!" Shane's voice calls out.

Celia's surprised to see him emerging from a run-down shed behind the cottage. He's got on jeans and one of his dark tees with the sleeves ripped off—giving clear view of several tattoos inked from his wrists to his shoulders. But his attention is clearly focused on what's in his hands: a dusty fishing pole he's brushing off.

"Friday night fishing tonight," Shane's saying while pulling a rag from his back pocket and wiping the handle. "With my brother."

Still Celia hasn't said a word. Not one. Not a hello. Not that she's glad Shane will spend time with his brother. She just can't, not with that damn lump in her throat.

"What's wrong?" Shane asks, looking up at her now.

Celia shakes her head. She tries to shake her shoulders, too. To shake off this horrible emotion that's taken hold. "I thought I could do this," she manages to say. "But it's so hard."

"*Do* this?"

"You're leaving tomorrow." She gives him a teary smile. "I came to say goodbye."

Shane sets down his fishing pole. "Oh, Celia," he says, coming closer.

"The whole way here? I thought of things you've told me about life on the Atlantic Ocean. Your lobster tales about rogue waves washing over you. All your stories of the boys on the boats, and working together at sea." She turns up her hands. "*Dirty days,*" she barely whispers, fighting ... okay, fighting a sob. "You helped me through many memories of my own."

"Why don't we go on the beach here? No one's around and we can talk." He walks right to her and rubs her arms. "Come on. You and Aria."

"She's asleep."

"I've got an umbrella and chair set up there." He hitches his head toward the little private beach down beyond his small yard. "I'll carry the stroller over so she can nap seaside?"

Celia knows her words will be few now. There's no other way to get through this farewell intact. So she only nods.

Shane lifts the baby's stroller then. Quietly, he tells Celia, "Grab another chair from the shed."

Celia heads over there, swiping at her eyes while she's in the cool shadows of that shed. Cobwebs hang in the corners; sunlight glances on the dusty gear—lawn equipment, rusted bicycles, faded beach umbrellas. She takes a couple of deep breaths, whispering to herself, "*Get it together.*" Finally, she picks up a faded sand chair and walks down a narrow path to the small strip of beach. It's just enough, that beach. Quiet and private enough for their last words coming now. When she steps onto the sand, Shane is gently setting Aria's stroller in the shade beneath his umbrella.

Watching, Celia can't help it, the way she just stops there. Stops on the sand and takes it all in: the small waves of Long Island Sound lapping at the beach; the motorboat cruising by out on the open water; the neighbor's lanterns lining a rock wall behind the yard; Shane.

Shane, so carefully adjusting the stroller.

Shane, looking back at Celia standing on the sand.

Shane, stepping out from beneath his umbrella and motioning her closer.

Celia slips off her sandals, then picks up the sand chair leaning against her leg and walks to him. When she stops, he reaches over and tucks her hair behind an ear; strokes the side of her face such that she presses it into his strong hand. "From that first night in the rowboat, when you helped me with the flowers?" she asks.

Shane barely nods, and just watches her.

"You've … Well, you've been so kind to me. And really, I didn't know what to make of it. Because I was conflicted, Shane, after hearing so many rumors and stories about you."

His voice is quiet. "Those have a way of getting around on the sea breezes, Celia."

Again, she says nothing. Just purses her lips, looks away to blink back hot tears stinging her eyes, then gives him a small smile.

"Here. Sit." He lifts her chair and opens it on the other side of the umbrella pole, away from her sleeping baby. "You were one of the biggest surprises here for me, too. Caught me a little off guard, you did," he says as he sits in his own chair.

Celia walks behind the umbrella, drops her sandals on the sand and drags her chair right up against his. But it's just too hard to collect herself, so she tries a different tactic: changing the subject after sitting down. "So. Friday night fishing? You mended fences with Kyle?"

"We're getting there," Shane tells her. "What Kyle saw as a cruel exclusion from our father's estate? It was all misinterpreted from the actual fact that there *was* no estate."

"*Nothing?*"

"Not a dime. After years of medical bills, and losing work while caring for our mother, our father ended up nearly destitute. When he died, Kyle and I were in our twenties. Unfortunately, my brother thought *I'd* sucked my father's bank account dry. Awful words got tossed around that separated us before we could just cool down and talk. Hear each other out."

Shane pauses, looking at the summer-blue water of the Sound, then taking a breath of the salt air. Celia figures he's doing one thing—trying to cure some brother rift that's ailing him still.

"His words that did it back then? That had me believe we were done?" Shane quietly asks. "I mentioned it to you last week, the way Kyle pinned our father's death on me."

"Oh, Shane," she says, stroking his arm beside her. Her fingers trace along the dark ink of a few swirling tattoos.

"Yeah. I didn't cause that death. And Kyle knows it *now*. Knows I actually gave Dad the best final months a guy could want, sitting harborside. Bullshitting with the old salts in Maine while he waited for my boat to come in. Repairing lobster pots." Again, Shane just breathes. "Ease, for our old man. And he deserved it," he says. "But that year when he died? That year actually broke me, Celia."

"*Broke* you?"

"Completely. It was the year I lost everybody. Everybody in my life, gone. One after the other after the other."

"The love of your life? Maris?"

Shane nods. "My father, several months later."

"And Kyle."

"A helluva trifecta. Everyone I cared about? Gone." He snaps his fingers. "Just like that."

"I didn't realize … Well, losing *everyone* all at once … There are just no words."

"No."

"Sounds like your own dirty year?"

"Absolutely. I was at my lowest point."

"It must've been like, I don't know, stepping off a cliff."

"Pretty close. Throwing myself into lobstering out on the Atlantic was the only thing that kept *me* from going under. It kept me alive."

Celia hears it. Shane's not tiptoeing around some truth here. There's no cloaking one truth with another. She gets it. If it weren't for lobstering, Shane wouldn't be here today.

"Maybe I didn't try hard enough back then," he goes on, "to reach out to Kyle. Doesn't matter, though. Because this week? *This* was the time. We talked two nights ago. Right here on my back porch. And it worked."

"Why *now*, do you think?" Celia asks. "And not then?"

"We see life differently now. Fifteen years of time softened the edges."

"Will you keep in touch?"

Shane looks at her and nods. "Hope to."

And he says nothing else. Just lets that hope sail in a slight breeze lifting off the water. They sit there while lazy waves lap onshore, and a seagull soars down from the sky and settles on the neighbor's rock wall. Minutes pass like that. The sand is warm on her bare feet. The sea air barely moves.

"I have something for you," Celia finally says. She digs the wrapped sea glass out of her tote. "These are from my walks on Stony Point Beach. And Little Beach, too." She holds out the netted glass. The muted greens and blues and whites show through. "For your happiness jar."

～

Shane takes the sea glass. His fingers touch the various pieces through the netting. He can feel the salt, the brine of the sea, on the pieces. Working the ocean's magic, dulling the sharp edges. He looks at Celia beside him. Her auburn hair is down; her gentle eyes watch him. She's dressed in blue today—a blue sleeveless blouse over her faded denim cutoffs. Silver studs are in her ears; sadness in her smile.

He looks a little longer, touches her hair, her neck. Isn't Celia herself the sea glass that softened the edges of his past two weeks here at Stony Point? He takes her hand and lifts it to his mouth. Pressing his lips against the back of her hand for a long moment, his eyes actually drop closed when he does. Then he lowers his arm and simply holds her hand on the sand chair armrest. Long Island Sound spreads out before them. The sun is high in the sky, its rays glistening in sparkles on the blue water. Shane knows. He knows just what they are. Celia sang about them the other day, her voice capturing just what he's feeling right about now. "Ocean stars," he says, squeezing her hand and looking at her.

Celia looks from the water, to him, and only nods.

～

"She's sound asleep," Celia says minutes later when she checks on Aria in her stroller. "So lulled by those easy waves, the warm air."

"The best kind of sleep."

"I wish she slept like this last night. Aria was so fussy, I was up half the night. Feeding her, changing her. Rocking her."

Shane looks over at Celia. "You're both tired today, then," he quietly says.

Celia bends and touches her sleeping baby, then returns

to her sand chair. "I was really taken aback earlier. Right when I got here," she says when she sits beside Shane again.

"Taken aback?" he asks.

Celia nods. "By my own heart. We talked before about your dirty year?"

"When I lost everyone."

"Right. For *me*, this is truly a dirty day. It's as difficult as can be." She draws her knees close and wraps her arms around them. "This goodbye? It's as uncharted and choppy as those waters on the Atlantic. I mean, what am I going to …" Then, nothing. Celia only shakes her head. And pauses. "*I've really got to go now*," she whispers instead, while suddenly standing up and trotting to the water.

"Wait." Shane slips off his boat shoes and follows her to the shallows. She wades in, letting the cool water try-try-try, he's sure, to cool her heart.

"Celia." He comes up behind her and turns her to him.

Celia waves him off. "Oh, you'll think I'm being all emotional. That I can't handle this. Can't handle anything."

He tips his head and squints at her in the sunlight. "I don't think that at all," he says, his words slow, and serious. "This is *not* easy on me, either."

The way he says that, with some anger in his tone, gets Celia to look at him. The best she can, anyway, while fighting her tears. "It's just that … Never mind," she says. "You'll think I'm being corny."

"Celia." He takes her arm and gives a little shake. "Say it."

"Okay." She inhales that salt air as though she can't get

enough. "Okay. To me? To me, we're like two ships that passed in the night. And now we have to go our own ways."

That anger laced in his voice moments ago, or the impatience, or regret? That same emotion fills Celia's words, enough that he steps closer.

"There's no … being together," she says, motioning between them. "Because it can *never* work, with us. You, the lobsterman fighting the Atlantic Ocean most days. And me, about to open a little beach inn five hours away. Not to mention, you've got too much of a past here and no one would even understand, or support this."

They stand ankle-deep in the Sound. Lapping waves break around them. When Celia looks away, Shane quickly puts his hand on her face and turns her toward him.

"*Don't,*" she whispers.

"Don't what?"

"Don't say whatever bullshit you're about to tell me."

"It's not bullshit." Shane takes her hands in his. "And we're not saying goodbye, Celia. At some point, at some time, we'll see each other again."

"Maybe, maybe not." She turns away and sloshes through the water, giving it a little kick as she does. "Regardless," she tells him when she turns again, "you're leaving tomorrow. Your bungalow will be locked up, your bags packed. You'll drive beneath that stone trestle—"

"With one of three things." Shane steps closer. His eyes never, not for one blessed second, leave hers. "I think you know which."

Celia reaches out and touches his light brown hair. Her

fingers stroke a lock of it, and run down his jaw. "I have to get back."

Shane nods, then follows her to their chairs on the beach. They're quiet now, both really feeling this goodbye. Celia checks on her baby before Shane picks up the stroller and carries it across the sand. Gently, very gently, he sets it down on the pathway beside the painted steps to his back porch. "*Be good for your mom*," he whispers, leaning close to sleeping Aria. "*She's a special lady.*"

But it's what he sees when he turns that finally unhinges him. Celia has sat herself on a porch step. She watched him whisper to her baby, and now silent tears run down her cheeks. It's obvious she's given up on trying to stop them.

"I'm going to miss you, Shane Bradford," she says. "Right here," she adds, patting her heart.

Shane climbs a few steps and sits beside her, saying nothing. But he turns his head to watch her. Her pretty hair shines beneath the afternoon sun. And her eyes, they glisten.

A minute passes before she reaches over and touches his face. When she does, he takes her hand in his and kisses it once, then again. His other hand reaches around her neck as he leans closer and kisses her face, too. Her cheek, her eyes, her mouth. Both his hands cradle her tear-streaked face as the kiss lengthens, as they both hold on to this moment slip-slipping away. It happens then, the way he chokes back some sadness of his own while kissing her. While hearing Celia murmur his name between kisses before she stops. Stops and touches his forehead, his cheek.

"*Safe travels*," she whispers.

"No, no. Wait." Shane leans close, holding her hand again, drawing his fingers through hers. "Can I see you tonight? I'm fishing with my brother, but afterward, maybe?" He looks at her. "We could grab a late dinner or—"

Celia is shaking her head. "It's best we don't."

"But Celia—"

"*No, Shane*," she quietly insists.

So he leans in and kisses her once more. "Listen. If you ever need anything, you find me."

"What?"

"Give me your phone."

So she does. She pulls her cell phone from her tote and hands it to him.

"If you ever, *ever* want to meet up," he says, typing his phone number and address into her contacts, "I live in a little fishing village called Rockport. There's a deck on my house, overlooking the docks. It's a nice place to sit and chew on life. You and your daughter are *always* welcome." He hands her the phone. "You know." His voice drops so low, she leans closer to hear. "If Stony Point gets to be too much. Or," he says, dragging a hand through his hair and feeling a little desperate himself now, "Or if you just need a change. You come to Maine."

"Okay." She barely nods. "*Okay*," she whispers this time, then stands and looks down at him. Her fingers alight on his shoulder. "It's good you came here when Lauren invited you."

Shane squeezes her fingers on his shoulder before she

walks to the baby's stroller and starts slowly pushing it. But she turns back once more, those silent tears still on her cheeks. "You did the right thing," she says.

Shane watches Celia from the stoop. He knows it'd be worse to walk her out front. So he just sits there on that porch step. Sits there and watches her go.

⁓

But when she must be halfway down Sea View Road, Shane knows something. Yes, when several long, now-quiet moments pass, he knows. Something rare happened between them. Something that can't be denied.

It's enough to get him off those porch steps and heading to the small beach where they'd just sat. He lifts Celia's netted sea glass off the sand chair and joggles it while looking out at Long Island Sound. The sea glass pieces clink together, and his thoughts are a pure mess. Finally, still holding the sea glass, he returns to his back porch. In the shade beneath the overhang, he takes his happiness jar off a crate and sets it on the old worn table where he and Celia had their grinder lunch. And their ice-cream desserts. Glasses of wine. Touches, words. After carefully opening the jar's lid, he stops and looks out to the distant water. It's the only way to quell the sudden knot in his throat.

"*Cures what ails you,*" he hoarsely whispers while wiping the back of his hand across an eye and taking a long breath of salt air. In a minute, or five or ten—he's not really sure—but after glancing in the direction of a faraway little guest cottage behind a grand beach inn, Shane loosens the twine around the netting.

But he stops then and sits at the table before pouring the sea glass into his open hand. The pieces are cool on his skin, and smooth with the touch of the sea. After folding the twined netting and tucking it into his pocket, he finally does it. A few at a time, he sprinkles each piece of Celia's sea glass into his happiness jar.

# twenty-three

### *Friday Evening*

THEY SAY FAMILIARITY BREEDS CONTEMPT. Now that's one saying Kyle would fight tooth and nail. Especially on these Friday fishing nights. Here, familiarity is like a slice of heaven. He sits on a boulder and takes in the familiar sights and sounds below. The early evening moon is just barely visible in the twilight-blue sky. Small waves lap at the rocks and tidal pools nearby. And when a distant foghorn moans, Kyle looks out at a light mist rising over the rippling Sound.

All of it familiar. Calming. His senses have memorized everything about Friday night fishing, ingraining it right into his soul.

But there's a new sound tonight, too. And this one's not bad, either. It's the sound of Shane's voice giving Evan a lesson in Fishing 101. They stand further down on the rocks, closer to the water. Evan's been completely mesmerized by his uncle ever since learning that he's a lobsterman. Holding a fishing rod now, Evan stands beside Shane and listens.

Kyle listens, too. From his vantage point higher up on the rocks, he hears only bits and pieces of Shane's instructions. But the tone? Caring and patient.

*Let's tie a hook on your line …*
*Got to attach your weight and bobber, too …*
*Get your hook baited. Easy now …*
*Cast your line …*

When Evan lifts his rod up over his shoulder, Shane stops him.

*You like to play baseball, Ev?*
*Cast your line side-armed, like a pitcher throwing the ball …*
*Atta boy …*
*And when you hook that fish, remember how to pull it in …*
*Pump and lift the rod while reeling.*

Evan pays attention to every word the lobsterman tells him, which gets Kyle to shake his head. Oh, if his son only knew their trials and tribulations. Maybe it's better this way, though. It's nice to have a hero in your life.

The thing is, for Kyle? That hero's pretty much been Jason Barlow, who's gotten Kyle through his share of situations. He wonders if Jason will show up tonight. Figures it can't hurt to text the guy. *You on for Friday night fishing?* he types. *Saved you a boulder. Fair warning, Shane's here too. But it's good, bro. I'll fill you in later.*

Kyle turns then, when he spots Nick climbing over the rocks. He's seriously ready to fish, holding his fishing rod and wearing his mesh sporting vest. Each vest pocket is stuffed with bobbers, hooks, spare line and scissors.

"Yo, guys," Nick calls out as he approaches Shane and Evan first. "Hey, hey! Who do we have here? A new pup in the group?" he asks while mussing Evan's dark moppy hair. "Sup, dude?"

"My uncle's teaching me how to fish," Evan says while reeling in some line.

"All right!" Nick high-fives Evan, nods to Shane, then heads over to Kyle. "Getting your boy started early. That's good, Kyle."

"Never too young to fish," Kyle tells him.

"Ain't that the truth." Nick sets down his fishing rod and takes a long breath of that salt air. "I just clocked out after a long day of monitoring Stony Point vacationers."

"Everyone behaving?" Kyle asks.

"A few minor infractions. They're getting pretty crafty the way they sneak food on the beach." Nick picks up his rod and baits his hook. "What's biting this fine evening?"

"The usual. Stripers. Porgy. Hear the fluke are getting better, too."

"You ever fish for blue crab?" Shane calls back to Kyle.

"Shit. Not in a long time," Kyle tells him. "Been years."

"Let's do it," Nick says, giving Kyle a shove. "We could try it one of these Fridays."

"Yeah, I could go for some blue crab." Kyle baits his

line, liking the idea more and more. "Catch some fresh for dinner. Steamed and dipped in warm garlic butter?"

"Oh man, sweet," Shane tosses back.

"Hey. Where is everybody?" Nick asks.

"Jason's busy tonight." Kyle steps lower on the rocks. It's the least he can do, cover for his friend. Because it looks like Barlow's not showing—or answering his text. Truth is, Kyle doesn't have a clue *where* Jason is—in his life, in his head. All Kyle knows is that Jason's in a bad way, if their oil-change talk was any indication. Friday night fishing, and Stony Point in general? It's just not the same without Jason here.

"That dude's always busy," Nick is saying. "And what about my boss?"

"Cliff? Heard he's going out with Elsa later."

"Wooing must've resumed," Nick says while tying a lure on his line. "Friday night date, maybe."

"Seems it. And Matt's in Martha's Vineyard with the fam." As he says it, Kyle casts his line, sending it whistling out over the water. The sun is just going down, the horizon violet now.

"All right. Well, I'm going to try my luck fishing with your son." Nick takes his gear and climbs lower on the rocks to where Evan fishes with Shane.

"Good luck," Kyle calls out. "My kid will whoop your butt."

When Shane looks back then, Kyle motions him over. Together they walk across the rocks to the beer-and-food cooler. Shane snaps open a can of beer while Kyle grabs some chow.

"What're these?" Shane asks when Kyle hands him a mini sandwich.

"Pinwheels. Made with flatbread."

"Safe to eat? No hot-pepper surprise in there?"

"Nah. You're good. There's turkey, fresh spinach, cheese, mustard."

"Damn. Not bad, bro," Shane says around a mouthful. "And your boy's a natural, on the water, fishing. Reminds me of how—"

"Neil was. Yeah, I know." Kyle swigs his beer, then grabs a turkey pinwheel for himself. He waves the food toward Evan, fishing with Nick. "Evan's a good kid. Couldn't ask for a better son," he says.

"No shit. Glad I got to spend some time with him tonight. You've got a great family. And with all the gang around again, too?" Shane lifts his beer in a slight toast. "That vow renewal must've meant a lot."

Kyle bites into his pinwheel. "Meant everything, Shane," he says around the food.

"Dad! *Dad!*" Evan calls from the lower rocks. "Uncle *Shane!*"

Nick spins around. "Bring the net! Evan's got a big one!"

"All *right!*" Shane reaches for the net, slapping Kyle's shoulder as he does, then heads down the rocks. "You're a true fisherman, Ev," he says. "Right from the get-go."

"Yoo-hoo!" a woman calls out twenty minutes later. Her voice cuts right through a peaceful fishing lull, when Kyle wonders if it's the fishing that draws the guys here, or the lulls. The lapping waves. The cooler evening air. The sunset sky. He looks over and sees Elsa approaching.

"Hey! No women allowed here Friday nights," Kyle calls back as he makes his way over to her. "You're crashing our boys' club," he says with a wink when he takes her hand and helps her cross some of the rocks.

"You fellas might change your mind about that. I've got the perfect *catch*." She opens an insulated tote. "Raspberry-cheesecake pots."

Kyle ventures a look at whatever delectables she packed in there. "Oh, *Marone*," he says while lifting out a tiny jar filled with layers of graham cracker, and cheesecake, and raspberries. "You are *amazing*."

"Bring it on, Elsa!" Nick tosses down his fishing pole and heads in her direction.

"I'm on my way out," Elsa says as she lifts another jar. "But I bumped into Lauren at the grocery store this morning. She mentioned there'd be a special visitor fishing here tonight. And I didn't want to miss you, Shane."

Shane takes Evan's fishing pole and sets it down before they both head back across the rocks. "Appreciate that, Elsa," Shane tells her. "I was going to swing by your place tomorrow morning, to say goodbye."

"Oh, you'll be so busy packing up. And I'm sure there's a mile-long cleanup checklist on your refrigerator." She pauses to give Evan a plastic spoon with his bottled cheesecake. "So I was wondering if you had five minutes for a beach walk?"

"For you? Always." He takes Elsa's tote from her and gives it to Kyle. "And hey, Evan." Shane walks over to the boy and claps his back. "Man the sea while I'm gone, would you?"

They walk along the sunset beach. Shadows grow long now. The sun has sunk below the horizon.

"I just have a few minutes," Elsa begins. She pulls close a light cardigan draped over her shoulders. "Cliff's waiting for me. We're going out to dinner tonight."

"Well, I'm glad you caught me, Elsa."

"And I'm glad *you* stopped at the Ocean Star Inn two weeks ago, when you spent your first nights here. You left quite an impression on me."

"Same here. And I thank you for that," Shane tells her. "You were really gracious with my arrival that weekend— when I needed it the most. I might not have stayed on at Stony Point if not for your hospitality."

"And look at you now," she tells him, giving his hand a quick squeeze. "Friday night fishing with your *brother!*"

Shane nods. "I truly wish you and Celia the very best with your inn's grand opening. It's coming up. Labor Day weekend, no?"

"It is. We're really excited for it and can't believe it's finally happening." When a gentle breeze lifts off the water,

212

Elsa brushes a wisp of hair from her face. "And what's next for you, Shane? A couple of weeks out on the Atlantic?"

"Not yet. I'll be eking out the summer season close to shore, my favorite time of year. Won't be on the big boats until later in the fall. Those are the two-week trips, and a whole different lifestyle. But right now? The work's with local Maine lobstermen. Start before sunup, back home at night most of the time."

"Home *every* day?"

"Here and there." Shane picks up a flat stone and skips it out over the evening water. "Me and the boys refer to these days as smooth sailing. We relish being on the calm sea late summer. And being home more often."

Elsa stops him right there. "In that case, I would love to extend an invitation to you, Shane. *If* you can make it, no pressure, to the inn's ribbon-cutting ceremony next Friday night."

"Now that's very nice of you. But are you *sure*, Elsa? After my last invite crashed an event?"

"Yes, I'm sure. Everyone will be here, and under *much* better circumstances this time around. I'm hoping, at least."

"Me, too," Shane says as they start walking again. "Sometimes things come up on the boats and my schedule changes, but I'll tell you what. I'll do my best to be there. No promises, but save a seat for me?"

"Oh, I will."

Shane nods to Cliff waiting over on the boardwalk. "Ah, the commissioner. Your date, I believe?"

"It is. I have to run, Shane," Elsa says. But before

leaving, she steps close and gives him a warm hug. "*Dio ti benedica*," she whispers. "God bless you."

Shane backs up a step. "Appreciate that."

"You be safe," she tells him. "And whether you make it here next week or not, there's always a room for you at the Ocean Star Inn."

Shane watches as Elsa crosses the beach toward Cliff. "I'm sure I'll take you up on that," Shane calls after her. When she waves back, he adds, "Someday."

# twenty-four

### *Friday Night*

JASON WALKS INTO THE CAPTAIN'S Lounge and stops near the hostess station. He looks into the restaurant at the dark wood square tables and ladder-back chairs. Most are filled tonight, with couples, friends, families dining together. Wall sconces cast dim light in the room, which is painted sea-foam green above a white chair rail, and paneled in ocean-blue planks below. White-framed photographs of various ships and seaports hang above that chair rail wrapping around the room. Except for the back wall. That wall is filled end to end with floor-to-ceiling windows looking out onto Long Island Sound.

Which is where he spots Elsa and Cliff, already sitting at a window table while considering their menus. Silverware and napkins are set out before them, as are three glasses of water. Elsa's dressed in black skinny pants and a black tank top, with a fitted sand-colored cardigan over it. A silky scarf is loosely tied at her neck, too.

Okay, and the first clue she's upset? She didn't come alone.

Second clue? She's so upset, when Jason crosses the dark hardwood floor and winds his way around other patrons and tables, Elsa does not stand up to greet him. Cliff does, though.

"Nice to see you, Jason," he says while shaking Jason's hand.

"Cliff." Jason clasps Cliff's arm, then walks around him toward Elsa. He squeezes her shoulder, than takes a seat across from her.

"Jason," Elsa says then. "I'm glad you came."

"Of course. It seemed important, from your text message the other day," he tells her while settling in his seat. "How are you tonight?"

"I'm okay." Elsa slightly shrugs. "You?"

"I'm fine, Elsa."

"Good, good," Cliff says while moving aside a menu. "But I'll tell you. *We* had a rough start getting here tonight. I swear, ever since losing my lucky domino, I've been having odd problems. If only I could find that good-luck charm of mine—"

"What's the problem now?" Jason asks.

"Been investigating some animal, maybe? Beneath the Stony Point Beach Association trailer."

"An animal? Like what?" Jason asks. "Because the last thing you need is mice, or some rodent setting up house there."

"There's been this scratching, skittering kind of sound coming through the floor," Cliff explains. "Mostly at night, when it's quiet. I pointed out to Elsa some spots where it appears the animal dug a small opening to get beneath the trailer."

"Maybe a raccoon?" Jason asks. "Or an opossum?"

Cliff shakes his head. "No, not that big of a hole. So something smaller."

"Okay, gentlemen," Elsa interrupts. "We've established that we're all relatively fine, and that some pesky animal lives beneath Cliff's temporary home."

"Elsa," Cliff quietly says while giving her hand a pat. "It's just small talk."

"And it's enough." Elsa pulls her chair in closer.

So Jason picks up a menu, opens it, then closes it and sits back in his chair. It's obvious that Elsa, of all people, is going to be the one holding him accountable for what he did—leaving his wife. And for where he's living—Ted Sullivan's cottage. And for any perceived slight or atrocity she sees fit in all of it. Here it all comes.

In the low lighting, Elsa leans forward and squints across the table at him. "You don't belong here," she says, motioning to the crowded tables around them. A waitress passes by holding an overloaded dinner tray. "On a Friday night? You belong out on the rocks, Jason, fishing with the guys."

Jason simply sips from a glass of iced water.

"And I hear it's a small crew fishing tonight," Cliff adds. "Nick told me earlier he's catching up with Kyle and Evan there."

Though Jason nods, he can't even picture it. Can't picture being in the frame of mind to sit on some random boulder. Can't picture digging into whatever cuisine Kyle packed from the diner; can't picture having a cold beer; or casting his fishing line out over Long Island Sound; or shooting the breeze with Shane—who's apparently fishing, too, according to Kyle's text. No, Jason hasn't been picturing much of anything lately.

A waiter approaches before they say more. "Welcome to The Captain's Lounge, folks. Dinner tonight?"

"Any specials?" Cliff asks.

"We've got a broiled bluefish filet, choice of two sides. Also have a New York strip steak, with potato and vegetable. And mussels over linguine, with a white wine sauce." He eyes the table. "Celebrating something? Someone's birthday? Anniversary?"

"No. No celebrations tonight," Jason tells him.

"Very well, then." Their waiter holds his pencil to order pad. "What can I get you?"

"I'll have the grilled salmon," Elsa says.

"Excellent choice." Their waiter jots down her order. "Has a nice lemon dill sauce. Comes with rice pilaf and steamed zucchini with oil and garlic."

"I'll have the same," Jason tells the waiter. "But swap the rice with sweet potato fries."

"Got it. And you, sir?" the waiter asks Cliff.

Cliff quickly opens the menu, drags his finger down a page and motions for Elsa's reading glasses. Holding the leopard-print frames in front of his eyes, he spots what he wants. "Lobster mac and cheese, with a Caesar salad."

"And something to drink? A bottle of wine for the table?"

"Draft beer," Jason tells him.

"Make that two," Cliff puts in.

Elsa thinks a moment. "Wine spritzer."

"Very good." The waiter collects their menus, saying, "I'll bring warm bread in a minute."

As he hurries off, their table quiets. Jason hears only the noise of the restaurant: silverware on plates; voices softly talking; chairs scraping. Until finally, it's obvious Elsa just can't hold back.

"You're breaking my heart, Jason Barlow. You know you're like a son to me. So tell me what's wrong."

"What's wrong?" Jason asks. "More like, what's right these days?"

"We heard about Maris being engaged to Shane all those years ago," Cliff says.

Elsa sits back as the waiter leaves a breadbasket and plate of butter tabs on the table. "Water under the bridge, that old engagement."

"I'm not convinced of that, Elsa." Jason takes a thick slice of bread and butters it.

"So you packed and left? Just like that?" Elsa presses. "You're running away?"

"Not running away. More like getting *out* of the way. There's a difference."

Cliff reaches for a bread slice, too, and spreads butter on it. "Jason," he says, then bites off a hunk of bread.

"We're not badgering you. Just trying to make sense of things," he manages around the food.

"And I'm not going to give you a blow-by-blow of my marriage." Jason lifts his buttered bread. "I just needed space, okay? And since I've left," he continues before taking a bite of his bread, "everybody, and I mean *everybody*—from Kyle to Paige to Shane even, and now you two—has been out to see me."

Elsa tips her head, eyeing him. "Everybody except Maris."

"We've talked. But you're right. She hasn't been to Ted's."

Elsa clasps Jason's arm. "Well," she says, her voice soft, "what happens when people love you is this. They don't let go without a fight. So Maris talked to *me*, too."

Jason sits back with a long breath, bread still in hand. "Listen. It's been a rough summer, Elsa. Different things have been chipping away at me."

"We all have things we deal with," Elsa says as their waiter delivers their drinks. But she doesn't miss a beat and keeps talking. "History. A past. You know that. So let the people around you help you through, Jason."

"We all *do* have a history," Jason repeats. "True. But when it's kept *secret* it becomes a problem," he says with a glance at Cliff. Oh, don't they both know Jason's referring to Cliff's secret identity as little lost Sailor—the boy for whom a man gave his life trying to rescue.

"And Elsa," Cliff reminds her. "Secrets in a *marriage* are a whole other animal."

As he says it, their dinners are delivered. Suddenly the table is loaded with salmon platters and side dishes. Warm plates are set down. Water glasses are refilled.

"You know something?" Cliff stands and sets his lobster mac and cheese back on the waiter's tray. "Think I'll have mine outside on a patio table."

"Here." The waiter reaches for his salad and drink, setting both on his tray. "Let me help you, sir," he says as Cliff drops his napkin and silverware on the tray, too.

"Cliff." Elsa reaches for his arm. "Are you sure?"

He bends and leaves a kiss on Elsa's cheek. "I think it's best. It'll give you some private time to talk with Jason." Cliff glances at their waiter heading for the outdoor patio. "I have to call my son, Denny, too. He left a message about a car show coming up he wants to go to."

"Okay, then," Elsa tells him.

Cliff pats Jason's shoulder, turns and follows the waiter outside.

⁓

Elsa watches Cliff go before opening her napkin in her lap. She says nothing while she does. Says nothing as she squeezes a lemon wedge over her grilled salmon. Says nothing while she forks off a flaky piece, chews it and sips her wine spritzer, too. As far as Jason can tell, she'll say nothing now until he explains himself.

"Elsa," he begins. "Shane this, Maris that. Histories, secrets." Jason waves his fork. "Maris and I *have* talked. What came of it is that I asked her to fix some issues with her past. To *deal* with them, or else they'll haunt her. Haunt us. Because honestly? I can't live in a haunted marriage." He forks off a piece of salmon. "I've got enough ghosts in my life."

"Which is the one thing you're not mentioning ... that it's also the ten-year anniversary of a very dark *day* in your life," Elsa reminds him. "And no one understands better than me that grief subsides, but it also rears its ugly head. Don't forget, it's been a year since I lost my son, Salvatore."

Jason, with a mouthful of zucchini, nods. "One year's different," he manages around the food. "It's hell, I know that. But at ten years, it's a different kind of hell."

"Really."

"They say it gets easier? Over time and all that?" Jason shakes his head.

"You're not finding that to be true?"

"No. Because one day, more of my life will be without my brother, instead of with him. Neil's long gone."

Elsa takes another bite of salmon and watches Jason. "So you're isolating yourself. And from the looks of you, I can see why. It's obvious."

"And why's that?"

"You don't want people to see you like this."

"Like what?"

"Emotional? Sad? I don't know." Elsa leans closer in the shadowy room. "Defeated by it all?" she quietly asks.

Jason tips his head, watching her. "Defeated?"

Elsa nods. "It's too much this year. *Too* sad. And what I'm seeing very clearly—from my vantage point?"

Jason sets down his fork and turns up his hands, giving Elsa the floor.

"Shane Bradford became your perfect crutch."

"Oh, you've got—"

"The answer, is what I've got." The angrier Elsa gets, the lower her voice drops. "Shane came into town at *just* the right time, didn't he? The right time for you to blame your emotional frame of mind on *him*. On his past with Maris." She hesitates then. "On an old engagement ring? Please, Jason."

Jason looks away, then back at Elsa. Seconds pass. He drags a knuckle across the raised scar on his jaw. "Maybe you should leave," he finally says.

"Like *hell*." Elsa pulls her chair in closer to the table. She loosens the silky scarf around her neck. And never takes her eyes off his. "You're going to do it, Jason. And you *know* it," she adds, pointing a stern finger at him. "You're going to push Maris away. Get divorced. Go your separate ways. Have her leave Stony Point. I *see* it this time. And you and I *both* know damn well what this all is."

"Which I'm sure you're about to tell me."

"Survivor's guilt."

Jason says nothing. He just breathes. Just hears the dishes and silverware clattering around him in the dimly lit room. The voices. And his own angry heart beating.

"Maris is *desperate*," Elsa goes on. "So she told me private things. Things you are *not* to hold against her."

"Like what?"

"She told me *you* were driving the motorcycle the day your brother died, okay? That you were together, so close, at the end. You felt Neil's very last breath. Heard his last words."

*Jay*, Jason remembers now, sitting there in the shadows. *Hey, Jay*, Neil had said as his arm reached forward, pointing to the approaching car's reflection in the motorcycle's mirror.

"Maris told me the details, Jason." Elsa sips her wine. "How you felt Neil's body against yours before he was thrown from the bike. But she also told me something else. That you struggle ... because you feel you *should've* been watching behind you to see that car in time. That *you* believe your brother's death is your fault."

It's all Jason can do to keep his tone level in the restaurant. "You're blowing things out of proportion." He drags a hand through his hair. "My staying at Ted's has nothing to do with that. I really just needed some *space*, for Christ's sake."

Elsa brushes off his words and turns a little sideways in her chair. "It's obvious that you have not slept in days. You're losing weight. Not eating," she says with a nod to his picked-at grilled salmon. "And *I'm* here to remind you, Mr. Barlow," she says, her voice barely above a whisper, "that you have a *beautiful* life, one that you're ruining because you don't think you deserve it."

"Don't *deserve* it?"

She gives him a small smile with a shrug. "I know what you must think ... Why Neil, and not *you*, that day? Why didn't Neil deserve to live, and *you* die?" She silently stares at him. Several seconds pass as she lets that one question sink in. Lets it hit him hard. Makes him face it. "Survivor's guilt."

But Jason won't have it. Won't let Elsa deliver her verdict without a rebuke. "And I'm telling you it *is* Shane." Now? Now *he* leans close, drops his head for a moment, then looks directly at his aunt-through-marriage. "And, yes. It was the wrong time for him to show up here. Because not only does Shane have some unfinished past with my wife. Not only did he screw over Kyle, back in the day. But he, but he …" And that's it. Jason just stops to catch his breath.

"But he *what*, Jason?"

"He sold Neil *his* motorcycle."

Elsa, well, what can she do except close her eyes and shake her head in disbelief.

"It's true," Jason says, nodding. "The Harley Neil and I were on? The one *I* was driving? It was Shane's, before he sold it to my brother."

"Still," Elsa says, searching for the words now. "Shane didn't cause that accident. You know that."

"You're right, he didn't. It's just that where Shane goes, so goes trouble."

"Look." Elsa's voice is still low in the busy restaurant. "You're a man who was strong enough to, pardon me, but strong enough to stand on his *own* two feet and stare *down* life. You went and *met* the enemy. You *met* Ted Sullivan. And … and you made *peace* with him."

"I did."

"And your life's gone on since then. Now you're married to my niece, are at the top of your game restoring beautiful beach homes, *and* are the host of a wonderful television show. A good life." She sips her wine, leans closer and continues.

"But this summer, at ten years, *you* feel it came with a price—your brother's life. Which is survivor's guilt. So you're sabotaging all of it, to make it topple."

Jason can see it on Elsa's face, some restraint as she tries to get through to him. Sees her attempt to keep her voice down.

"You don't feel worthy, I suppose, of this incredible life you built *after* the wreck. A wreck that ended Neil's life, but *not* yours. And maybe it's easier to cope with the survivor's guilt if you take your life down a notch—"

"Elsa …" Jason begins, without any fight in his voice.

"No," Elsa continues. "What's next? Lose *Castaway Cottage*, too? Get that show covering the *esteemed* Fenwick place cancelled—before it even airs?"

Jason sits back, takes a breath, watches Elsa. He lifts his napkin and wipes his mouth first, then a bead of perspiration. His appetite's gone; a wave of nausea passes over him. "I'll be back," he tells her, then goes to the men's room. When the door closes behind him, he walks past the urinals, past the stalls and goes straight to a sink. Feeling sick, he right away turns on the faucet, cups his hands beneath it, bends and scoops handful after handful of water on his face, his neck. Finally, he straightens, drags his wet hands through his hair and sees his reflection in the mirror. Sees the ashen skin, the three days' worth of whiskers, the shadows.

And takes in some damn truth that Elsa just tossed his way.

When Jason walks back to the table, Cliff is there again. He and Elsa are getting ready to leave. Elsa is collecting her handbag, folding her napkin on the table. Jason sits across from the two of them.

"Jason," Cliff says. "If we can't convince you to go back home, is there anything else we can do?"

"What do you mean?" Jason asks.

Cliff shrugs. "Well, it seems that your coming here to dinner tonight is some sort of admission that you need help."

"And we all love you," Elsa tells him, then finishes the last of her wine. "Listen. One year ago, I was ready to leave Stony Point—for good. Had my inn listed for sale, bags practically packed."

Jason nods.

"I was all done," Elsa admits. "I just couldn't go on there. And you *knew* it, too. But it was *you* who convinced me to stay. Remember that morning last year? On the little dock when we were going to move Sal's rowboat?"

Jason thinks of that morning he found Elsa on the dock. Her body shuddered with tears and gasps as she fully realized her son's death. In the late-summer sunshine, Jason quietly sat with her, put his arm around her shoulders, let her lean into him and simply weep.

"I often think of the beautiful story you told me that morning. Your father's story of that poor soldier walking through the swamp in Vietnam one night. The soldier prayed, quietly chanted—over and over again—the Hail Mary. He thought he was *done*. That it was the end of his life that night. But it wasn't. Your father's unit *heard* that soft chant, recognized the prayer and saved the man. That lost soldier prayed to Mary, seeking his *Stella Maris* one awful night at war." Elsa takes Jason's hand. "You're lost, too," she whispers. "But you *have* your Maris."

"And no one said I won't be back, Elsa."

"From what I'm seeing?" She shakes her head. "You keep this up and you're too far gone." She stands and hooks her purse on her shoulder. "Neil's Memorial Mass is this Sunday. And it's really not wise for you to be alone that day. Maris will be there at the church. I'll be there."

"And we want to see *you* there, Jason," Cliff says as he and Elsa stand to leave.

Jason says nothing. He just stands too, and hugs Elsa, who leaves a kiss on his cheek and walks out of the restaurant with Cliff.

⌒

Outside the big window at his table, the sky is black. Jason can't distinguish it from Long Island Sound—also there, beneath the sky. Inside, his table is quiet now. He sits there, looking out at the night. When he leans a forearm on the table, there's a painful throb near his elbow. He twists his arm around to see that nasty bruise, from when he took a fall out of bed.

"All set here?" his waiter asks moments later. He picks up the remaining dishes on the table. "Would you like any of this packed for you?" he asks, motioning to all the salmon and zucchini still on Jason's plate.

"No."

"Okay, then."

"I'll have another draft, when you get a chance."

As though the waiter knows that whatever went down at this table was bleak, he promptly delivers the glass of beer, wordlessly setting it on a paper napkin.

Jason sits there, by the window. He says nothing to the waiter, who turns and leaves. In a minute, he picks up his beer and takes a long swallow. At the square tables near him, diners talk, eat. The wall sconces throw soft light on the shadowy room. But Jason only looks at the darkness outside. Beyond the outdoor patio, the harbor water is black. A few moored boats cast pools of golden light on the rippling waves. Occasionally Jason lifts his beer glass for another sip, but other than that, does not move. Does not look around. Just angles his chair toward the window and keeps his eye on the night.

# *twenty-five*

### **Saturday at Dawn**

KYLE STANDS IN HIS TINY en-suite bathroom. The pedestal sink leaves barely enough room for his razor and shaving cream. But he manages. There's somewhere he's got to be, and hopefully he's not too late. The rising sun is just starting to edge the blinds with pale light. Standing there in his pajama bottoms, Kyle drags the razor down his cheek. And remembers the conversation from the other night on Shane's porch.

*No estate to lock you out of, bro ... Nothing there ... Barely enough to pay Dad's funeral expenses.*

"Shit," Kyle quietly says as he rinses his razor beneath the running water. It still sucks, thinking of the years lost between him and his brother, all over a painful misunderstanding. Sucks, too, knowing he then lost his vow renewal ceremony because of that very misunderstanding. After talking things out with Shane a few nights ago, Kyle went home exhausted by the whole conversation. Later that night, he sat with Lauren on their front porch. With the twinkle lights glimmering and water lapping at the bay across the street, he told her the truth of *everything*. That his father died practically destitute, after years of medical bills accumulated during their mother's illness. Even Shane had no idea their father was broke back then. Not until the morning their father stood on the front stoop with a suitcase in hand and begged a ride to Maine.

Now Kyle can't get it all out of his head. With every hurried drag of that razor along his jaw, certain things he told Lauren that night play over and over …

⁓

*Tempers were short back then*, Kyle began. He and Lauren sat side by side on their little porch sofa, and she held his hand as he talked.

> *Emotions taut. Especially for Shane, who'd been floored by Maris' broken engagement.*
> *Devastated.*
> *So everything was compounded.*
> *And misread.*
> *Misunderstood.*
> *No money. No estate.*
> *Couldn't get through to each other.*
> *Never knew. My brother took care of Dad right to the end.*

That line in particular got to Kyle. He'd *blamed* Shane for their father's death—only to find out the opposite. Only to learn that Shane did right by their father, giving him a place to live when the man had nowhere else to turn. And their father's last days were actually sweet, lived out by the sea with Shane. Out of the whole rift, the whole estrangement, *that's* the fact toughest to swallow—the stinging, wrongful blame Kyle leveled at his brother fifteen years ago. In the privacy of Kyle's home on the bay, he cried when he admitted that to Lauren.

Fought tears, too, when he said he needed to fix things, in many ways. First, he told Lauren he *had* to share the truth with everybody. That they should have a boardwalk meeting so Kyle could straighten everything out. Could admit he'd been wrong about Shane. He'd take the hit for messing up the past fifteen years, and let the chips fall where they may. The truth might even help Jason and Maris resolve *their* problems.

*Truth?* Lauren had asked.

*That Shane's not here to cause trouble, to pursue Maris, to disrupt lives. He's here because he was invited to make peace. And it's up to me, Ell, for that to happen,* Kyle had said. *Because I started the whole mess with that one damn bonfire fifteen years ago, when I said that Shane wronged me. Stole from me. Screwed me over. I believed all that, too. Stupid fool that I was, I got everybody to burn my brother's name and write him off as dead. To never speak of Shane Bradford again.* Kyle couldn't say any more then, couldn't get any more words past the painful lump in his throat.

*Okay,* Lauren agreed while lightly stroking his arm on

the porch sofa. *Okay. You do have to come clean. But not until after Neil's Memorial Mass this weekend. Let's get through that first.*

They just sat there then. Lauren continued to stroke his arm, which calmed him. He must've closed his eyes because the next thing he knew, he felt Lauren's lips light on his face, his mouth.

*I love you, Kyle,* she murmured. *It's going to be okay.*

⁓

So now, at the crack of dawn Saturday morning, Kyle believes that—believes that things will be okay. He felt that last night, too, fishing on the rocks with Shane. After rinsing off his razor and wiping down the sink, he puts on cargo shorts and a short-sleeve button-down, then stands at his dresser. *And* he has a plan.

"What are you doing?" Lauren asks, squinting over at him from the bed. Her voice is groggy with sleep. "It's so early, Kyle. And I thought Jerry's opening up the diner."

"He is." Kyle lifts his wallet from his dresser and puts it into his shorts back pocket. "I have something else to do."

Lauren sits up beneath the sheet and straightens her satin nightshirt. "You're going to see your brother before he leaves, aren't you?"

"I am." Kyle walks to the bed, bends and kisses Lauren's sleep-mussed hair.

"You better hurry then," she whispers. "He's probably taking off first thing."

Kyle nods and returns to the dresser for his keys. But he

stops for a moment. Late or not, he's painfully aware of why this reconciliation with his brother came about. It just took him a long, difficult two weeks to accept it.

So he turns back to the bed. "Thanks, Ell, for inviting Shane here. You know, and pushing for that second chance." Kyle touches her shoulder and is quiet for a second, until her hand clasps his. "You were right all along."

# twenty-six

## Minutes Later

KYLE WALKS THE SANDY BEACH roads to Shane's cottage. Though the sun is just coming up, the day is warm already. And his memories, they surface like the misty heat waves rising off the damp morning pavement. Visions of his childhood waver in and out of focus. Of course they would. These are the same roads, decades ago, that he and Shane pedaled their bikes on, racing around curves, skidding on sandy patches. The same roads they skateboarded a few summers as kids. On their boards, they'd totally break ordinances and glide off onto a paved footpath or clatter across the planked boardwalk. They'd set up makeshift ramps on the road in front of their blue cottage. Using the street as their runway, they'd get up enough speed to attempt various flip tricks off those jerry-rigged skateboard ramps.

As teenagers, these were the same streets they'd *walk*,

meeting up with the gang on the boardwalk during hot summer afternoons. The same streets they walked again on summer nights, most often headed to Foley's back room, then maybe Little Beach afterward. Get a little lit, have a little fun. Hook up, start some trouble.

Memories wavering … rising with each gritty step Kyle takes to Shane's front door. Once there, Shane tells him to meet him around back, on the porch. That he'll bring out coffee.

So Kyle heads down the planked walkway around the bungalow. He hears gulls crying on the bluff. A train whistle floats through the morning air like a silver ribbon of sound. That's the one, that train whistle he hears now while standing on Shane's back porch, that gets to him the most.

That brings Kyle back to being fourteen years old with not a care in the world.

That reminds him what it's like having a brother.

~

*The railroad tracks ran over an embankment rising off the sand on Back Bay. That sloping hill was built up with large stones, perfect for them to scale and get to the top.*

*"Listen!"*

*They froze on the railroad tracks, the four of them: Kyle, Shane, Jason and Neil. Any one of them could've uttered the word. Didn't matter who said it. What mattered was that it meant danger—that one word. It meant to pay attention. To stop walking on the rails and just feel for the vibration, gauging how close the train was.*

*This one evening, the very last time they walked the tracks, the sun was low in the sky; shadows were long. It was that dusky hour that amped up their teenaged bravado. They were invincible, after all. Young and bold. They'd spent the past hour keeping their balance while walking the steel rails. Or they'd walk four abreast while challenging each other to see who'd break off first when a train came. They'd nearly reached the trestle at Stony Point's entrance when it happened.*

*"Listen!"*

*This time on the tracks, they all waited to actually see the train before they jumped off and scrambled down the embankment. Kyle grabbed his brother's arm at the last second and tumbled down the brush-covered sloping hill with him. Their hoots and hollers filled the air long after the speeding train thundered past—whistle blowing, train chugging, windy dust rising.*

*"Let's go back up," Neil had said.*

*"What?" they all asked, still catching their breath.*

*"Come on," Neil insisted as he climbed the embankment again. But he turned around and stopped then. "When my father was in 'Nam, he said soldiers put coins on the railroad tracks. Thought they might derail the VC trains."*

*They all got quiet then. Because what if it worked? What if they put coins on the tracks here and sent the train over the embankment?*

*"And what happened?" Shane asked. "Did the trains crash?"*

*"Nah." Neil headed up to the tracks again. "But my dad has lots of flattened coins from the war in his dresser drawer."*

*So suddenly they were soldiers. Suddenly Neil and Jason drew them into their imaginary jungles, and swamps, and hilltops waiting*

237

to be won in battle. They moved aside leafy brush. Swatted at mosquitoes. Neil grabbed a large rock to mark beside the tracks where they'd eventually leave their copper pennies, or silver quarters. This way, it would be easier to find the flattened coins later. Then they all dug in their shorts pockets for any leftover ice-cream change. Neil warned them the enemy was close at hand, so they all quieted. The evening turned urgent. The buzzing cicadas became jungle insects. Long twilight shadows concealed the imagined VC soldiers.

"What do you have?" Jason quietly asked Kyle when he stepped onto the tracks. They were right near the trestle, and a beach guard stood duty down below.

"Shane," Kyle whispered loudly, yanking his brother close. "Give me some money."

Shane dug into his pocket and pulled out a nickel. Just one nickel.

"Quick!" Neil said. "The train's coming! We've got to take down the VC."

They glanced further down the tracks, then hurried to a straightaway section. Kyle took his and Shane's one nickel and set it on the steel rail, close to the quarter Jason and Neil laid down.

After setting Neil's marker-rock against the rails, they did it. They ran for their lives. Because wasn't there some part of them that believed those measly coins would send the oncoming locomotive right off the rails and crashing down the embankment. The explosion would be deafening. Fire would roar. So they blindly stumbled over large stones tripping them, and through the overgrown weeds and branches slapping at them, to wait out their fate.

Until it happened. Until the tracks hummed and a passenger train sped past, horn blowing, metal screeching. The four of them ducked for cover, hands over their heads as they crouched in the brush. Kyle's *heart pounded, and when he looked over at Shane, he was white as a ghost.*

*But they'd survived. And there was no derailment. Quickly, they ran back to the tracks and dug through stones and scrubby grass there until spotting their flattened coins in the fading sunlight.*

*"Hey! You boys up there!" a voice suddenly called out. It was old Commissioner Lipkin. He stood at the bottom of the embankment and shone a flashlight up to the tracks. "What are you doing there?"*

*"It's the VC! The VC!" Jason hissed as he ran along the tracks.*

*"He's got a grenade," Neil added.*

*They all ducked, then, and scattered. Kyle couldn't remember ever running faster, feeling the enemy tailing him. He looked back to Shane, who was far behind him. So he stopped.*

*"Hurry up, soldier," Kyle told him. "Hold on," he said, turning and letting his kid brother grab onto the back of his tee. Together they ran along the tracks, wordlessly, their chests heaving with desperate breaths; their feet occasionally stumbling. After about a quarter mile, they all veered off into the shadows, safe from the enemy. Safe from the gunfire and grenades and hidden traps in the brush. They ended up coming off the tracks right where they'd started, at Back Bay. In the waning light, they slid down the stone embankment and through wispy dune grass to the little beach there, where they all collapsed at the water's edge. Their breathing was labored. Their muscles ached. But they were safe, sitting together beside the lapping waves of the sea.*

~

Now Kyle looks out at Long Island Sound from where he stands on Shane's back porch. The rising sun is golden at the horizon, leaving a swath of light on the dark water. When the train whistle fades, he takes a long breath of the salt air, remembering gulping that same air when they hit the beach that train-track night. Jesus, he and Jason had been fourteen; Shane and Neil only twelve. Over two decades have since passed.

Kyle turns then, seeing old crates on the porch, and the whitewashed bench. He spots what looks like one of Elsa's happiness jars sitting atop the painted table. Elsa must've given it to Shane during his stay at the inn. Curiosity gets the best of Kyle, so he walks over and picks up the glass jar. Holding it up to the light of the sunrise, he looks inside it. On top of fine sand is a clump of dried and tangled seaweed. Several pieces of smooth sea glass are scattered on the sand, too. And there … there's a perfect skipping stone. A sailor's knot diamond ring. And an ice-cream punch card from Scoop Shop.

Every one of them, Kyle's sure, attached to some memory from these past two weeks. Some he can figure himself—like the engagement ring, and the skipping stone. Others are a mystery. He sets the glass jar down and walks away, toward the half-wall. But he turns back before getting there. Turns back while pulling his wallet from his pocket. Because one more thing really needs to be in Shane's happiness jar.

Kyle digs through his wallet, moving aside notes and tiny papers in one of the side pockets until he finds it. Until he slips out the flattened nickel he's kept tucked in there, behind some tattered photos of his kids. For all these years, that nickel's gone wherever he has.

He looks at it now in the golden light of morning. Rubs his thumb over the dull gray surface. Feels the tiniest of nicks and dings in the coin, each one left behind by the weight of a train one long-ago summer night.

And he does it.

He quickly returns to Shane's happiness jar, opens it and sets the flattened nickel on the sand. His fingers move the coin to right where it should be, leaning against the glass side. Satisfied, Kyle twists on the lid and sets the jar back on the table.

Just then, the screen door squeaks and Shane shoulders his way through, holding two steaming cups of coffee.

"I'm glad you stopped by, Kyle."

# twenty-seven

### Saturday Midmorning

KITCHEN COUNTERS WIPED CLEAN," SHANE quietly reads an hour later. He drags a finger down the cottage checklist on the fridge. "*Stovetop sponged off. Refrigerator emptied.*"

Yes, he did it all—some late last night, after fishing. The rest before Kyle even arrived earlier. Now the little beach bungalow's floors are mopped and vacuumed. Dresser drawers all emptied. Bed stripped and remade. Bathroom sink, toilet and shower cleaned.

Done, done, done.

It's time to leave.

Funny, he'd never thought when he arrived two weeks ago that this hour, this minute, this moment would be so difficult. Being here at Stony Point was a lot like being out at sea for two weeks. He occasionally lost his footing when the boat rocked; there were stormy nights; a few rogue waves crashed over the deck. But there was more, too. The

242

seas calmed. By the last few days, the salt air was more soothing than stinging. The two weeks were a journey that set his life on a different course. Because there's Kyle now. And his niece and nephew. A difficult past righted with Maris. A new friend in Elsa.

And there's Celia.

All people he's about to leave behind. That's the hard part. The part that makes him want to hightail it out of here as quickly as possible to avoid prolonging this sudden sadness he's feeling.

After scanning the shelves near the kitchen sink, he double-checks the refrigerator, then grabs his happiness jar from the back porch and walks into his bedroom. Kyle helped him load just about everything into his truck earlier, after they had coffee together. Now Shane gives one last look around the bedroom—at the bed, its light quilt hanging evenly; at the old paned windows, their sills needing a fresh coat of paint; at the rag rug on the floor; at the antique wooden dresser and tarnished mirror. The red sailboat he and Kyle set afloat all those years ago leans against the mirror. Shane picks up the toy boat, runs a hand over the faded white canvas sails, touches a piece of old salty string dangling from the mast. Carefully then, he places the boat in a cardboard carton and tucks crumpled newspaper around it—leaving space for only his happiness jar. Picking that up, he notices something new in it, leaning against the glass. So he lifts the jar and takes a look.

And looks more closely, raising a finger to the glass. It's a flattened nickel. The gray metal is dull, and thin. A few scratches and tiny nicks are ingrained in the coin, which is more oval now, than round. That's what a speeding train will do to a nickel on the tracks.

Well. There's only one flattened nickel that's ever been in Shane's life, and only one person who'd leave it in his jar. He shakes his head, still feeling Kyle's hand slapping his shoulder in their *take-care* hug an hour ago.

Nestling the Mason jar in the same carton as the toy boat, Shane knows this is it. He's done here—so he gets going. He puts on a faded denim shirt over his sleeveless tee, sets his newsboy cap on his head, then zips up the last duffel on his bed. And takes a quick breath. It's time. He hefts the box and duffel out through the living room— passing the hanging glass fishing floats he'd dusted off; the gray rattan sofa where he comforted Celia one rainy day; the silver tin pitcher filled with dried beach grasses. He goes outside and loads his duffel and carton in the truck, then walks the planked pathway around back one more time.

And isn't it true … The last look is always the sweetest, or the saddest. After climbing the painted porch steps two at a time, he leans on the half-wall and takes in the sight of Long Island Sound. A sea breeze lifts off the water and glances his skin, bringing its hint of salt water and waves and innate rhythm. That's what it all comes down to, life. Rhythms inherent in every day, every decision. The high tide and the low, day in, and day out.

In a minute, Shane gives a nod. It's getting late. So he checks that the porch door is locked before heading down the planked walkway again, to the front door. After locking that, he tucks the keys inside an old fishing buoy hanging from the railing—just like the cottage checklist requests. With the little beach bungalow buttoned up tight, he gets in his pickup and backs out of the driveway, ready to head home.

⁓

Slowly cruising the cottage-lined streets, Shane drives toward the stone railroad trestle. But there's still one item of business to tend to before driving *beneath* that trestle. He maneuvers his pickup around a speed barrier, and passes shingled cottages and painted bungalows. The day's going to be perfect here, with the sun rising high in a clear August sky. Which only makes it harder to leave.

When he approaches the Stony Point Beach Association trailer, he hits his blinker and turns into the gravel parking lot. Some of the sliding windows are open on the white, flat-roofed trailer. Cliff might be around, so Shane's got to be quick if he wants to make a clean exit. With his truck idling, he finds a pen and scrap of paper in the glove box and whispers to himself while writing Cliff's note.

*"I really needed the luck, Commissioner. Sorry if you lost any."*

After signing his name, he pulls Cliff's scuffed-up black domino out of his denim shirt pocket. Carefully, he wraps both the lucky domino and his note in the sea glass netting from Celia. After tying it with twine, he gets out and leaves the small package in Cliff's mailbox, flips up the red flag, then gets back in his truck and leaves.

And suddenly, there it is. It could almost seem like that stone railroad trestle is defying him as he approaches it. Stay, or go. Come into this little beach world one way, or drive far away from it, the other. The trestle's brown stone walls rise on either side of the road, forming a short dark tunnel beneath the tracks. It's a sight as welcome upon arrival as it is dreaded upon departure.

"*The trestle giveth, and the trestle taketh away,*" Shane whispers.

He tips his newsboy cap at Nick standing guard there before driving into the shadows beneath the stone bridge. After turning onto Shore Road in the direction of the highway, he rolls down his window. Anything, Shane will do *anything*, to get that last breath of sweet salt air here.

He also glances in the rearview mirror often as he drives.

As the cottages and bait shops and ice-cream shacks give way to farm stands and country homes.

As the sound of crying gulls and breaking waves recedes.

As the silver-shingled cottages and painted bungalows, the sandy boardwalk and rocky ledge at the end of the crescent-moon-shaped beach fade to nothing behind him.

# twenty-eight

## Saturday Afternoon

THEY WALK AMONG LIGHTS. THERE are chandeliers and sconces. Pan fixtures and entranceway lamps. Exterior post lanterns and nautical lanterns. There are even old streetlamps and subway lights. Jason knew that Rick's architectural salvage yard would have more than enough to choose from. Something might work well for the Fenwick job.

Having Carol and Mitch Fenwick here to select just the right fixture also makes for an interesting *Castaway Cottage* segment. So his producer, Trent, has the cameraman capture it all, panning the entire room of lights of every kind. Many of them are plugged in and turned on, casting a warm glow on the antique wood-paneled ceiling in this part of the old brick building.

All Mitch and Carol have to do is pick out one large lamp. It'll hang in the third-floor cupola-style room of their

247

stilted cottage-on-the-beach. *Easy enough*, Jason thought—until the Fenwicks arrived.

"I was thinking maybe a ship lantern," Mitch says. He wears a tan utility shirt—loose at the collar and cuffed at the wrists—over casual black pants and leather sandals. His faded blond hair is pulled into a tiny, low ponytail, and he draws a hand down his goatee as he surveys the fixtures. *And* clears his throat. "Since the cottage is right *on* the water," Mitch goes on, "some maritime illumination would suit it."

So they browse the old nautical lanterns—many handmade with detailed craftsmanship. There are brass lanterns, and tin. Salt-coated, and showing the pitted-and-tarnished wear of harsh seaside conditions. Others are polished to a dull sheen. There are bulkhead lights and running lights of various colors.

"The red running lights are port lights. Green or blue, starboard," Rick explains.

Carol points out a large masthead light. Its brass-and-copper casing is aged to a beautiful patina.

"That one's from the early 1900s. But it can be converted to an electrical fixture," Rick tells them. He points to the two separate wicks in the original oil burner. "I've got a guy who can take care of that for you."

"Hmm," Carol says, eyeing the lantern. Wearing a crochet sweater over a fitted navy tank top and ripped shorts, she holds a finger to her chin. "What do you think, Dad?"

"Well, I like that it's historical, dating back a century or so," Mitch adds. He dabs at a bead of perspiration running along his temple. "And it picks up on the coastal feel of the cottage."

Jason unclips a measuring tape from his belt. "Lantern's seventeen inches high, top to bottom. But with the securing hoops extended, add about ten inches to that."

"Where's the light fixture going?" Rick asks.

"You've seen their place, Rick," Jason reminds him. "When we installed the beach binoculars on the deck?"

"Oh, sure. Nice digs. The last-standing cottage on the beach."

"That's the one," Jason says while double-checking the lantern measurements. "The light will hang in the third story belvedere."

"Wait. The *what?*" Trent asks. "Belvedere?"

"Yeah," Jason explains as the cameraman moves in front of him to capture this exchange. "It's Italian, for beautiful view. A belvedere is an upper room on a structure, like a cupola, or a lookout. It's built to take advantage of a significant view."

"*Belvedere,*" Mitch muses. "I like the sound of that."

"Mr. Barlow." Carol looks at Jason from beneath her long blonde bangs. "Question. Wasn't your blueprint design for the cottage's *belvedere,*" she says, air-quoting the word, "inspired by an actual lighthouse image Neil sketched?"

Jason nods. "It was." He taps his extended measuring tape on the antique masthead light. "So installing this in the upper-level room? With the longer windows in the redesign, your lantern here will seriously give the space the same lighthouse *feel.*"

"Which is important to us." Mitch pauses to clear his throat once more. "Especially since my wife's family spent many days *looking out* for her father, Gordon."

"Who would've been Mitch's father-in-law," Jason explains to Rick. "*And* Carol's grandfather. But Gordon died in the sixties, during a hurricane. Tried to save a neighbor's son who went missing in the storm. Gordon ventured out in a rowboat looking for the boy, and lost his life somewhere on those storm waters."

"Is that right?" Rick asks. "So your place has quite a history attached to it."

"Sure does," Mitch says, nodding slowly.

"And with that masthead light," Jason tells them, "the belvedere will look like a beacon on the beach when it's illuminated."

"Just what we hoped for," Carol adds.

Once she and Mitch confirm the brass-and-copper fixture as their choice, Jason wraps up the segment and arranges the light delivery with Rick.

"*Excellent*," Mitch tells him, shaking Jason's hand afterward. "And thanks for your assistance here today."

"No problem. You did good, Mitch. You know, in front of the camera."

"Yeah, well ..." Carol admits. "I made him listen to a guided meditation podcast at the cottage earlier."

"Not a bad idea," Jason says.

"Calmed me down some," Mitch agrees, then swipes another bead of perspiration from his forehead. "And I'll be meeting with Elsa, too. Said she's got a few on-camera pointers. Little tricks to relax."

"That's great." Jason checks his dinging cell phone, then pockets it. "You set something up, then."

Mitch nods. "I did. For early next week."

"Elsa's a pro, and knows all the ins and outs of filming now," Jason assures him while walking Mitch and Carol toward the exit. He glances back to his producer, who's talking with the cameraman still. "Listen, I'm going to help Zach and Trent pack up the production gear. You guys are free to leave," he tells the Fenwicks as they head for the door.

The surprising thing, though, is that when Jason walks outside twenty minutes later, Mitch and Carol are still hanging around the salvage yard. They're browsing chipped garden statues and weathered fountains in an area beside the parking lot.

"Jason!" Mitch calls out as he catches up with him. "Wanted to ask you something."

Jason walks with the two of them through the parking lot. "What's up? You see something there you're interested in?" he asks, hitching his head to the garden décor behind them.

"No. Carol and I were wondering, well, why don't you and Maris stop by for a cookout tonight?" Mitch asks. "We'd love to have you. Talk about what's coming up the pike with our demo."

"And it'd be good to chill before the reno actually begins," Carol says, putting on her green-tinted circle sunglasses.

"Thanks, you two. Appreciate it, but ah ... tonight probably won't work."

"You *sure?*" Mitch presses. "Summer's winding down, and it'll be a nice evening."

"Dad! I think they're busy." Carol shrugs at Jason. "And already have plans, I'm sure."

Jason veers off to his SUV parked beside the Fenwick vehicle. "Some other time, definitely."

"Just thought you might like a night sitting out on the deck seaside," Mitch tells him. "You look a little tired, my friend."

"Won't argue that. It's the heat, *and* it's been a long week." Jason opens the SUV liftgate and tosses in his measuring tape, along with the lantern invoice. Problem is, tired doesn't begin to cover how he's feeling. Even Trent commented earlier, cuffing Jason's jaw and asking him if he was under the weather. "Plus I've got something going on in the morning," Jason mentions now. "Memorial Mass, for my brother."

"Is that right?" Mitch asks from behind him.

"Yeah," Jason says over his shoulder while closing the liftgate. "My sister and I usually arrange one, every summer."

"And where might that be?" Mitch asks.

"St. Bernard's. Not too far from Stony Point."

"Oh, sure," Mitch says, squinting through the afternoon sunlight. "Been there a few times."

Carol walks around to the passenger side of her father's safari-style vehicle. "Big crowd going?"

"Everybody," Jason tells them.

Mitch steps up into his vehicle's driver seat, buckles the safety belt and casually hooks a hand on an upper grab handle. "Kyle, too? And his wife?"

"Should be." Jason gets into his SUV and lowers the window.

From his own open-air seat, Mitch calls out, "Good. That's good."

"He and Lauren must be doing better, then," Carol says while settling into her passenger seat.

"Definitely." Jason starts up his vehicle. "They are."

"I like Kyle! He's all right." Mitch raises his hand through his vehicle's open top and waves as he and Carol cruise out of the parking lot.

~

Jason has the same thought when he gets to Ted Sullivan's cottage later that evening and finds a wrapped meatloaf dinner from Kyle waiting in an insulated case on the stoop. With heating instructions. *And* a chilled fruit parfait dessert, no less. Yep, Kyle's all right.

Thinks it again, too, twenty minutes later, after washing up and feeding the dog, then heating Kyle's diner dinner and bringing it outside to the teak deck table. He's not sure when he last ate. Was it really hours ago, at lunch? Hell, when he drags a forkful of that diner meatloaf through gravy and mashed potatoes, it all just about melts in his mouth. Gets his eyes to drop closed, too, as he sits back

253

and relishes the food, the quiet. "You *are* all right, Kyle," he says, then slides his cell phone closer. He finally gets around to responding to Kyle's Friday night fishing text—a day late. Sends a thumbs-up emoji for the dinner, too.

As he continues slicing his fork through the meat, and scooping up beans and potatoes, an offshore breeze blows. It carries the sound of waves breaking across the street, on the beach. Those waves seem choppy tonight. Over and over, they roll onto the beach, rhythmically. The water splashes, and hisses in retreat.

Jason just eats. Just sits alone, the only sound being those distant waves on Sea Spray Beach, or his own fork and knife clinking on the dish, or the dog chewing on a rawhide bone beneath the deck table.

# twenty-nine

### Saturday Night

"YOU SURE YOU DON'T WANT help cleaning up?"
Elsa asks. She lifts her light cardigan from the back of a
kitchen chair and slips it on. "I don't mind."

Maris wipes a pan with a dishtowel at the sink. "It's
enough that you came for dinner," she says. "*And* brought
your sun-dried tomato pesto."

"Oh, I was happy to. Especially with your stove being
on the fritz."

"Only three burners work now on that old thing."

"At least you got the penne cooked, so dinner was nice."
Elsa lifts her tote to her shoulder. "You really don't need
my help here?"

Maris dries her hands on the towel, then shoos Elsa off.
"You're so busy getting ready for the inn's grand opening."
She gives Elsa a quick hug, whispering, "*Go! Have a cup of
tea and get some rest.*"

"Okay, then." Elsa pulls her golf cart key out of her tote.

"Just text me when you get home, so I know you made it safely," Maris tells her while walking her to the slider.

"Of course. And you call me if you need anything."

"I will, Aunt Elsa. Let me put on the deck light. It's dark out now."

After Maris hits the light switch, Elsa gives her another hug. "I'll see you tomorrow at Mass. I'm sure Jason will be there, so maybe you can talk."

"We'll see." Maris crosses her arms in front of her and fiddles with a turquoise cuff on her wrist. "The wall he built this time is so high, Elsa, I'm not sure either of us can get over it."

Elsa shakes her head. "Don't say that. Because even if Jason's afraid to let you in, Maris, he *needs* you."

"But when you marry someone, you *commit* to letting them in."

"I know, dear. I know." After squeezing Maris' hand, Elsa opens the slider screen. She heads down the deck stairs to her golf cart in the driveway.

Maris goes outside to the deck, too, and waves goodbye as Elsa drives off. When she turns back inside to the kitchen, she shuts off the deck light and clears their wineglasses from the table. After rinsing them, she drops some food scraps into the garbage disposal, then loads the last few plates into the dishwasher. That done, she takes a damp dishrag and wipes off the dingy, faded countertops; taps shut a sticking painted cabinet; opens the temperamental oven door to check inside it, then presses that old door tightly closed.

The whole time, with each wipe, each drawer closed, each item returned to the refrigerator—salad dressing and Parmesan—Maris does something else. She remembers Elsa's words said over their quiet dinner at the kitchen table. With each forkful of penne, each taste of salad and sip of wine, Elsa told her all about having dinner with Jason the night before.

*He looked tired. Didn't say too much, either*, and
*I told him Shane actually became his perfect crutch*, and
*This is more about Neil than anything else*, and
*Survivor's guilt is behind it all, I truly believe that.*

But most concerning is Elsa's genuine worry about Jason now. *That* surprises Maris, the way her aunt's initial anger at Jason's leaving has changed.

*I really tried to get through to him last night. And even though he looked tired, that didn't bother me as much as this. Jason just seems lost this summer. Incredibly lost.*

*Lost?* Maris had asked.

To which Elsa nodded. *And he doesn't want you, or anyone, to see him this way. So I think he's using the whole situation between you and Shane as his excuse to be alone right now.*

That's the thought that bothers Maris the most, the idea of Jason being lost. She knows he's struggled in the past to find his way through situations, around thoughts. But he *always* found his way.

So now to be *lost?*

Maris shuts off the ceiling light in the kitchen, leaving on only the low light over the sink. As she does, she wonders how she and Jason could possibly have gone from reading his sweet paper wish just two weeks ago—to this. To solitude. To being apart.

Suddenly, nothing is more important than finding that wish. She runs upstairs and rummages through the valet on his dresser. It's got to be here, somewhere. She brushes aside some change, a dentist appointment card, a business card with a phone number scribbled on the back.

*There.* There it is, the wish Jason wrote a year ago on a tiny scrap of paper, rolled it up and tied it with twine. They all did that evening. All wrote private wishes that were sealed since then in Elsa's wish jar.

They'd opened those wishes together two weeks ago— when Elsa summoned everyone to dinner after the vow renewal fell apart. One by one, each wish was read—some to cautious smiles, some to tears.

Maris unrolls Jason's paper now and reads his familiar handwriting. *More jukeboxes dances with my wife.* That's it. That was his heart's desire.

When she goes back downstairs in the shadowy house now, she stops at the jukebox. Its silver trim glimmers in the low light. She stands there looking at the record selections before choosing one. It's the same song she and Jason danced to, two weeks ago. A song whose strains of violin and saxophone fill the quiet house. A song about leaving someone behind. About missing sweet loving.

Oh, isn't she doing just that tonight, with a broken heart, too.

Because Maris can't help but feel that her and Jason's slow dance two weeks ago, in the misty light of the jukebox, might very well have been their last.

∽

It's the one place Jason can usually count on. The driftline. The hard-packed sand below the seaweed line running across the beach. Damn, Neil even named his novel that. *Driftline.* There's no other ground on earth that feels like it. In all the years since his accident, it's the one place that cradles Jason's gait. Eases his steps, his mind.

But the beach at Sea Spray is different. He walks it now. Here, the packed sand is gritty, rather than smooth. It's rockier than Stony Point. The waves are bigger, too, such that tonight they sound jarring when they break onshore beside him. Though Maddy doesn't seem to notice the difference. The German shepherd runs ahead and barks into the salty breeze. Jason's sure she's just relieved to be walking the beach with him again.

Tonight, a crescent moon hangs over the dark Sound. That slice of moon casts little light on the water, the beach. But there's enough for Jason to spot a good-sized piece of driftwood washed up on the sand. He picks it up, holding it in one hand and slapping the stick in his other. Finally, he stops and looks out at Long Island Sound. A few wispy clouds pass in front of that slice of moon. The muted moonlight leaves a pale swath of silver on the rippling waves. Some lights also shine from boats anchored offshore—fishermen, maybe. Or pleasure boats moored for the night. Those boat lights reflect on the water, dropping streaks of gold on it.

Jason looks out into the darkness for a long while, until he turns, pulls his arm back and flings that driftwood as hard as possible. His whole body wrenches with some anger that propels the heavy stick far over the dark water, beneath the night sky.

As soon as that driftwood leaves his hand, though, and is spinning airborne, he can't get a breath. His chest just won't fill. His lungs suck at the sea air, to no avail. The harder he tries, the tighter his chest clamps in on itself. He bends then, puts his hands on his knees and tries to relax his muscles. But, nothing. So he looks around and walks into the shadows where he sits on the sand. Just sits, his arms hung over his knees, his chest heavy. The dog lopes over, sniffing at his shoulders as Jason drags his hands through his hair, tips his head way back and desperately gasps.

*Jay*, he hears in that sound.

Jason struggles for another breath, panicking at the thought that he actually might pass out. Not enough air is getting to his lungs.

*Jay … breathe, damn it.*

As he tries, Maddy whines beside him in the shadows.

*Come on, you've been running, and fighting*, Jason hears his brother's voice then. *Fight or flight. Do like Dad told us. Remember?*

When Jason gasps another breath, the dog circles around him, before dropping on her belly in the sand.

*You're in the jungle, Jay,* Jason hears, then shakes his head.

*You damn well are!* A wave crashes below on the beach, right as more whispers come. *And if you can't breathe, you can't get out of the jungle.*

Jason's sweating now. Perspiration runs down his temples as his breaths are too shallow for comfort.

*Think of Dad, when he trained us, man. Tactical breathing, like he did in 'Nam. Clear your body, clear your mind,* come the words, as rhythmic as the tides. *Clear your mind.*

Maddy whines again, then rests her muzzle on her extended front paws.

Jason closes his eyes, and tries, *tries* to clear his mind. To not have a cyclone of thoughts spinning through it—the accident ten years ago; Neil, his hand pointing to the fast-approaching car in the mirror as he warned, *Jay. Hey, Jay.* Jason's jeans, hooked onto the bike. Shane: *What are you doing marrying my fiancée?* The bike spinning, a soundless ripping burning through his leg. Maris: *The ring, it's just a nautical knot. Nothing happened between me and Shane.* Jason: *Neil tossed me the keys.* Neil: *You drive.* Maris: *Let your brother go and live, Jason.* Jason: *You quit your denim design while married to me.* Maris: *Finishing Neil's book.* Jason: *My vow is to walk with you, talk with you, touch you, be with you.* Maris: *My friend, my confidante, my love. Always.* Jason: *Always.* Shane: *I'm telling you don't fuckin' blow it.*

*Good. Clear it out,* he hears then as a wave retreats with a hissing sound across the sand. *Remember what Dad told us when I got caught in that rip? That time at Hammonasset Beach?*

Jason remembers. He remembers sitting on the sand like he's doing right now. Sitting there one long-ago summer day; Neil coughing and spitting out water; Jason beside him taking panicked breaths at how close Neil came to drowning.

*Breathe, boys*, his father insisted. *With me! Inhale through your nose.* Silence, then, *Do it! In, two … three … four.*

When they did, barely, their father told them they *must* control what they can, and that's their breathing. *Hold, two … three … four. Exhale, two … three … four.*

Over and over, slowly inhaling, holding, slowly exhaling. He guided them again, and again, and would *not* let them quit.

In a breeze that rustles the dune grasses behind Jason now, he hears Neil. The words are the same, the insistence as direct as their father's.

*Inhale, two … three … four.*

And Jason slowly does. Once. Then holds.

*Exhale, two … three … four.*

He doesn't stop. Inhale, hold, exhale. Slower, deeper, counting, the numbers ticking off in his mind.

In time, the pressure in his lungs lightens. His chest lifts easier. As it does, his dog stands, paces, then sits and watches him again. Jason reaches over and gives Maddy's shoulder a rub. Still, through each turn of a sea breeze, and with each breaking wave splashing on the beach, Jason keeps listening for the count. Continues that simple tactical exercise to keep him breathing. To calm him. Keep him alive. It kept his father alive, in the jungles of Vietnam.

In the misty night, the two voices blur then—Neil's and his father's. But in the rhythm of the waves, over and over, Jason makes out the deep intonations. The quieting rhythm. The low tones of the two men counting, somehow.

Eventually, sitting beneath that crescent moon on the dark beach and working through the count, Jason does it. He gets that long, necessary breath that fills his lungs. That signals him his panic has turned.

# *thirty*

### Sunday Morning

JASON BRUSHES THROUGH THE FEW hung clothes he has at Ted's. Usually he wears a suit to Neil's Memorial Mass. Only the best for his brother. But he has no necktie here, no summer suit hanging in the closet. So a blazer over his casual outfit—chambray button-down, dark khakis and leather boat shoes—will have to do.

An hour later, he walks alone through the parking lot of St. Bernard's Church. Its cedar shingles are weathered driftwood gray by the salty air of Long Island Sound. This morning, the bottom third of the church's stained glass windows are tilted open so that a sea breeze might find its way inside the warm building.

Jason walks into the church, passes the holy water font without dipping in his fingers, and takes a seat in a rear pew. He kneels there, head bowed, hands clasped on the pew in front of him. In the past, he'd find the same spiritual connection to the soul standing at the edge of the sea as he did facing an altar. He'd ask the same questions of the ocean that he asked of God. Bowed his head in prayer, at both.

Today? Today he can't even bless himself. Because what's the point? What's the point of beginning some random prayer? Is the Lord hearing him lately? Does He hear Jason pray for his marriage? Pray to somehow find his way back to Maris?

Has God *ever* heard his prayers that Neil didn't suffer at the time of his death—his body flung from that bike upon impact, then tossed like a limp rag.

Has *anyone* above heard his prayers for Ted Sullivan, who bears unwarranted guilt and a heavy burden on his innocent shoulders?

Jason can't be certain the Lord hears any of it.

One thing he *is* certain of, though, as he raises his head and glances around the church. Every friend and family member hears him. Because each and every one of them is here. Paige and Vinny. There's Elsa and Cliff, sitting behind Eva, Matt and Taylor. Maris sits beside her sister. There's his best man Kyle, with Lauren, over on the side. Nick's here. Trent. But this one surprises him: Mitch and Carol sit in a pew, a few rows down.

Every one of them, it seems, hearing what Jason's not sure the good Lord ever does.

Ceiling fans slowly paddle above her. Sitting in a wooden pew, Maris barely feels the air stir. Nothing seems to cool down this summer. While fanning herself with a folded church bulletin, she hears the soft footsteps of people arriving for Mass. Some genuflect before moving into a pew. The scent of the sea drifts in through the open stained glass windows—she's aware of that, too. And there's a Mason jar filled with blessed seawater beside a vase of beach grasses on a table near the altar. Elsa's touch, Maris is sure.

She takes this all in while listening to Eva whispering harshly beside her. Her sister's auburn hair is streaked blonde. Oh, Maris can't help but notice *that* as Eva sends a few squinted glares at her through her long, sideswept bangs. And any relaxing, any good vibes from Eva's Martha's Vineyard getaway? Apparently they've evaporated into the summer air now. Because before the Mass begins, Eva leans close and tosses around her indignant words. Through it all, through Eva's hushed, *How could you not have told me?* Maris tries to remain calm. As Eva quietly demands, *Who does Jason think he is?* and *I've really had it with him this time*, Maris slightly nods. Tries to get a word in edgewise. Tries to placate her infuriated sister. Even as the pews in front of them fill, Eva keeps at it, whispering, *When did this happen? Where's he staying? For how long? What do you mean, he took the dog?*

Until finally, Elsa leans forward in the seat behind them, uttering a stern *Shh!* Then, well then she points upward while mouthing, *God.*

266

Which effectively muzzles Eva's rant. So instead, she silently looks around the church—side to side, front to back. In a minute, her sharp elbow nudges Maris as she points out Jason sitting alone in a rear pew.

~

Jason waits for it, for the one line that's all he's ever had. He listens throughout the Mass as parishioners stand, sit, kneel. Waits for that line through *Glory to God*, through the readings and the Gospel. He hears the priest's low voice, his words as fluid as a stream flowing over smooth stones. Recognizes the solemn intonations that haven't changed throughout time. And so Jason's sure the intonations were the same at his brother's funeral, which he missed—being critically injured and treated in the hospital. He missed the blessed words granting Neil eternal rest. Missed the words pleading for perpetual light to shine on his brother. Missed the words asking God to have mercy on Neil and to welcome him into His kingdom.

Instead, Jason has one line. It's what brings him to this Mass each year. Hearing the line that he's got memorized. That he knows exactly where it falls in the Mass.

It's the line that gets to him, every summer. Gets to him—because he couldn't somehow attend his own brother's funeral. Laid up in a hospital bed, Jason couldn't somehow be wheeled into church for even an hour.

It's the line that has him bow his head.

Finally, the line's here.

JOANNE DEMAIO

"For all our departed brothers and sisters who have gone to their rest in the hope of rising again. Especially today for Neil Barlow, for whom this Mass is offered, we pray to the Lord."

As the parishioners around him murmur, *Lord, hear our prayer*, Jason, too, forms those words. He owes his brother that much.

And there it is—*owes* Neil.

Jason remembers Elsa's words from the other night. Remembers her pointed accusation that he's experiencing survivor's guilt—which explains why he walked out of a beautiful life this year. Because he didn't think he *deserved* that life.

Her observation unsettled him ever since she voiced it.

*I know what you must think,* Elsa had ventured. *Why Neil, and not you, that day? Why didn't Neil deserve to live, and you die?*

And as the priest continues at the altar, his voice rising and dipping, Jason listens for some answer to those questions that, yes, Elsa nailed.

But there are no answers. No explanation cloaked in Catholic symbolism that might alleviate Jason's guilt. No words explaining the death of Neil over his own death.

Instead Jason hears from the priest the same tone his father often used, talking about the Vietnam War. If anyone had reason to feel survivor's guilt, it *was* his father. If he were alive, what would *he* say to Jason now? How would his father allay Jason's guilt that yes, he survived and Neil didn't. That Jason grabbed the keys when Neil tossed them and actually *drove* the bike that fateful day. How could one

268

choice decide a life? *Did* Jason decide the life? If he'd said no, if he'd insisted Neil drive, would it have changed their fate? Or not?

Could his father find a parallel from the trenches in the jungle? A parallel from the time he held a lit cigarette to a dying man's lips? From the time he listened to another soldier's last description of his girl back home? How did his father make sense of his survival when comrades right next to him perished?

*Damn it*, what words could his father find—and surely, he would—that might set Jason's troubled mind at ease?

That would dispel Elsa's accusation.

That would free him.

⁓

Jason looks up now as the Eucharist is prepared at the altar. And though he listens, the priest is not who Jason watches. No, now he's watching *Maris*, instead. She's dressed entirely in navy—from the sleeveless button-down blouse to the cropped navy pants. Her brown hair is in a low twist, and her gold star pendant hangs from a braided chain around her neck. He sees all this because she's actually standing, reaching for her purse, and leaving her pew. Discreetly, she walks the length of the aisle toward the rear of the church.

Which is when he stops watching her. Because he knows that in mere moments, Maris will slip in beside him. She'll be gentle, murmuring something, her voice a salve. So he simply waits as the parishioners around him recite the Lord's Prayer, and shake hands, and nod, in signs of peace.

It happens, then. Happens like he knew it would. He feels Maris step into the pew beside him; glances at her so close. They wordlessly kneel, both of them, when the Communion procession begins.

Which is when her hand covers his and she leans closer. Her whispered breath reaches his ear. *"You can walk away, Jason. You can leave Stony Point. But you can't stop me from loving you."*

He says nothing. Does nothing. Doesn't even look at her, lest he choke up on some emotion he won't see coming.

Maris squeezes his hand then, before standing and getting in line for Communion.

Jason stands, too, following behind her as they walk down the aisle. Nearing the altar, he hears the priest's low voice again while he administers the Sacrament.

"The Body of Christ." Over and over, "The Body of Christ. The Body of Christ."

When Maris steps forward to receive Communion, Jason stands back, watching until she turns, vaguely blesses herself and walks back to the pew.

"The Body of Christ," the priest says, placing the Eucharist in Jason's cupped hand.

*"Amen,"* Jason whispers, lifting the wafer to his mouth and returning down the aisle. Maris walks in front of him, her purse slung over her shoulder, her hands clasped. What surprises him, though, is what she does next. It's exactly what *he* did three years ago, the first summer she attended

Neil's Memorial Mass. The summer they started dating.

That day, Jason walked up the aisle after receiving Communion—and didn't turn into their pew. He did what Maris does right now. She walks straight past their pew and straight out of the church.

Jason watches her go, but doesn't follow. Doesn't hurry to catch up as she pushes open the heavy church door and steps alone into the sunshine outside. Instead, he turns into his pew, kneels during the Communion hymn, drops his head and closes his eyes.

# thirty-one

### *Minutes Later*

IF ANYONE DIDN'T YET KNOW that he and Maris had separated, they sure as hell know it now. Because more than anything—more than hearing sympathetic words about Neil and getting warm hugs outside after the Mass—Jason gets this. From everyone. He gets questions about Maris.

Starting with Elsa. "Jason? Is Maris okay?"

Then Lauren *and* Paige. "Where's Maris?" And, "Did she go ahead to help set up for brunch?"

Even Nick asks where Jason's better half took off to.

When Mitch and Carol approach, it's the first thing Mitch asks. "Where's your wife?" Mitch glances around at the parked cars. "Thought I saw Maris inside the church."

"Maris," Jason begins. And stalls. "Well, the thing is, she had to …"

As he's talking, Jason spots Eva in the crowd. His sister-

272

in-law's making a beeline straight for him. She's wearing a fitted striped sheath, holds a straw clutch—and looks spittin' mad. A suspicion confirmed when she pulls Jason aside before he can say any more to Mitch.

"*Jason Barlow*," Eva hisses after apologizing to the Fenwicks for whisking him away. Her hand grips his arm as they walk. It's an iron grip, right on the bruise he got hitting his arm on the nightstand the other morning. "I am *so* mad at you, I made Matt take Tay to the car so she wouldn't hear me."

"Eva." Jason stops beneath the shade of a nearby maple tree, and rubs that bruise. "Let's not get into this right now. Not a good time."

Eva steps close and directly faces him. "It's *never* a good time for you. And … and Maris walked out of the Mass!" She glances at the crowd lingering in the parking lot, then whips back to him. "I get home from Martha's Vineyard and find out you and my sister are *done*? I knew things were shaky, but," she says, jabbing his shoulder with each of her next three words. "Not. This. Bad."

"Eva." He takes those rigid fingers in his hand and gives a quick squeeze. "I *said*, not now."

Eva squints at him, her eyes dropping to his dark khakis and tan blazer over a faded chambray shirt, the sleeves of both folded back. "I should've known you left. Look at you, left to your own devices without your wife. You need a good shave. A haircut. You have circles under your eyes. And *seriously*? No tie for this Mass?"

"Eva!" Lauren suddenly calls out as she approaches.

"Wait a minute, Eva. Jason. Where's Celia?" As she asks, Lauren lifts her sunglasses, turns and squints out at the parking lot. "Did I miss her?"

Elsa, following behind Lauren, looks out at the parking lot, too. "I thought Celia was with *you*, Lauren."

"And I thought she was with *you*, in the church?" Lauren asks Elsa.

"No ..." Elsa trails off, looking at Eva and Jason then.

"Maybe she didn't want to bring Aria to the Mass," Eva says as the women crowd beneath the maple tree. "Sometimes it's hard with an infant."

"Especially if the baby gets fussy," Paige adds when she joins them. "Have you heard anything, Jason? You know, since everyone really comes here today for you."

"No." He checks his text messages and shrugs his shoulders. "Nothing."

"Huh. I was sure she'd be here." Lauren pulls her cell phone from her purse and presses the phone to her ear. "I'm calling her, but there's no answer."

"Well, she probably just got tied up with something. Or else Aria's tired today and needed a morning nap," Eva assures her, looping arms with Lauren as they walk toward their cars. *And* as Eva throws one last glare over her shoulder at Jason.

"I hope that's all it is," Paige says while heading through the parking lot with Elsa.

Jason watches them all go, hearing snatches of their talk—Elsa, this time. "Cliff's driving me, so I'll text Celia on the way. Maybe she's meeting us at the diner." Hurrying to where Cliff waits by his car, Elsa calls back one last thing. "We'll see you at brunch, Jason!"

〜

Kyle watched it all, from a distance. He could just imagine the words spewed at Jason: Eva's rant as she defended her sister; Lauren's and Paige's cautious questions about Maris' whereabouts; even Nick's casual remark tossed Jason's way. Kyle stood leaning against Jason's SUV and witnessed every gesture, every glare, every question. The only interruption to the show came from Mitch. He swung by to say hello and shake Kyle's hand before heading to the diner for brunch.

Now Kyle crosses his arms, still leaning on that SUV. Jason's approaching, switching his keys from one hand to the other as he slips out of a tan blazer.

"What are you doing, guy?" Jason asks when he spots Kyle.

Kyle doesn't move. He just stands there, arms still crossed. "Making sure you don't bail on brunch."

"I'm on my way there." Jason turns, and with Kyle, watches the others closing their car doors and one by one taking off for the diner. "So you're good to go, too."

"I saw Maris leave the church before," Kyle offhandedly says, instead of taking off.

"It's obvious everyone did, from the questions they shot at me."

"She head over to The Dockside?" Kyle asks, squinting through the sunlight at Jason.

"Don't know."

"Really. Things still that bad?"

Jason, with that blazer draped over an arm, simply turns up his hands.

So Kyle knocks on the locked SUV passenger door. "Open up, and make room for me."

"What about your wife?" Jason asks. "She waiting for you?"

"Told Lauren I'm hitching a ride with you. Let's get a move on." He knocks on the SUV door again.

So Jason unlocks the vehicle, then walks around to the driver's side and gets in, too. He sits back with a long breath and recuffs his denim shirtsleeves.

"Want a smoke?" Kyle asks right away, tapping a cigarette from an open pack.

"Jesus, didn't we quit these together for New Year's? Made a pact at The Sand Bar?"

"Sure did. That was before we knew how bad this year would get."

Jason looks at Kyle, shakes his head and plucks out the cigarette. When Kyle holds up a lighter, too, Jason lights the smoke and takes a long drag before starting up the truck.

"You're looking fatigued," Kyle tells him through a cloud of smoke after lighting his own cigarette. "You okay, man?"

Jason checks traffic before pulling out onto Shore Road. "Eh. Things are hitting me harder than I thought they would this summer."

"Okay, fine. I can get that. Question is, what are you going to do about it?"

"Nothing." Jason takes another drag of his cigarette. "What can I do?"

"For starters? Rest. Which it looks like you haven't been. And eat right, to keep your energy up. You finish all my dinner last night?"

"The meatloaf. Yeah. Cleaned the plate."

"And the parfait? You have that, too?"

Jason nods. "Good stuff, Bradford."

"Made that parfait special for you. Used full-fat Greek yogurt. It's been proven to help increase production of dopamine. You know, the feel-good shit." He flicks an ash out the window, then looks at Jason. "Guess it didn't help?"

"I'll leave the diagnosis to you, Doc," Jason says, grabbing his sunglasses off the visor and putting them on.

So Kyle sits back and they quietly cruise to the diner, where Jerry and Rob are setting up the brunch. Shore Road's busy this Sunday morning. Cars are pulling out in front of them, signaling and turning, coming and going. Maybe because summer's almost done, and people are grabbing at what's left of it. Jason drives past a calm inlet, where a few rowboats are being paddled. The marsh grasses have that late-August look to them, all golden and sweeping. Beyond the marsh, shingled cottages look silver beneath the summer sun.

"Shane left," Kyle mentions then, breaking the scenic-drive quiet.

Jason just throws Kyle a look.

"For real this time," Kyle insists. "His two-week rental was up."

"Or his two weeks of raising hell, depending."

"Yep. He'll be back to the boats now."

A second passes before Jason tells him, "Maybe he's better off."

"Look. I really have to fill you in on some stuff. A lot went down with me and Shane this week."

"Well, we're five minutes from the diner. So you better get talking."

"Nah, not now." Kyle waves him off. "Another time, all right?"

Minutes pass, during which Jason says nothing. So Kyle finishes his smoke before tossing the butt out the window. "Seriously, bro?" he says, worried about Jason now. "This isn't like you." He looks over at him when they stop at a red light. "I've always kind of thought of you like a boxer."

"A boxer?"

"Yeah. Throwing one-two punches through every round that comes your way."

"That's just life, Kyle," Jason says while accelerating after the traffic light changes. "Dealing with things. Everybody does it."

"Maybe. But hell, you've had more than your fair share." Kyle holds out his hand, folding down a finger with each incident. "The motorcycle accident. Losing your brother, *and* half your leg. Getting that second prosthesis. A brief pain meds addiction. Corporate work in the city. Facing

278

memories at Stony Point three years ago when you finally came back. Getting serious with Maris when she was spoken for, by Scott. Convincing her to stay. Losing Sal. Making peace with Ted. And two weeks ago, fighting like the *dickens* to pick up me and Lauren on one of our darkest days. Hell, that's twelve rounds by my count."

Jason takes a drag of his cigarette and just keeps driving, slowing to turn into the diner's parking lot.

"So yeah," Kyle goes on. "You're like this tough-as-nails boxer who's taken so many hits. Some really nasty, too." He glances at the people arriving for brunch. Already the guests are walking around his roped-off patio area. Elsa, Cliff, Matt, Nick, *everybody*. They're picking out tables, talking, pointing to the distant harbor. "The thing is," Kyle says to Jason, his voice low as he turns to him in the SUV. "You've got to get *up*. Because in this latest round, it's like you're down for the count. And the ref's standing over you, yelling, *Seven … Eight*."

"Listen, Kyle. I get it, the whole boxer thing. And fighting off my opponents." Jason tosses his cigarette out the window and shuts off the engine. "But this time around? I don't know." He looks over at the brunch crowd gathering. "This time around … maybe it just feels easier to stay down on the mat."

# thirty-two

**Late Sunday Morning**

ALL CELIA WANTS IS THIS one day.

One day with Shane before he gets back to lobstering. A Sunday by the sea.

It's why she packed food, baby gear and a diaper bag before settling Aria in the car very early this morning.

Then they hit the road.

The destination is programmed into her cell phone; the directions occasionally come through the speaker. Getting on the highway, she drives north, up the East Coast. City gives way to country, which gives way to rural. The sea of blue she's accustomed to changes to a sea of green. Green forests, green mountains, as far as the eye can see. While on the highway, there are signs that encourage her to keep going. *Welcome to Massachusetts. Welcome to New Hampshire.*

The entire trip, Celia stops frequently to care for Aria. She feeds her and changes her diaper at various roadside rest areas. When Aria gets fussy, and during one long crying spell in her car seat, Celia exits the highway into one small town or another. She finds a place to park, then walks outside with her daughter while rubbing her back and talking softly. It helps calm the baby to breathe the fresh country air. That's one thing Celia notices. The further north they travel, the fresher the air seems. Crisper. She inhales deeply while standing at a scenic lookout. While sitting at a picnic table outside a tourist stop.

Until finally, she drives past the sign she'd been seeking: *Welcome to Maine*. After over five hours of driving, that one sign makes the trip worthwhile. From here, her destination is only a hop, skip and a jump away. And when she continues on, the first thing she does is roll down her window to breathe that clear, Maine air.

Yes, this is all she wants. This one day.

Nearing Rockport, the sights are exactly as Shane had described one recent evening. She can almost hear his words telling her about his favorite fish shack restaurant in a local brick building. Or his description of the shops and galleries housed in clapboard-sided two-stories painted rich colonial colors. Brightly striped awnings extend over the storefronts.

"Look!" Celia slows the car when she rounds a bend in Rockport. "Look, sweetie," she says again to her daughter while pointing to a building the color of silver sea fog. There are crisscrossed windowpanes. A tall, peaked front and wide white trim give the structure a grand feel. "An honest-to-goodness *opera* house. Imagine the actual *arias* that must've been sung there!"

This one day. Yes. That's all Celia wants.

Already she's glad she's here. That for this one day, she'd driven beneath the Stony Point trestle and taken twenty-four hours of Sunday for herself.

*Anytime,* Shane had told her. *If you ever need anything, you find me … You come to Maine.*

He has no idea how those few words reached her. How they stirred something inside her.

Or else, Shane *did* know. Shane, with his seafaring ways, his honest outlook.

So she ventures through town and finds the harbor near where he lives. The water here is blue as can be. Wild white roses climb among rocky ledges. There are lobster traps stacked on the docks and sailboats bobbing in the calm water.

What it all is, Celia thinks, is a haven. Peace, with no prying eyes. No whispers behind shingled walls, paned windows. No questions. No judgments.

No, Celia couldn't sit in Mass this morning for so many reasons, those included. Couldn't chat with Lauren; couldn't ask about Jason and Maris; couldn't scroll through Eva's Martha's Vineyard photos; couldn't sit next to Elsa and pretend the past two weeks hadn't happened. No, not today.

Not on this one day.

So she came to Maine with Aria instead. Celia wants to see exactly where Shane landed back then. See something of his life, *here.* Driving the narrow town roads, she finally spots his street, and his tiny shingled home up ahead. A few faded buoys hang beside the door of the charming harbor house. She slows and pulls into the gravel driveway, stopping right behind his pickup truck.

"We're here," she says over her shoulder to Aria. "At Shane's."

Before getting out, Celia takes a deep breath of the pungent salt air, presses her hair back and looks more closely at this place Shane calls home. The coastal house's shingles are weathered to a pretty silver. And there's a wide granite step leading to a screened front door. It's all very casual, very welcoming. The door and window trim are painted a soft blue color, one Celia imagines to be a shade of the Atlantic Ocean. Beneath the paned window beside the front door, red geraniums spill out of a window box painted that same shade of blue.

Finally, Celia opens her car door, gets out and loops a fabric baby-sling over her shoulders. Standing there and squinting against the bright sun, she can see the docks beyond Shane's house. More lobster traps are stacked there, and past those, a scenic harbor leads to the great blue sea.

And already, she's smiling. Just like that.

Just for one day.

Leaning into the car again, Celia lifts Aria from her baby seat and tucks her into the soft sling she wears. "We'll have a nice day here with Shane," she tells Aria while settling her into the sling's fabric, "before he goes out on the lobster boat tomorrow." Holding the baby close, Celia walks up the granite step to the front door. When she quickly knocks, yes, she's still smiling. Her breath catches, though. Damn it, she's nervous.

But, nothing happens. There are no footsteps from inside. No one calling out, *Be right there*. No Shane. So she glances over at his pickup, then takes a peek in through the paned window.

"Oh, look," she tells Aria, turning the baby toward the window. "There's his red sailboat. Do you know he used to play with that boat when he was just a boy?" Slightly bouncing the baby, she squints to see further inside. It's shadowy, but there, on a table near the window, she also can't miss his happiness jar. The way the sunlight shines inside, it glimmers right on her pieces of sea glass that he must've sprinkled over the sand.

"Hmm," Celia softly says to Aria. She brushes aside a few wisps of her daughter's dark hair. "Maybe he went out for something. Or took a walk somewhere, because his truck's here."

Stepping down the granite step, she walks alongside the house and looks for the deck that he spoke of. *You and your daughter are always welcome … It's a nice place to sit and chew on life*, he'd told her.

And he wasn't kidding. When Celia rounds the corner to the back of the house, there it is. The deck—and what a deck it is. Sitting there, you'd have a clear view of the docks, the harbor. There are lobster boats out on the water, and sailboats. Seagulls swoop and cry. The sky is blue, the water bluer. And the sun perfectly drops ocean stars right on the rippling waves.

"Hello!" a voice suddenly calls out.

Celia turns to see a man approaching. He looks to be about forty and wears a baseball cap over dark hair curling beneath it.

"You looking for Shane?" he asks.

"Yes. Yes, I am," Celia says while turning to him.

The man steps closer. He's got on a plaid short-sleeve button-down loose over long cargo shorts. "You just missed him, I'm afraid."

"Oh." Celia lightly joggles Aria in her arms. "Do you know if he'll be back soon?"

"Don't think so. Took his duffel and asked me to water his window boxes. I'm his neighbor," the man says, vaguely pointing to a nearby home, its shingles painted a dark red. "Believe he'll be back and forth for the next week, at least. Out lobstering."

"Today? He left *today*?"

"That he did."

"Oh, *shoot*. I just assumed he'd leave on *Monday*. The start of the workweek, and, well I guess …" Celia turns and eyes Shane's house, which she now sees is all closed up. And of course his truck *would* be here if he was headed out on a lobster boat from right on these docks.

"No, his crew's setting out today. Good weather and all, gettin' a head start on the week," the man tells her. "Something important going on? Need to get a message to Shane?"

Celia turns back to this neighbor. The guy's nice enough, and seems to want to help. "No," she says, shaking her head.

"I'm just a friend. Stopped by for a little visit. But that's okay," she adds with a small smile.

"All right, then." The neighbor gives an easy shrug, takes off his cap and squints at her. "You know ... I'm sorry. I didn't get your name?"

"Celia."

"And who's this little one?"

Celia lightly pats the baby's head. "This is Aria."

"Well, Celia," the neighbor says while giving the baby's foot a gentle squeeze. "You just *might* be able to catch Shane, though."

"What?" Celia shifts Aria in her hold.

"If you hurry."

"You think so? But, how?"

"Over on the harbor." The man points out a distant boat tied to a pier. The large vessel is painted dark green. Several rows of lobster traps are stacked five-high on deck. "That's the boat Shane's headed out on, right there."

# thirty-three

### Moments Later

IT'S ALL CELIA CAN DO to stop looking at that one boat as she wills it to stay docked. But she *has* to tear her eyes away if she'll ever safely reach it. Still, the entire time she straps Aria into her car seat, backs the vehicle out of Shane's driveway, and drives the short cut-through to the docks, her eyes keep returning to that one sight. To that one green boat stacked high with lobster pots. If Shane hasn't boarded yet, maybe he has time for even a quick coffee. A few words.

In mere minutes, her car's tires crunch over stone and dirt in the harbor parking lot. A few heaves in the ground jostle the car. As she looks for a place to park, Celia also spots Shane standing on a further dock. Can't miss him, actually, with that newsboy cap he wears. So there's still time; he's not yet left port. But she feels the clock ticking. Ticking away precious minutes, seconds. Her heart especially sinks the moment Shane hoists up his packed duffel because, oh, she knows what that moment means. Standing there in his jeans and a loose button-down over a tee, he raises those arms of his and throws that duffel on the deck of the lobster boat. His departure is imminent. Celia knows it; feels it as she turns the car into a parking space.

By the time she gets out, Shane's swung around to board the waiting boat. And there are no other lobstermen hanging around on the docks. No one running along, waving a hand to hold up the boat. It looks like Shane's the last man to board. So Celia unbuckles Aria.

*Tick, tick.*

Seconds pass as she fumbles with the car seat harness.

*Tick, tick.*

More seconds as Celia lifts the baby out of the car. When she straightens and tucks Aria into her strap-on baby sling again, she hears distant men's voices. They're friendly, calling out to one another. *Throw the line and let's get the hell out of here!* And, *Throttle up, Captain!*

*Tick, tick.*

Now, as she slips Aria's legs securely through the sling fabric, now comes the rumble of the boat's engine.

Carefully holding Aria close, Celia half walks, half trots along the dock. If she can just have a few *minutes* with Shane, enough time to tell him about her trip here, and that she thought, well … She thought he'd be home for a day, at least. That he wouldn't be on the water so soon. The wooden boards shift and creak beneath her hurried step.

Water sloshes beneath the dock. A seagull perched on a roped piling squawks and flaps its wings as she rushes past.

Now, Celia slow-trots. That green boat is still a ways down, but if she's not mistaken, it's also pulling away. There won't even be time to tell Shane she thought they'd sit on his deck and have a lazy day together. She quickens her pace as the lobster boat churns through the calm water. Its engine chugs along; several men gather on deck. It's harder to see as the vessel heads toward the channel out to sea. But she can still clearly make out Shane on board. With one hand supporting Aria in the sling around her shoulders, Celia raises her other hand to shield the sun from her eyes.

But it's no use. She's too late—the boat's leaving port. There's no reason to continue along the dock. She's just too late. So Celia slows her step, and gradually stops. Stops and watches the lobster boat depart. It leaves a frothy white wake in the blue water behind it.

It's too much, all too much. The weight of being just *minutes* too late actually surprises her. There was no time to even say a few words to Shane. To tell him she had to see him again. To touch his jaw. To wish him a safe trip. To wave little Aria's hand at him.

Nothing.

As she stands there, she watches Shane on deck with the boys. One thing is obvious by the backslapping, by the laughter and talking going on. The crew is really glad to have him aboard ship again after his two weeks away.

But somehow, after those same two weeks, and after all this today—the packing and food prep and rest stops and driving, driving, driving—it's more than Celia can take, watching that boat chug through the harbor.

So she simply turns and walks away. Crosses the same dock she just trotted over minutes ago. Passes the same prickly seagull sitting on a roped piling. Hears the same creaking boards beneath her sandaled feet. Slows her step, strokes Aria's dark hair and whispers in her ear. Murmurs words about the pretty boats, and the sparkling water, and the salt air. Presses a kiss to the side of Aria's head, all while closing her eyes against stinging tears.

One day—the one day she'd hoped for—long out of reach now.

~

As soon as he does it, as soon as Shane heaves his packed duffel onto the boat's deck, it happens. The past two weeks are gone from his thoughts. As well they have to be. The Atlantic Ocean shows no mercy for distractions, for carelessness. One wrong move on a boat pitching on the sea can be deadly. One trip-up on an uncoiling rope, one inattentive moment looking away from the hauler, and he could end up at the *bottom* of that deep sea—caught up in the wayward line of some lobster trap. So the thud of his duffel hitting the deck triggers the necessary lobstering frame of mind. Focused. Sharp. Diligent. Aware.

And then there are the greetings from the boys.

*Yo, Shane! Good to see you*, said with a hearty backslap.

*Made it back in one piece, did ya?* asked with a cuff to the shoulder.

*You won't believe the stunt the greenhorn pulled,* said with a quick headlock. *Toppled the pots, almost lost a damn finger.*

Shane bullshits with them for a minute or two, then picks up his duffel. These late-August days are his favorite part of every summer. There's the rocking motion of the boat as it starts moving through the harbor. A bell buoy clangs; gulls swoop overhead; a distant lighthouse rises from the rocky shores. Calm, peaceful. He can breathe easy. Taking it all in now, it's as familiar as home itself.

Still, like he always does before going to store his things below deck, Shane gives one last look back toward his home on land. It's a routine from which he never veers, knowing it could very well be the last time he sees that shingled house near the docks—the ocean is that temperamental. And his house is the sight he likes to keep in his thoughts as the boat heads out. So after inhaling a deep breath of that salt-soaked air right on the water, he swings around for his one last look home.

But before he can see his house, there's something else. *Someone* else.

A woman. Shit, his eyes must be playing tricks on him. He take a cautious step toward the rear of the boat to be sure. And squints through the sunlight. It *is*. It's *Celia*. He *knows* it is. Her auburn hair is down, held back by sunglasses propped on her head as she shields her eyes and looks toward his boat. She's got on cropped white pants and a sleeveless denim blouse. And of course, little Aria is strapped to her in a baby sling.

Shane works his way around the stacked lobster pots for a better look. Carefully, he turns sideways and squeezes through, his one hand holding his duffel, the other hand running along the pots to keep steady as he gets through the tight space. Still, there's some doubt. Really? Celia's *here*? In Maine? It doesn't make sense.

God damn it, how many traps are loaded on this boat? It's taking too long to get past them. A sharp corner of one trap snags on his shirt. As he breaks away, Shane also knows that he and the boys will be baiting and sending every one of these stacked and towering lobster pots overboard. He knows that they'll eventually haul them back up, full and dripping, from the sea. Knows that he'll be gone for days, far out on Penobscot Bay.

But not yet. Shane finally squeezes past the last of the traps and gets to an open space near the stern. There, he tips up his cap and takes a good look at the woman on the docks—the woman just turning away now. She walks slowly, her face tipped down to the baby's ear. He recognizes that gesture. Celia's *always* whispering into Aria's ear, telling her some sweet nothing, or pointing out a seagull, or a flower.

Well. There's only one reason Celia Gray is here in Rockport, Maine. Shane knows it. Believes it. She'd driven over five hours north and come to the docks looking for *him*. Problem is, there's not a blessed thing he can do about it now. No way in hell will the captain stop the boat; no way can Shane put his job at risk asking him to. Bad enough he just missed two weeks of work. He can only hope that everything's all right with Celia.

Watching her, he thinks she still *might* turn around. Might stop and give one last look back. He could at least wave then. Make some vague connection. Maybe see her face, *and* see that she's okay. He considers calling out her name, but she'd *never* hear him over the sound of the boat's engine, over the sloshing water as the vessel slowly maneuvers around idle lobster boats and several sailboats anchored in the harbor.

So Shane just watches and waits. Drops his heavy duffel and leans against a secured stack of lobster traps. Crosses his arms and doesn't take his eyes off Celia as she walks further and further away. With each passing second, the boat puts more distance between them. There's still time though, *and* that shred of hope that she'll turn. That she'll glance back over her shoulder and look out over the calm harbor water. Give him a brief glimpse at her face.

That's all he wants—one reassuring glimpse. And he *won't* turn his back on that possibility.

But, nothing. Minutes tick by. Not a glance from Celia; not even a hesitation as she walks across the docks, passes the boats moored there, and heads toward the distant parking lot. *No, no*, Shane thinks. If he'd only had the chance to talk to her, he'd have pressed his house key into her hand. Insisted she and Aria rest from the long trip. Stay for a day, at least—or even until he got back.

Instead, he sees her walking to her car.

The boat's really chugging along now; deeper water slaps at the hull. The harbor grows smaller as the boat moves past a rocky coast. Behind him on deck, voices rise above the thrumming engine as the guys talk about their weekend, rib each other. Eventually, Shane hears one voice directed at him.

*Bradford, let's go!*

But as the lobster boat makes its way to open waters, he does not move. Doesn't bend and pick up his duffel. Doesn't go below deck to store his gear. Does not take his eyes off of Celia.

He just stands there, looking across the lengthening span of water between her and the boat. Looking past moored vessels the lobster boat leaves in its wake.

He watches only Celia holding Aria close.

Celia walking away.

Shane doesn't budge, not one bit.

And he won't, either. Not until Celia is long out of his sight.

The beach friends' journey continues in

# SALT AIR SECRETS

The next novel in The Seaside Saga from

New York Times Bestselling Author

# JOANNE DEMAIO

# Also by Joanne DeMaio

**The Seaside Saga**
(In order)
*1) Blue Jeans and Coffee Beans*
*2) The Denim Blue Sea*
*3) Beach Blues*
*4) Beach Breeze*
*5) The Beach Inn*
*6) Beach Bliss*
*7) Castaway Cottage*
*8) Night Beach*
*9) Little Beach Bungalow*
*10) Every Summer*
*11) Salt Air Secrets*
*—And More Seaside Saga Books—*

**Summer Standalone Novels**
*True Blend*
*Whole Latte Life*

**Winter Novels**
*Eighteen Winters*
*First Flurries*
*Cardinal Cabin*
*Snow Deer and Cocoa Cheer*
*Snowflakes and Coffee Cakes*

For a complete list of books by *New York Times*
bestselling author Joanne DeMaio, visit:

Joannedemaio.com

# *About the Author*

JOANNE DEMAIO is a *New York Times* and *USA Today* bestselling author of contemporary fiction. The novels of her ongoing and groundbreaking Seaside Saga journey with a group of beach friends, much the way a TV series does, continuing with the same cast of characters from book-to-book. In addition, she writes winter novels set in a quaint New England town. Joanne lives with her family in Connecticut.

For a complete list of books and for news on upcoming releases, visit Joanne's website. She also enjoys hearing from readers on Facebook.

**Author Website:**
Joannedemaio.com

**Facebook:**
Facebook.com/JoanneDeMaioAuthor

Made in United States
Orlando, FL
11 July 2024

48832825R00189